SUPERNATURAL
STORIES

KINGFISHER
An imprint of Larousse plc
Elsley House, 24-30 Great Titchfield Street
London W1P 7AD

First published by Kingfisher 1995
2 4 6 8 10 9 7 5 3 1 (hardback)
2 4 6 8 10 9 7 5 3 1 (paperback)

A CIP catalogue record for this book
is available from the British Library

ISBN 1 85697 322 0 (hardback)
ISBN 1 85697 211 9 (paperback)

Printed and bound in Great Britain by
BPC Paperbacks Ltd
A Member of
The British Printing Company Ltd

SUPERNATURAL
STORIES

CHOSEN BY
WILLIAM MAYNE

ILLUSTRATED BY
MARTIN SALISBURY

Kingfisher

CONTENTS

INTRODUCTION

WILLIAM MAYNE

Y OU'D THINK THE SUPERNATURAL might have faded away by now, since we know everything. However, the more we know the less natural it seems, with electrons or quarks or diplons (as some of them used to be called) hurtling around backwards through time at critical moments in their lifestyles. Because there are those moments that bend reality, or our idea of it, we need the notion of the supernatural to give us a way of thinking about them.

But it is more than a way of thinking. There is something almost like a taste on the tongue when we hear some things: the party of walkers on the Lakeland fells, late one night, bright moonlight, catching up to another walker, walking along with him, talking about ghosts; but of course not believing in them at all. "You don't?" asked their new companion, turning into a puff of mist and sinking into the heather. You can put it out of your mind; but next time, in broad daylight, how quickly do you catch up to the figure walking ahead over the moor?

And we find meaningless odd paragraphs here and there, about things we still know well, and whose behaviour we ordinarily understand.

> At another time one of his shoe-strings was observed (without the assistance of any hand) to come of its own accord out of its shoe and fling itself to the other side of the room; the other was crawling after it, but a maid espying that, with her hand drew it out, and it strangely *clasp'd* and *curl'd* about her hand like a living *eel* or *serpent*.

I have read recently that parts of the atom that we can't even think about act in just that way.

So how about the supernatural being the actual natural, and what we usually think of as the natural being rather a poor copy. There are plenty of things we cannot see with our eyes or hear with our ears, but which are certainly there: ultra-violet rays, infra-red for remote controls, X-rays, γ-rays; so why not a powerful parallel universe?

> A naval officer visited a friend in the country. Several men were sitting round the smoking-room fire when he arrived, and a fox-terrier was with them. Presently the heavy, shambling footsteps of an old dog, and the metallic shaking sound of his collar, were heard coming up the stairs.
> "Here's old Peter!" said the visitor.
> "*Peter's dead!*" whispered his owner.
> The sounds passed through the closed door, heard by all; they pattered into the room; the fox-terrier bristled up, growled, and pursued a viewless object across the carpet; then the hearth-rug sounded a shake, a jingle of a collar, and the settling weight of a body collapsing into repose.

I was there, for a moment or two. Something was there last night, in the wall at the foot of the bed. It will be somewhere else tomorrow night. Houses are never at rest. Electrons are pacing back and forth.

And if electrons run backwards in our world are they at the same time running forwards in another? Are we supernatural to that world, or is it supernatural to ours? How many of them are there? Are electrons running crabwise, up and down, corner-ways, in half a dozen different directions that this world does not have?

And have we called them something different in times past?

> Fairies! I went into a farmhouse to stay a night, and in the evening there came a knocking in the room as if someone had struck the table.

I jumped up. My hostess got up, and "Good-night," says she, "I'm off."

"But what is it?" says I.

"Just a poor old fairy," says she; "Old Nancy. She's a poor old thing; been here ever so long; lost her husband and her children; it's bad to be left like that, all alone. I leave a bit o' cake on the table for her, and sometimes she fetches it, and sometimes she don't."

Well, we believe in fairies, or we don't believe in fairies, but no matter what we think about them they are existential, they have a place in our minds; we know what we are talking about, what we are believing in, what we are not believing in. And, come to think of it, it's only in the last hundred years that we have believed electrons existed, that anything was smaller than an atom. Somebody even had to make up the word itself, but now we are certain of it. And it's stranger than that, because the heart of the atom is, for comparison, as big as a bean in a room, and the electron is like a speck of dust that never comes closer than outside the window. All that space is empty; so why don't we fall into our own internal spaces?

It's the supernatural that holds us together, or apart, however you like to think of it. So be careful how you treat electrons: it's bad enough if you insult a fairy.

After the offence given to them the fairies took the greatest revenge on the family, and each member of it always seemed as if he or she saw some dreadful appearance in the distance that terrified them. They were never able to express what it was, but it drew them down too much. In the end the neighbours turned away from them, because of the ill-luck that came on everything that family touched.

Of the six children, they grew from birth withered and old, with the thinnest crooked fingers. It was clear they were fairy changelings. The blacksmith said they should be put on the anvil and the trouble beaten from them with a hammer, and drawn from them with hot pincers; and the wise women said they should be dragged through the fire. But none of that was done, and in the end they all dwined and perished, and the revenge was not over until all the family had gone that way and the house fired and the ashes thrown on the stream.

Alongside our belief that the atom is hollow, that time runs the wrong way, alongside our look inside, we are looking outside too. We are seeing the vast distances of our own universe (where the sun is like a bean and the planets dust outside the window), and the distances of a size we cannot imagine, but which might lead us not only to other ways of living and being, but to huger ones than can now be dreamed of or described.

Perhaps, at the end of knowledge, we shall see what is really there, where time always runs backwards, and from where the new holy terrors of the future (or is it the past?) will descend on us, the aliens of each others' fancies.

All the same, keep hold of your common reality, and perhaps it will be the supernatural; perhaps there will be ways of staying in charge, places where we shall show through to those other worlds:

The seventh son of a seventh son, in addition to his natural powers, can wield others: if an earthworm is put into his newborn hand, and if he holds it until the worm dies, the child will not only charm away disease but be able to charm all the bogles of the sky.

Keep practising to be the seventh son of a seventh son. It can be done.

ZERO HOUR

RAY BRADBURY

O H, IT WAS TO BE SO jolly! What a game! Such excitement they hadn't known in years. The children catapulted this way and that across the green lawns, shouting at each other, holding hands, flying in circles, climbing trees, laughing. Overhead the rockets flew, and beetle cars whispered by on the streets, but the children played on. Such fun, such tremulous joy, such tumbling and hearty screaming.

Mink ran into the house, all dirt and sweat. For her seven years she was loud and strong and definite. Her mother, Mrs Morris, hardly saw her as she yanked out drawers and rattled pans and tools into a large sack.

"Heavens, Mink, what's going on?"

"The most exciting game ever!" gasped Mink, pink-faced.

"Stop and get your breath," said the mother.

"No, I'm all right," gasped Mink. "Okay I take these things, Mom?"

"But don't dent them," said Mrs Morris.

"Thank you, thank you!" cried Mink, and boom! she was gone, like a rocket.

11

Mrs Morris surveyed the fleeing tot. "What's the name of the game?"

"Invasion!" said Mink. The door slammed.

In every yard on the street children brought out knives and forks and pokers and old stovepipes and can-openers.

It was an interesting fact that this fury and bustle occurred only among the younger children. The older ones, those ten years and more, disdained the affair and marched scornfully off on hikes or played a more dignified version of hide-and-seek on their own.

Meanwhile, parents came and went in chromium beetles. Repairmen came to repair the vacuum elevators in houses, to fix fluttering television sets or hammer upon stubborn food-delivery tubes. The adult civilization passed and repassed the busy youngsters, jealous of the fierce energy of the wild tots, tolerantly amused at their flourishings, longing to join in themselves.

"This and this and *this*," said Mink, instructing the others with their assorted spoons and wrenches. "Do that, and bring *that* over here. No! *Here*, ninny! Right. Now, get back while I fix this." Tongue in teeth, face wrinkled in thought. "Like that. See?"

"Yayyyy!" shouted the kids.

Twelve-year-old Joseph Connors ran up.

"Go away," said Mink straight at him.

"I wanna play," said Joseph.

"Can't!" said Mink.

"Why not?"

"You'd just make fun of us."

"Honest, I wouldn't."

"No. We know *you*. Go away or we'll kick you."

Another twelve-year-old boy whirred by on little motor skates. "Hey, Joe! Come on! Let them sissies play!"

Joseph showed reluctance and a certain wistfulness. "I *want* to play," he said.

"You're old," said Mink firmly.

"Not *that* old," said Joe sensibly.

12

"You'd only laugh and spoil the Invasion."

The boy on the motor skates made a rude lip noise. "Come on, Joe! Them and their fairies! Nuts!"

Joseph walked off slowly. He kept looking back, all down the block.

Mink was already busy again. She made a kind of apparatus with her gathered equipment. She had appointed another little girl with a pad and pencil to take down notes in painful slow scribbles. Their voices rose and fell in the warm sunlight.

All around them the city hummed. The streets were lined with good green and peaceful trees. Only the wind made a conflict across the city, across the country, across the continent. In a thousand other cities there were trees and children and avenues, businessmen in their quiet offices taping their voices, or watching televisors. Rockets hovered like darning needles in the blue sky. There was the universal, quiet conceit and easiness of men accustomed to peace, quite certain there would never be trouble again. Arm in arm, men all over earth were a united front. The perfect weapons were held in equal trust by all nations. A situation of incredibly beautiful balance had been brought about. There were no traitors among men, no unhappy ones, no disgruntled ones; therefore the world was based upon a stable ground. Sunlight illumined half the world and the trees drowsed in a tide of warm air.

Mink's mother, from her upstairs window, gazed down.

The children. She looked upon them and shook her head. Well, they'd eat well, sleep well, and be in school on Monday. Bless their vigorous little bodies. She listened.

Mink talked earnestly to someone near the rose-bush – though there was no one there.

These odd children. And the little girl, what was her name? Anna? Anna took notes on a pad. First, Mink asked the rose-bush a question, then called the answer to Anna.

"Triangle," said Mink.

"What's a tri," said Anna with difficulty, "angle?"

13

"Never mind," said Mink.

"How you spell it?" asked Anna.

"T-r-i – " spelled Mink slowly, then snapped, "Oh, spell it yourself!" She went on to other words. "Beam," she said.

"I haven't got tri," said Anna, "angle down yet!"

"Well, hurry, hurry!" cried Mink.

Mink's mother leaned out of the upstairs window. "A-n-g-l-e," she spelled down at Anna.

"Oh, thanks, Mrs Morris," said Anna.

"Certainly," said Mink's mother and withdrew, laughing, to dust the hall with an electro-duster magnet.

The voices wavered on the shimmery air. "Beam," said Anna. Fading.

"Four-nine-seven-A-and-B-and-X," said Mink, far away, seriously. "And a fork and a string and a – hex-hex-agony – hexagon*al*!"

At lunch Mink gulped milk at one toss and was at the door. Her mother slapped the table.

"You sit right back down," commanded Mrs Morris. "Hot soup in a minute." She poked a red button on the

kitchen butler, and ten seconds later something landed with a bump in the rubber receiver. Mrs Morris opened it, took out a can with a pair of aluminium holders, unsealed it with a flick, and poured hot soup into a bowl.

During all this Mink fidgeted. "Hurry, Mom! This is a matter of life and death! Aw—"

"I was the same way at your age. Always life and death. I know."

Mink banged away at the soup.

"Slow down," said Mom.

"Can't," said Mink. "Drill's waiting for me."

"Who's Drill? What a peculiar name," said Mom.

"You don't know him," said Mink.

"A new boy in the neighbourhood?" asked Mom.

"He's new all right," said Mink. She started on her second bowl.

"Which one is Drill?" asked Mom.

"He's around," said Mink, evasively. "You'll make fun. Everybody pokes fun. Gee, darn."

"Is Drill shy?"

"Yes. No. In a way. Gosh, Mom, I got to run if we want to have the Invasion!"

"Who's invading what?"

"Martians invading Earth. Well, not exactly Martians. They're – I don't know. From up." She pointed with her spoon.

"And *inside*," said Mom, touching Mink's feverish brow.

Mink rebelled. "You're laughing! You'll kill Drill and everybody."

"I didn't mean to," said Mom. "Drill's a Martian?"

"No. He's – well – maybe from Jupiter or Saturn or Venus. Anyway, he's had a hard time."

"I imagine." Mrs Morris hid her mouth behind her hand.

"They couldn't figure a way to attack Earth."

"We're impregnable," said Mom in mock seriousness.

"That's the word Drill used! Impreg – That was the word, Mom."

"My, my, Drill's a brilliant little boy. Two-bit words."

"They couldn't figure a way to attack, Mom. Drill says – he says in order to make a good fight you got to have a new way of surprising people. That way you win. And he says also you got to have help from your enemy."

"A fifth column," said Mom.

"Yeah. That's what Drill said. And they couldn't figure a way to surprise Earth or get help."

"No wonder. We're pretty darn strong." Mom laughed, cleaning up. Mink sat there, staring at the table, seeing what she was talking about.

"Until, one day," whispered Mink melodramatically, "they thought of children!"

"*Well!*" said Mrs Morris brightly.

"And they thought of how grown-ups are so busy they never look under rose-bushes or on lawns!"

"Only for snails and fungus."

"And then there's something about dim-dims."

"Dim-dims?"

"Dimens-shuns."

"Dimensions?"

"Four of 'em! And there's something about kids under nine and imagination. It's real funny to hear Drill talk."

Mrs Morris was tired. "Well, it must be funny. You're keeping Drill waiting now. It's getting late in the day and, if you want to have your Invasion before your supper bath, you'd better jump."

"Do I have to take a bath?" growled Mink.

"You do! Why is it children hate water? No matter what age you live in children hate water behind the ears!"

"Drill says I won't have to take baths," said Mink.

"Oh, he does, does he?"

"He told all the kids that. No more baths. And we can stay up till ten o'clock and go to two televisor shows on Saturday 'stead of one!"

"Well, Mr Drill better mind his p's and q's. I'll call up his mother and—"

Mink went to the door. "We're having trouble with guys like Pete Britz and Dale Jerrick. They're growing up. They make fun. They're worse than parents. They just won't believe in Drill. They're so snooty, 'cause they're growing up. You'd think they'd know better. They were little only a coupla years ago. I hate them worst. We'll kill them *first*."

"Your father and me last?"

"Drill says you're dangerous. Know why? 'Cause you don't believe in Martians! They're going to let *us* run the world. Well, not just us, but the kids over in the next block, too. I might be queen." She opened the door.

"Mom?"

"Yes?"

"What's lodge-ick?"

"Logic? Why, dear, logic is knowing what things are true and not true."

"He *mentioned* that," said Mink. "And what's im-pression-able?" It took her a minute to say it.

"Why, it means –" Her mother looked at the floor, laughing gently. "It means – to be a child, dear."

"Thanks for lunch!" Mink ran out, then stuck her head back in. "Mom, I'll be sure you won't be hurt much, really!"

"Well, thanks," said Mom.

Slam went the door.

At four o'clock the audio-visor buzzed. Mrs Morris flipped the tab. "Hello, Helen!" she said in welcome.

"Hello, Mary. How are things in New York?"

"Fine. How are things in Scranton? You look tired."

"So do you. The children. Underfoot," said Helen.

Mrs Morris sighed. "My Mink too. The super-Invasion."

Helen laughed. "Are your kids playing that game too?"

"Lord, yes. Tomorrow it'll be geometrical jacks and motorized hopscotch. Were we this bad when we were kids in '48?"

"Worse, Japs and Nazis. Don't know how my parents put up with me. Tomboy."

"Parents learn to shut their ears."

A silence.

"What's wrong, Mary?" asked Helen.

Mrs Morris's eyes were half closed; her tongue slid slowly, thoughtfully, over her lower lip. "Eh?" She jerked. "Oh, nothing. Just thought about *that*. Shutting ears and such. Never mind. Where were we?"

"My boy Tim's got a crush on some guy named – *Drill*, I think it was."

"Must be a new password. Mink likes him too."

"Didn't know it had got as far as New York. Word of mouth, I imagine. Looks like a scrap drive. I talked to Josephine and she said her kids – that's in Boston – are wild on this new game. It's sweeping the country."

At this moment Mink trotted into the kitchen to gulp a glass of water. Mrs Morris turned. "How're things going?"

"Almost finished," said Mink.

"Swell," said Mrs Morris. "What's *that*?"

"A yo-yo," said Mink. "Watch."

She flung the yo-yo down its string. Reaching the end it – It vanished.

"See?" said Mink. "Ope!" Dibbling her finger, she made the yo-yo reappear and zip up the string.

"Do that again," said her mother.

"Can't. Zero hour's five o'clock. 'Bye!" Mink exited, zipping her yo-yo.

On the audio-visor, Helen laughed. "Tim brought one of those yo-yos in this morning, but when I got curious he said he wouldn't show it to me, and when I tried to work it, finally, it wouldn't work."

"You're not *impressionable*," said Mrs Morris.

"What?"

"Never mind. Something I thought of. Can I help you, Helen?"

"I wanted to get that black-and-white cake recipe – "

The hour drowsed by. The day waned. The sun lowered in

the peaceful blue sky. Shadows lengthened on the green lawns. The laughter and excitement continued. One little girl ran away, crying. Mrs Morris came out the front door.

"Mink, was that Peggy Ann crying?"

Mink was bent over in the yard, near the rose-bush. "Yeah. She's a scarebaby. We won't let her play, now. She's getting too old to play. I guess she grew up all of a sudden."

"Is that why she cried? Nonsense. Give me a civil answer, young lady, or inside you come!"

Mink whirled in consternation, mixed with irritation. "I can't quit now. It's almost time. I'll be good. I'm sorry."

"Did you hit Peggy Ann?"

"No, honest. You ask her. It was something – well, she's just a scaredy pants."

The ring of children drew in around Mink where she scowled at her work with spoons and a kind of square-shaped arrangement of hammers and pipes. "There and there," murmured Mink.

"What's wrong?" said Mrs Morris.

"Drill's stuck. Half-way. If we could only get him all the way through it'd be easier. Then all the others could come through after him."

"Can I help?"

"No'm, thanks. I'll fix it."

"All right. I'll call you for your bath in half an hour. I'm tired of watching you."

She went in and sat in the electric relaxing chair, sipping a little beer from a half-empty glass. The chair massaged her back. Children, children. Children and love and hate, side by side. Sometimes children loved you, hated you – all in half a second. Strange children, did they ever forget or forgive the whippings and the harsh, strict words of command? She wondered. How can you ever forget or forgive those over and above you, those tall and silly dictators?

Time passed. A curious, waiting silence came upon the street, deepening.

Five o'clock. A clock sang softly somewhere in the house in a quiet musical voice: "Five o'clock – five o'clock. Time's a-wasting. Five o'clock," and purred away into silence.

Zero hour.

Mrs Morris chuckled in her throat. Zero hour.

A beetle car hummed into the driveway. Mr Morris. Mrs Morris smiled. Mr Morris got out of the beetle, locked it, and called hello to Mink at her work. Mink ignored him. He laughed and stood for a moment watching the children. Then he walked up the front steps.

"Hello, darling."

"Hello, Henry."

She strained forward on the edge of the chair, listening. The children were silent. Too silent.

He emptied his pipe, refilled it. "Swell day. Makes you glad to be alive."

Buzz.

"What's that?" asked Henry.

"I don't know." She got up suddenly, her eyes widening. She was going to say something. She stopped it. Ridiculous. Her nerves jumped. "Those children haven't anything dangerous out there, have they?" she said.

"Nothing but pipes and hammers. Why?"

"Nothing electrical?"

"Heck, no," said Henry. "I looked."

She walked to the kitchen. The buzzing continued. "Just the same, you'd better go tell them to quit. It's after five. Tell them—" Her eyes widened and narrowed. "Tell them to put off their Invasion until tomorrow." She laughed, nervously.

The buzzing grew louder.

"What are they up to? I'd better go look, all right."

The explosion!

The house shook with dull sound. There were other explosions in other yards on other streets.

Involuntarily, Mrs Morris screamed. "Up this way!" she cried senselessly, knowing no sense, no reason. Perhaps she saw something from the corners of her eyes; perhaps she smelled a new odour or heard a new noise. There was no time to argue with Henry to convince him. Let him think her insane. Yes, insane! Shrieking, she ran upstairs. He ran after her to see what she was up to. "In the attic!" she screamed. "That's where it is!" It was only a poor excuse to get him in the attic in time. Oh, God – in time!

Another explosion outside. The children screamed with delight, as if at a great fireworks display.

"It's not in the attic!" cried Henry. "It's outside!"

"No, no!" Wheezing, gasping, she fumbled at the attic door. "I'll show you. Hurry! I'll show you!"

They tumbled into the attic. She slammed the door, locked it, took the key, threw it into a far, cluttered corner.

She was babbling wild stuff now. It came out of her. All the subconscious suspicion and fear that had gathered secretly all afternoon and fermented like a wine in her. All

21

the little revelations and knowledges and sense that had bothered her all day and which she had, logically and carefully and sensibly, rejected and censored. Now it exploded in her and shook her to bits.

"There, there," she said, sobbing against the door. "We're safe until tonight. Maybe we can sneak out. Maybe we can escape!"

Henry blew up too, but for another reason. "Are you crazy? Why'd you throw that key away? Damn it, honey!"

"Yes, yes, I'm crazy, if it helps, but stay here with me!"

"I don't know how in hell I *can* get out!"

"Quiet. They'll hear us. Oh, God, they'll find us soon enough —"

Below them, Mink's voice. The husband stopped. There was a great universal humming and sizzling, a screaming and giggling. Downstairs the audio-televisor buzzed and buzzed insistently, alarmingly, violently. *Is that Helen calling?* thought Mrs Morris. *And is she calling about what I think she's calling about?*

Footsteps came into the house. Heavy footsteps.

"Who's coming in my house?" demanded Henry angrily. "Who's tramping around down there?"

Heavy feet. Twenty, thirty, forty, fifty of them. Fifty persons crowding into the house. The humming. The giggling of the children. "This way!" cried Mink, below.

"Who's downstairs?" roared Henry. "Who's there?"

"Hush. Oh, nonononono!" said his wife weakly, holding him. "Please, be quiet. They might go away."

"Mom?" called Mink. "Dad?" A pause. "Where are you?"

Heavy footsteps, heavy, heavy, very *heavy* footsteps, came up the stairs. Mink leading them.

"Mom?" A hesitation. "Dad?" A waiting, a silence.

Humming. Footsteps towards the attic. Mink's first.

They trembled together in silence in the attic, Mr and Mrs Morris. For some reason the electric humming, the queer cold light suddenly visible under the door crack, the

22

strange odour and the alien sound of eagerness in Mink's
voice finally got through to Henry Morris too. He stood,
shivering, in the dark silence, his wife beside him.

"Mom! Dad!"

Footsteps. A little humming sound. The attic-lock
melted. The door opened. Mink peered inside, tall blue
shadows behind her.

"Peekaboo," said Mink.

BUBBLING WELL ROAD

RUDYARD KIPLING

Look out on a large scale map the place where the Chenab river falls into the Indus fifteen miles or so above the hamlet of Chachuran. Five miles west of Chachuran lies Bubbling Well Road, and the house of the *gosain* or priest of Arti-goth. It was the priest who showed me the road, but it is no thanks to him that I am able to tell this story.

Five miles west of Chachuran is a patch of the plumed jungle-grass, that turns over in silver when the wind blows, from ten to twenty feet high and from three to four miles square. In the heart of the patch hides the *gosain* of Bubbling Well Road. The villagers stone him when he peers into the daylight, although he is a priest, and he runs back again as a strayed wolf turns into tall crops. He is a one-eyed man and carries, burnt between his brows, the impress of two copper coins. Some say that he was tortured by a native prince in the old days; for he is so old that he must have been capable of mischief in the days of Runjit Singh. His most pressing need at present is a halter, and the care of the British Government.

These things happened when the jungle-grass was tall; and the villagers of Chachuran told me that a sounder of pig had gone into the Arti-goth patch. To enter jungle-grass is always an unwise proceeding, but I went, partly because I knew nothing of pig-hunting, and partly because the villagers said that the big boar of the sounder owned foot long tushes. Therefore I wished to shoot him, in order to produce the tushes in after years, and say that I had ridden him down in fair chase. I took a gun and went into the hot, close patch, believing that it would be an easy thing to unearth one pig in ten square miles of jungle. Mr Wardle, the terrier, went with me because he believed that I was incapable of existing for an hour without his advice and countenance. He managed to slip in and out between the grass clumps, but I had to force my way, and in twenty minutes was as completely lost as though I had been in the heart of Central Africa. I did not notice this at first till I had grown wearied of stumbling and pushing through the grass, and Mr Wardle was beginning to sit down very often and hang out his tongue very far. There was nothing but grass everywhere, and it was impossible to see two yards in any direction. The grass stems held the heat exactly as boiler-tubes do.

In half an hour, when I was devoutly wishing that I had left the big boar alone, I came to a narrow path which seemed to be a compromise between a native footpath and a pig-run. It was barely six inches wide, but I could sidle along it in comfort. The grass was extremely thick here, and where the path was ill defined it was necessary to crush into the tussocks either with both hands before the face, or to back into it, leaving both hands free to manage the rifle. None the less it was a path, and valuable because it might lead to a place.

At the end of nearly fifty yards of fair way, just when I was preparing to back into an unusually stiff tussock, I missed Mr Wardle, who for his girth is an unusually frivolous dog and never keeps to heel. I called him three times and said aloud, "Where has the little beast gone to?" Then I stepped backwards several paces, for almost under my feet a deep voice repeated, "Where has the little beast gone?" To appreciate an unseen voice thoroughly you should hear it when you are lost in stifling jungle-grass. I called Mr Wardle again and the underground echo assisted me. At that I ceased calling and listened very attentively, because I thought I heard a man laughing in a peculiarly offensive manner. The heat made me sweat, but the laughter made me shake. There is no earthly need for laughter in high grass. It is indecent, as well as impolite. The chuckling stopped, and I took courage and continued to call till I thought that I had located the echo somewhere behind and below the tussock into which I was preparing to back just before I lost Mr Wardle. I drove my rifle up to the triggers between the grass-stems in a downward and forward direction. Then I waggled it to and fro, but it did not seem to touch ground on the far side of the tussock as it should have done. Every time that I grunted with the exertion of driving a heavy rifle through thick grass, the grunt was faithfully repeated from below, and when I stopped to wipe my face the sound of low laughter was distinct beyond doubting.

I went into the tussock, face first, an inch at a time, my mouth open and my eyes fine, full, and prominent. When I had overcome the resistance of the grass I found that I was looking straight across a black gap in the ground. That I was actually lying on my chest leaning over the mouth of a well so deep I could scarcely see the water in it.

There were things in the water – black things – and the water was as black as pitch with blue scum atop. The laughing sound came from the noise of a little spring, spouting half-way down one side of the well. Sometimes as the black things circled round, the trickle from the spring fell upon their tightly-stretched skins, and then the laughter changed into a sputter of mirth. One thing turned over on its back, as I watched, and drifted round and

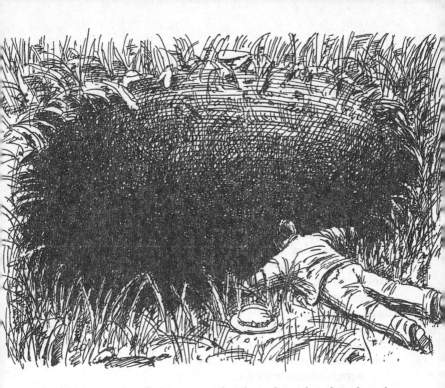

round the circle of the mossy brickwork with a hand and half an arm held clear of the water in a stiff and horrible flourish, as though it were a very wearied guide paid to exhibit the beauties of the place.

I did not spend more than half an hour in creeping round that well and finding the path on the other side. The remainder of the journey I accomplished by feeling every foot of ground in front of me, and crawling like a snail through every tussock. I carried Mr Wardle in my arms and he licked my nose. He was not frightened in the least, nor was I, but we wished to reach open ground in order to enjoy the view. My knees were loose, and the apple in my throat refused to slide up and down. The path on the far side of the well was a very good one, though boxed in on all sides by grass, and it led me in time to a priest's hut in the centre of a little clearing. When that priest saw my very white face coming through the grass he howled with terror and embraced my boots; but when I reached the bedstead set outside his door I sat down quickly and Mr Wardle mounted guard over me. I was not in a condition to take care of myself.

When I awoke I told the priest to lead me into the open, out of the Arti-goth patch and to walk slowly in front of me. Mr Wardle hates natives, and the priest was more afraid of Mr Wardle than of me, though we were both angry. He walked very slowly down a narrow little path from his hut. That path crossed three paths, such as the one I had come by in the first instance, and every one of the three headed towards the Bubbling Well. Once when we stopped to draw breath, I heard the Well laughing to itself alone in the thick grass, and only my need for his services prevented my firing both barrels into the priest's back.

When we came to the open the priest crashed back into cover, and I went to the village of Arti-goth for a drink. It was pleasant to be able to see the horizon all round, as well as the ground underfoot.

The villagers told me that the patch of grass was full of devils and ghosts, all in the service of the priest, and that men and women and children had entered it and had never returned. They said the priest used their livers for purposes of witchcraft. When I asked why they had not told me of this at the outset, they said that they were afraid they would lose their reward for bringing news of the pig.

Before I left I did my best to set the patch alight, but the grass was too green. Some fine summer day, however, if the wind is favourable, a file of old newspapers and a box of matches will make clear the mystery of Bubbling Well Road.

THE PICKTREE "BRAG"

MARY ARCHBOLD

"I NEVER SAW the Brag very distinctly, but I frequently heard it. It sometimes appeared like a calf, with a white handkerchief about its neck, and a bushy tail. It came also like a galloway, but more often like a coach horse, and went trotting along the lonin' afore folks, settin' up a great nicker and a whinney every now and then; and it came frequently like a 'dickass', and it always stopped at the pond at the lonin' ends and nickered and whinnied. My brother once saw it like four men holding up a white sheet. I was then sure that some near relation was going to die, which was true. My husband once saw it in the image of a naked man without a head. I knew a man, of the name of Bewick, that was so frightened that he hanged himself 'for fear on't'. Whenever the midwife was sent for, it always came up with her in the shape of a galloway. Dr Harrison wouldn't believe it; but he met it one night as he was going home, and it 'maist' killed him. He never would tell what happened, didn't like to talk about it, and whenever the Brag was mentioned, he sat 'trimilin' and shakin' by the fireside. My uncle had a white suit of clothes, and the first time he ever put them on he met the Brag, and he never had them on afterwards but he met with misfortune. Once, when he had his white suit on, he met the Brag (he had been at a christening), and being a bold sort of a man, he was determined to get on the Brag's back, but when he came to the four 'lonin' ends', the Brag 'joggled him so sore' that he could hardly keep his seat, and at last it threw him off into the middle of the pond, and then ran away, setting up a great nicker and laugh, just 'for all the world like a Christian'. But this I know to be true of my own knowledge, that when my father was dying, the Brag was heard coming up the lonin' like a coach and six, and it stood before the house, and the room 'shaked'; it gave a terrible yell when my father died, and then it went clattering and galloping down the lonin' as if 'yeven and yerth were coming together'."

A SCHOOL STORY

M. R. JAMES

TWO MEN in a smoking-room were talking of their private-school days. "At *our* school," said A., "we had a ghost's footmark on the staircase. What was it like? Oh, very unconvincing. Just the shape of a shoe, with a square toe, if I remember right. The staircase was a stone one. I never heard any story about the thing. That seems odd, when you come to think of it. Why didn't somebody invent one, I wonder?"

"You never can tell with little boys. They have a mythology of their own. There's a subject for you, by the way – 'The Folklore of Private Schools'."

"Yes; the crop is rather scanty, though. I imagine, if you were to investigate the cycle of ghost stories, for instance, which the boys at private schools tell each other, they would all turn out to be highly-compressed versions of stories out of books."

"Nowadays the *Strand* and *Pearson's*, and so on, would be extensively drawn upon."

"No doubt; they weren't born or thought of in *my* time. Let's see. I wonder if I can remember the staple ones that I was told. First, there was the house with a room in which a series of people insisted on passing a night; and each of them in the morning was found kneeling in a corner, and had just time to say, 'I've seen it,' and died."

"Wasn't that the house in Berkeley Square?"

"I dare say it was. Then there was the man who heard a noise in the passage at night, opened his door, and saw someone crawling towards him on all fours with his eye hanging out on his cheek. There was besides, let me think – Yes! the room where a man was found dead in bed with a horseshoe mark on his forehead, and the floor under the bed was covered with marks of horseshoes also; I don't know why. Also there was the lady who, on locking her bedroom door in a strange house, heard a thin voice among the bed-curtains say, 'Now we're shut in for the night.' None of those had any explanation or sequel. I wonder if they go on still, those stories."

"Oh, likely enough – with additions from the magazines, as I said. You never heard, did you, of a real ghost at a private school? I thought not; nobody has that ever I came across."

"From the way in which you said that, I gather that *you* have."

"I really don't know; but this is what was in my mind. It happened at my private school thirty odd years ago, and I haven't any explanation of it.

"The school I mean was near London. It was established in a large and fairly old house – a great white building with very fine grounds about it; there were large cedars in the garden, as there are in so many of the older gardens in the Thames valley, and ancient elms in the three or four fields which we used for our games. I think probably it was quite an attractive place, but boys seldom allow that their schools possess any tolerable features.

"I came to the school in a September, soon after the year 1870; and among the boys who arrived on the same day was one whom I took to: a Highland boy, whom I will call

McLeod. I needn't spend time in describing him: the main thing is that I got to know him very well. He was not an exceptional boy in any way – not particularly good at books or games – but he suited me.

"The school was a large one: there must have been from 120 to 130 boys there as a rule, and so a considerable staff of masters was required, and there were rather frequent changes among them.

"One term – perhaps it was my third or fourth – a new master made his appearance. His name was Sampson. He was a tallish, stoutish, pale, black-bearded man. I think we liked him: he had travelled a good deal, and had stories which amused us on our school walks, so that there was some competition among us to get within earshot of him. I remember too – dear me, I have hardly thought of it since then! – that he had a charm on his watch-chain that attracted my attention one day, and he let me examine it. It was, I now suppose, a gold Byzantine coin; there was an effigy of some absurd emperor on one side; the other side had been worn practically smooth, and he had had cut on it – rather barbarously – his own initials, G.W.S., and a date, 24 July, 1865. Yes, I can see it now: he told me he had picked it up in Constantinople: it was about the size of a florin, perhaps rather smaller.

"Well, the first odd thing that happened was this. Sampson was doing Latin grammar with us. One of his favourite methods – perhaps it is rather a good one – was to make us construct sentences out of our own heads to illustrate the rules he was trying to make us learn. Of course that is a thing which gives a silly boy a chance of being impertinent: there are lots of school stories in which that happens – or anyhow there might be. But Sampson was too good a disciplinarian for us to think of trying that on with him. Now, on this occasion he was telling us how to express *remembering* in Latin: and he ordered us each to make a sentence bringing in the verb *memini*, 'I remember'. Well, most of us made up some ordinary sentence such as

'I remember my father,' or 'He remembers his book,' or something equally uninteresting: and I dare say a good many put down *memino librum meum*, and so forth: but the boy I mentioned – McLeod – was evidently thinking of something more elaborate than that. The rest of us wanted to have our sentences passed, and get on to something else, so some kicked him under the desk, and I, who was next to him, poked him and whispered to him to look sharp. But he didn't seem to attend. I looked at his paper and saw he had put down nothing at all. So I jogged him again harder than before and upbraided him sharply for keeping us all waiting. That did have some effect. He started and seemed to wake up, and then very quickly he scribbled about a couple of lines on his paper, and showed it up with the rest. As it was the last, or nearly the last, to come in, and as Sampson had a good deal to say to the boys who had written *meminiscimus patri meo* and the rest of

it, it turned out that the clock struck twelve before he had got to McLeod, and McLeod had to wait afterwards to have his sentence corrected. There was nothing much going on outside when I got out, so I waited for him to come. He came very slowly when he did arrive, and I guessed there had been some sort of trouble. 'Well,' I said, 'what did you get?' 'Oh, I don't know,' said McLeod, 'nothing much: but I think Sampson's rather sick with me.' 'Why, did you show him up some rot?' 'No fear,' he said. 'It was all right as far as I could see: it was like this: *Memento* – that's right enough for remember, and it takes a genitive, – *memento putei inter quatuor taxos*.' 'What silly rot!' I said. 'What made you shove that down? What does it mean?' 'That's the funny part,' said McLeod, 'I'm not quite sure what it does mean. All I know is, it just came into my head and I corked it down. I know what I *think* it means, because just before I wrote it down I had a sort of picture of it in my head: I believe it means "Remember the well among the four" – what are those dark sort of trees that have red berries on them?' 'Mountain ashes, I s'pose you mean.' 'I never heard of them,' said McLeod; 'no, *I'll* tell you – yews.' 'Well, and what did Sampson say?' 'Why, he was jolly odd about it. When he read it he got up and went to the mantelpiece and stopped quite a long time without saying anything, with his back to me. And then he said, without turning round, and rather quiet, "What do you suppose that means?" I told him what I thought; only I couldn't remember the name of the silly tree: and then he wanted to know why I put it down, and I had to say something or other. And after that he left off talking about it, and asked me how long I'd been here, and where my people lived, and things like that: and then I came away: but he wasn't looking a bit well.'

"I don't remember any more that was said by either of us about this. Next day McLeod took to his bed with a chill or something of the kind, and it was a week or more before he was in school again. And as much as a month went by without anything happening that was noticeable. Whether or not Mr Sampson was really startled, as McLeod had thought, he didn't show it. I am pretty sure, of course, now, that there was something very curious in his past history, but I'm not going to pretend that we boys were sharp enough to guess any such thing.

"There was one other incident of the same kind as the last which I told you. Several times since that day we had had to make up examples in school to illustrate different rules, but there had never been any row except when we did them wrong. At last there came a day when we were going through those dismal things which people call Conditional Sentences, and we were told to make a conditional sentence, expressing a future consequence. We did it, right or wrong, and showed up our bits of paper, and Sampson began looking through them. All at once he got up, made some odd sort of noise in his throat, and rushed out by a door that was just by his desk. We sat there for a minute or two, and then – I suppose it was incorrect – but we went up, I and one or two others, to look at the papers on his desk. Of course I thought someone must have put down some nonsense or other, and Sampson had gone off to report him. All the same, I noticed that he hadn't taken any of the papers with him when he ran out. Well, the top paper on the desk was written in red ink – which no one used – and it wasn't in anyone's hand who was in the class. They all looked at it – McLeod and all – and took their dying oaths that it wasn't theirs. Then I thought of counting the bits of paper. And of this I made quite certain: that there were seventeen bits of paper on the desk, and sixteen boys in the form. Well, I bagged the extra paper, and kept it, and I believe I have it now. And now you will want to know what was written on it. It was simple enough, and harmless enough, I should have said.

"'*Si tu non veneris ad me, ego veniam ad te,*' which means, I suppose, 'If you don't come to me, I'll come to you.'"

"Could you show me the paper?" interrupted the listener.

"Yes, I could: but there's another odd thing about it. That same afternoon I took it out of my locker – I know for certain it was the same bit, for I made a finger-mark on it – and no single trace of writing of any kind was there on it. I kept it, as I said, and since that time I have tried various experiments to see whether sympathetic ink had been used, but absolutely without result.

"So much for that. After about half an hour Sampson looked in again: said he had felt very unwell, and told us we might go. He came rather gingerly to his desk, and gave just one look at the uppermost paper: and I suppose he thought he must have been dreaming: anyhow, he asked no questions.

"That day was a half-holiday, and next day Sampson was in school again, much as usual. That night the third and last incident in my story happened.

"We – McLeod and I – slept in a dormitory at right angles to the main building. Sampson slept in the main building on the first floor. There was a very bright full moon. At an hour which I can't tell exactly, but some time between one and two, I was woken up by somebody shaking me. It was McLeod; and a nice state of mind he seemed to be in. 'Come,' he said, – 'come! There's a burglar getting in through Sampson's window.' As soon as I could speak, I said, 'Well, why not call out and wake everybody up?' 'No, no,' he said, 'I'm not sure who it is: don't make a row: come and look.' Naturally I came and looked, and naturally there was no one there. I was cross enough, and should have called McLeod plenty of names: only – I couldn't tell why – it seemed to me that there *was* something wrong – something that made me very glad I wasn't alone to face it. We were still at the window looking out, and as soon as I could, I asked him what he had heard or seen. 'I didn't *hear* anything at all,' he said, 'but about five minutes before I woke you, I found myself looking out of this window here, and there was a man sitting or kneeling on Sampson's windowsill, and looking in, and I thought he was beckoning.' 'What sort of man?' McLeod wriggled. 'I don't know,' he said, 'but I can tell you one thing – he was beastly thin: and he looked as if he was wet all over: and,' he said, looking round and whispering as if he hardly liked to hear himself, 'I'm not at all sure that he was alive.'

"We went on talking in whispers some time longer, and eventually crept back to bed. No one else in the room woke or stirred the whole time. I believe we did sleep a bit afterwards, but we were very cheap next day.

"And next day Mr Sampson was gone: not to be found: and I believe no trace of him has ever come to light since. In thinking it over, one of the oddest things about it all has seemed to me to be the fact that neither McLeod nor I ever mentioned what we had seen to any third person whatever. Of course no questions were asked on the subject, and if they had been, I am inclined to believe that we could not have made any answer: we seemed unable to speak about it.

"That is my story," said the narrator. "The only approach to a ghost story connected with a school that I know, but still, I think, an approach to such a thing."

The sequel to this may perhaps be reckoned highly conventional; but a sequel there is, and so it must be produced. There had been more than one listener to the story, and, in the latter part of that same year, or of the next, one such listener was staying at a country house in Ireland.

One evening his host was turning over a drawer full of odds and ends in the smoking-room. Suddenly he put his hand upon a little box. "Now," he said, "you know about old things; tell me what that is." My friend opened the little box, and found in it a thin gold chain with an object attached to it. He glanced at the object and then took off

his spectacles to examine it more narrowly. "What's the history of this?" he asked. "Odd enough," was the answer. "You know the yew thicket in the shrubbery: well, a year or two back we were cleaning out the old well that used to be in the clearing here, and what do you supposed we found?"

"Is it possible that you found a body?" said the visitor, with an odd feeling of nervousness.

"We did that: but what's more, in every sense of the word, we found two."

"Good Heavens! Two? Was there anything to show how they got there? Was this thing found with them?"

"It was. Amongst the rags of the clothes that were on one of the bodies. A bad business, whatever the story of it may have been. One body had the arms tight round the other. They must have been there thirty years or more – long enough before we came to this place. You may judge we filled the well up fast enough. Do you make anything of what's cut on that gold coin you have there?"

"I think I can," said my friend, holding it to the light (but he read it without much difficulty); "it seems to be G.W.S., 24 July, 1865."

LA LLORONA,
THE WEEPING WOMAN

JOE HAYES

A Mexican folktale

THE STORY BEGINS long ago, when the city we call Santa Fe was a little village called La Villa Real de la Santa Fe de San Francisco de Asis. That was a long name for a tiny village. And living in that village was one girl who was far prettier than any other. Her name was María.

People said María was certainly the prettiest girl in New Mexico. She might even be the most beautiful girl in the world. But because María was so beautiful, she thought she was better than everyone else.

María came from a hardworking family, and they had one of the finest homes in Santa Fe. They provided her with pretty clothes to wear. But she was never satisfied. She thought she deserved far better things.

When María became a young woman, she would have nothing to do with the youths from Santa Fe and the nearby village. She was too good for them.

Often as she was walking with her grandmother through the countryside surrounding Santa Fe, she would say to her grandmother, *"Abuelita*, when I get married, I'll marry the most handsome man in New Mexico."

The grandmother would just shake her head. But María would look out across the hillside and go on. "His hair will be as black and shiny as the raven I see sitting on that *piñon* tree. And when he moves, he will be as strong and graceful as the stallion *Abuelito* has in his corral."

"María," the old woman would sigh, "why are you always talking about what a man looks like? If you're going to marry a man, just be sure that he's a good man. Be sure he has a good heart in him. Don't worry so much about his face."

But María would say to herself, "These old people! They have such foolish old ideas. They don't understand."

Well, one day, a man came to Santa Fe who seemed to be just the man María was talking about. His name was Gregorio. He was a cowboy from the *llano*, the plain, east of the mountains.

He could ride anything. In fact, if he was riding a horse and it got well trained, he would give it away and go rope a wild horse. He thought it wasn't manly for him to ride a horse that wasn't half wild.

He was so handsome that all the girls were falling in love with him. He could play the guitar and sing beautifully. María made up her mind. That was the man she would marry.

But she didn't let on. If they passed on the street and Gregorio greeted her, she would look away. He came to her house and played his guitar and sang. She wouldn't even come to the window.

Before long, Gregorio made up his mind. "That haughty, proud girl María," he told himself. "That's the girl I'll marry. I can win her heart!" So things turned out just as María had planned.

María's parents didn't like the idea of her marrying Gregorio. He won't make a good husband," they told her. "He's used to the wild life of the plains. He'll be gone on buffalo hunts and cattle drives, or drinking wine with his friends. Don't marry him."

42

Of course, María wouldn't listen to her parents. She married Gregorio. And for a time things were fine. They had two children.

But after a few years, Gregorio went back to his old ways. He would be gone for months at a time.

When he returned, he would say to María, "I didn't come to see you. I just want to visit my children." He would play with the children, and go off to the *cantina* to drink and gamble all night long. And he began to court other women.

As proud as María was, she became very jealous of those other women. And she began to feel jealous of her own children, as well, because Gregorio paid attention to them, but ignored her.

One evening, María was standing out in front of her house with her two children beside her when Gregorio came riding by in a hired carriage. Another woman sat on the seat beside him. He stopped and spoke to his children, but didn't even look at María. He just drove up the street.

At the sight of that, something just seemed to burst

inside María. She felt such anger and jealousy! And it all turned against her children.

She seized her two children by their arms and dragged them along with her to the river. And she threw her own children into the water.

But as they disappeared with the current, María realized what she had done. She ran along the bank of the river, reaching out her arms, as though she might snatch her children back from the current. But they were long gone.

She ran on, driven by the anger and guilt that filled her heart. She wasn't paying attention to where she was going, and her foot caught on a root. She tripped and fell forward. Her forehead struck a rock. And she was killed.

The next day her parents looked all over town for her. Then someone brought the word that her body lay out on the bank of the river.

They brought María's body back into Santa Fe, but because of what she'd done, the priest wouldn't let her be buried in the *camposanto*, the holy graveyard. "Take her out and bury her on the bank of the river!" he commanded.

So her parents buried her there on the river bank where she had been found. And many people in Santa Fe say they know exactly where she was buried, because a big building stands there today. It's called the New Mexico State Capitol!

But they also tell that the first night she was in the grave, she wouldn't rest at peace. She was up and walking along the bank of the river. They saw her moving through the trees, dressed in a long, winding white sheet, as a corpse is dressed for burial.

And they heard her crying through the night. Sometimes they thought it was the wind. But at other times they were sure they could hear the words she was saying: "*Aaaaaiii . . . mis hijos . . . ¿Donde estan mis hijos?*"

"Where are my children?" she cried. She went all up and down the banks of the river, through all the *arroyos* to the base of the mountains and back down.

Night after night they saw her and heard her. Before long, no one spoke of her as María. They called her by a name every boy and girl in New Mexico knows – *La Llorona*, the weeping woman.

And they told the children, "When it gets dark, you get home! La Llorona is out looking for her children. She's so crazy, if she sees you, she won't know if it's you or her own child. She'll pick you up and carry you away! We'll never see you again."

The children heed that warning. They may play along the rivers and *arroyos* during the daytime, but when the sun sets, they hurry home!

Many tales are told of children who narrowly escaped being caught by La Llorona. One is about a boy who didn't believe she existed.

"Do you believe that nonsense?" he would ask his friends. "That's just a story parents made up to frighten children."

One evening the boys were playing out on the bank of the river, and it began to grow late. "It's getting dark," the other boys said. "We'd better get home."

But not that one boy. "No," he said. "I'm having fun. I'll stay out here a while longer."

The other boys couldn't believe what they were hearing. "Aren't you afraid of La Llorona?"

"La Llorona!" he laughed. "There's no such thing."

The other boys went home and left that one boy by himself. He had a good time throwing sticks into the river and hitting them with rocks as they floated past. It grew dark. The moon rose.

Suddenly, the boy felt cold all over, as though an icy wind were blowing through his clothes. And all around him there were dogs barking. He looked around and saw a white shape coming toward him through the trees.

He tried to run, but somehow his legs had no strength in them. He couldn't move. He sat there trembling as the

45

shape drew nearer. And he could hear the high, wailing
voice, "*Aaaaiii . . . mis hijoooos . . .*"

Still he couldn't move. He crouched low, hoping she
wouldn't see him. But suddenly she stopped. "*Mi 'jo!*" she
cried, "my little boy!" And she came toward him.

His face was as white as the sheet that La Llorona was
wearing! But still he couldn't run. She approached him and

46

reached out her long fingers and took hold of his shoulders. When La Llorona's fingers touched his shoulders, it felt like icicles were cutting into his flesh!

Just then, when La Llorona was about to pick him up and carry him away, back in Santa Fe the cathedral bell started ringing, calling the people to Mass. When the church bell started to ring, La Llorona looked over her shoulder furtively, dropped the boy, and disappeared into the trees.

The boy sat there for a long time, gathering his strength and courage together. Finally he was able to run home.

When he got home, his mother was furious. "Where have you been?" she demanded. "You should have been home hours ago!"

The boy stuttered and stammered, "*M-M-Mama* . . . La Llorona!"

"Nonsense! Don't go making up stories about La Llorona. You should have been home a long time ago." She reached out to grab him. She was going to give him a good shaking.

But when she reached out to take hold of his shoulders, she noticed that on each shoulder there were five round, red marks – like five bloodstains. They had been left by La Lloronas fingers!

Then she believed him. She took that shirt and washed it over and over. She tried every trick she knew. But she could never remove those stains.

She carried that shirt all around the neighbourhood and showed it to the children. "Look here," she said. "You count these – one . . . two . . . three . . . four . . . five! Those stains were left by La Llorona's fingers. La Llorona can carry children away. When it gets dark, you get home!"

And you can be sure that the children in that neighbourhood got home when it got dark. But no one seems to know what became of the shirt, so who can say if the story is true?

BANG, BANG – WHO'S DEAD?

JANE GARDAM

THERE IS AN OLD HOUSE in Kent not far from the sea where a little ghost girl plays in the garden. She wears the same clothes winter and summer – long black stockings, a white dress with a pinafore, and her hair flying about without a hat, but she never seems either hot or cold. They say she was a child of the house who was run over at the drive gates, for the road outside is on an upward bend as you come to the gates of The Elms – that's the name of the house, The Elms – and very dangerous. But there were no motor cars when children wore clothes like that and so the story must be rubbish.

No grown person has even seen the child. Only other children see her. For over fifty years, when children have visited this garden and gone off to play in it, down the avenue of trees, into the walled rose-garden, or down deep under the high dark caves of the polished shrubs where queer things scutter and scrattle about on quick legs and eyes look out at you from round corners, and pheasants send up great alarm calls like rattles, and whirr off out of the wet hard bracken right under your nose. "Where've you been?" they get asked when they get back to the house.

"Playing with that girl in the garden."

"What girl? There's no girl here. This house has no children in it."

"Yes it has. There's a girl in the garden. She can't half run."

When last year The Elms came up for sale, two parents – the parents of a girl called Fran – looked at each other with a great longing gaze. The Elms.

"We could never afford it."

"I don't know. It's in poor condition. We might. They daren't ask much for such an overgrown place."

"All that garden. We'd never be able to manage it. And the house is so far from anywhere."

"It's mostly woodland. It looks after itself."

"Don't you believe it. Those elms would all have to come down for a start. They're diseased. There's masses of replanting and clearing to do. And think of the upkeep of that long drive."

"It's a beautiful house. And not really a huge one."

"And would you *want* to live in a house with—"

They both looked at Fran who had never heard of the house. "With what?" she asked.

"Is it haunted?" she asked. She knew things before you ever said them. Almost before you thought of them.

"Of course not," said her father.

"Yes," said her mother.

Fran gave a squealing shudder.

"Now you've done it," said her father. "No point now in even going to look at it."

"How is it haunted?" asked Fran.

"It's only the garden," said her mother. "And very *nicely* haunted. By a girl about your age in black stockings and a pinafore."

"What's a pinafore?"

"Apron."

49

"*Apron*. How cruddy."

"She's from the olden days."

"Fuddy-duddy-cruddy," said Fran, preening herself about in her tee-shirt and jeans.

After a while though she noticed that her parents were still rattling on about The Elms. There would be spurts of talks and then long silences. They would stand for ages moving things pointlessly about on the kitchen table, drying up the same plate three times. Gazing out of windows. In the middle of Fran telling them something about her life at school they would say suddenly, "Rats. I expect it's overrun with rats."

Or, "What about the roof?"

Or, "I expect some millionaire will buy it for a Country Club. Oh, it's far beyond us, you know."

"When are we going to look at it?" asked Fran after several days of this, and both parents turned to her with faraway eyes.

"I want to see this girl in the garden," said Fran because it was a bright sunny morning and the radio was playing loud and children not of the olden days were in the street outside, hurling themselves about on bikes and wearing jeans and tee-shirts like her own and shouting out, "Bang, bang, you're dead."

"Well, I suppose we could just telephone," said her mother. "Make an appointment."

Then electricity went flying about the kitchen and her father began to sing.

They stopped the car for a moment inside the propped-back iron gates where there stood a rickety table with a box on it labelled "Entrance Fee. One Pound."

"We don't pay an entrance fee," said Fran's father. "We're here on business."

"When I came here as a child," said Fran's mother, "We always threw some money in."

"Did you often come?"

"Oh, once or twice. Well yes. Quite often. Whenever we had visitors we always brought them to The Elms. We used to tell them about—"

"Oh yes. Ha-ha. The ghost."

"Well, it was just something to do with people. On a visit. I'd not be surprised if the people in the house made up the ghost just to get people to come."

The car ground along the silent drive. The drive curved round and round. Along and along. A young deer leapt from one side of it to the other in the green shadow, its eyes like lighted grapes. Water in a pool in front of the house came into view.

The house held light from the water. It was a long, low, creamy-coloured house covered with trellis and on the trellis pale wisteria, pale clematis, large papery early roses. A huge man was staring from the ground-floor window.

"Is that the ghost?" asked Fran.

Her father sagely, solemnly parked the car. The air in the garden for a moment seemed to stir, the colours to fade. Fran's mother looked up at the gentle old house.

"Oh – look," she said. "It's a portrait. Of a man. He seems to be looking out. It's just a painting, for goodness sake."

But the face of the long-dead seventeenth-century man eyed the terrace, the semi-circular flight of steps, the family of three looking up at him beside their motor car.

"It's just a painting."

"Do we ring the bell? At the front door?"

The half-glazed inner front door above the staircase of stone seemed the door of another shadowy world.

"I don't want to go in," said Fran. "I'll stay here."

"Look, if we're going to buy this house," said her father, "you must come and look at it."

"I want to go in the garden," said Fran. "Anyone can see the house is going to be all right."

All three surveyed the pretty house. Along the top floor of it were heavily-barred windows.

"They barred the windows long ago," said Fran's mother. "To stop the children falling out. The children lived upstairs. Every evening they were allowed to come down and see their parents for half an hour and then they went back up there to bed. It was the custom for children."

"Did the ghost girl do that?"

"Don't be ridiculous," said Fran's father.

"But did she?"

"What ghost girl?" said Fran's father. "Shut up and come and let's look at the house."

A man and a woman were standing at the end of the hall as the family rang the bell. They were there waiting, looking rather vague and thin. Fran could feel a sadness and anxiety through the glass of the wide, high door, the woman with her gaunt old face just standing; the man blinking.

In the beautiful stone hall at the foot of the stairs the owners and the parents and Fran confronted each other. Then the four grown people advanced with their hands outstretched, like some dance.

"The house has always been in my family," said the woman. "For two hundred years."

"Can I go out?" asked Fran.

"For over fifty years it was in the possession of three sisters. My three great-aunts."

"Mum – can I? I'll stay by the car."

"They never married. They adored the house. They scarcely ever left it or had people to stay. There were never any children in this house."

"Mum—"

"*Do*," said the woman to Fran. "Do go and look around the garden. Perfectly safe. Far from the road."

The four adults walked away down the stone passage. A door to the dining-room was opened. "This," said the woman, "is said to be the most beautiful dining-room in Kent."

"What was that?" asked Fran's mother. "Where is Fran?"

But Fran seemed happy. All four watched her in her white tee-shirt running across the grass. They watched her through the dining-room window all decorated round with frills and garlands of wisteria. "What a sweet girl," said the woman. The man cleared his throat and went wandering away.

"I think it's because there have never been any children in this house that it's in such beautiful condition," said the woman. "Nobody has ever been unkind to it."

"I wouldn't say," said Fran's mother, "that children were—"

"Oh, but you can tell a house where children have taken charge. Now your dear little girl would never—"

The parents were taken into a room that smelled of rose-petals. A cherry-wood fire was burning although the day

53

was very hot. Most of the fire was soft white ash. Somebody had been doing some needlework. Dogs slept quietly on a rug. "Oh, Fran would love—" said Fran's mother looking out of the window again. But Fran was not to be seen.

"Big family?" asked the old man suddenly.

"No. Just – just one daughter, Fran."

"Big house for just one child."

"But you said there had never been children in this house."

"Oh – wouldn't say never. Wouldn't say never."

Fran had wandered away towards the garden but then had come in again to the stone hall, where she stopped to look at herself in a long dim glass. There was a blue jar with a lid on a low table, and she lifted the lid and saw a heap of dried rose-petals. The lid dropped back rather hard and wobbled on the jar as if to fall off. "Children are unkind to houses,"; she heard the floating voice of the woman shepherding her parents from one room to another. Fran pulled an unkind face at the jar. She turned a corner of the hall and saw the staircase sweeping upwards and round a corner. On the landing someone seemed to be standing, but then as she looked seemed not to be there after all. "Oh yes," she heard the woman's voice. "Oh yes, I suppose so. Lovely for children. The old nurseries should be very adequate. We never go up there."

"If there are nurseries," said Fran's father, "there must once have been children."

"I suppose so. Once. It's not a thing we ever think about."

"But if it has always been in your family it must have been inherited by children?"

"Oh cousins. Generally cousins inherited. Quite strange how children have not been actually born here." Fran, who was sitting outside on the steps now in front of the open door, heard the little group clatter off along the stone pavement to the kitchens and thought, "Why are they going on about children so?"

She thought, "When they come back I'll go with them. I'll ask to see that painted man down the passage. I'd rather be with Mum to see him close."

Silence had fallen. The house behind her was still, the garden in front of her stiller. It was the moment in an English early-summer afternoon when there is a pause for sleep. Even the birds stop singing. Tired by their almost non-stop territorial squawks and cheeps and trills since dawn, they declare a truce and sit still upon branches, stand with heads cocked listening, scamper now and then in the bushes across dead leaves. When Fran listened very hard she thought she could just hear the swish of the road, or perhaps the sea. The smell of the early roses was very strong. Somewhere upstairs a window was opened and a light voice came and went as people moved from room to room. "Must have gone up the back stairs," Fran thought and leaned her head against the fluted column of the portico. It was strange. She felt she knew what the house looked like upstairs. Had she been upstairs yet or was she still thinking of going? Going. Going to sleep. Silly.

She jumped up and said, "You can't catch me. Bang, bang – you're dead."

She didn't know what she meant by it so she said it again out loud. "Bang, bang. You're dead."

She looked at the garden, all the way round from her left to her right. Nothing stirred. Not from the point where a high wall stood with a flint arch in it, not on the circular terrace with the round pond, not in the circle of green with the round gap in it where the courtyard opened to the long drive, and where their car was standing. The car made her feel safe.

Slowly round went her look, right across to where the stone urns on the right showed a mossy path behind them. Along the path, out of the shadow of the house, the sun was blazing and you could see bright flowers.

Fran walked to the other side of the round pond and looked up at the house from the courtyard and saw the portrait again looking at her. It must be hanging in a very narrow passage, she thought, to be so near to the glass. The man was in some sort of uniform. You could see gold on his shoulders and lace on his cuffs. You could see long curls falling over his shoulders. Fancy soldiers with long curls hanging over their uniform! Think of the dandruff.

"Olden days," said Fran, "Bang, bang, you're dead," and she set off at a run between the stone urns and into the flower garden. "I'll run right round the house," she thought. "I'll run like mad. Then I'll say I've been all round the garden by myself, and not seen the ghost."

She ran like the wind all round, leaping the flower-beds, tearing along a showering rose-border, here and there, up and down, flying through another door in a stone wall among greenhouses and sheds and old stables, out again past a rose-red dove-house with the doves like fat pearls set in some of the little holes, and others stepping about the grass. Non-stop, non-stop she ran, across the lawn, right turn through a yew hedge, through the flint arch at last and back to the courtyard. "Oh yes," she would say to her friends on their bikes. "I did. I've been there. I've been all round the garden by myself and I didn't see a living soul."

"A *living* soul."

"I didn't see any ghost. Never even thought of one."

"You're brave, Fran. I'd never be brave like that. Are your parents going to buy the house?"

"Don't suppose so. It's very boring. They've never had any children in it. Like an old-folks' home. Not even haunted."

Picking a draggle of purple wisteria off the courtyard wall – and pulling rather a big trail of it down as she did so – Fran began to do the next brave thing: to *walk* round the house. Slowly. She pulled a few petals off the wisteria and gave a carefree sort of wave at the portrait in the window.

In front of it, looking out of the window, stood a little girl.

Then she was gone.

For less than a flick of a second Fran went cold round the back of the neck. Then hot.

Then she realized she must be going loopy. The girl hadn't been in a pinafore and frilly dress and long loose hair. She'd been in a white tee-shirt like Fran's own. She had been Fran's own reflection for a moment in the glass of the portrait.

"Stupid. Loopy," said Fran, picking off petals and scattering them down the mossy path, then along the rosy flag-stones of the rose garden. Her heart was beating very hard. It was almost pleasant, the fright and then the relief coming so close together.

"Well, I thought I saw the ghost but it was only myself reflected in a window," she'd say to the friends in the road at home.

"Oh Fran, you are brave."

"How d'you know it was you? Did you see its face? Everyone wears tee-shirts."

"Oh, I expect it was me all right. They said there'd never been any children in the house."

"What a cruddy house. I'll bet it's not true. I'll bet there's a girl they're keeping in there somewhere. Behind those bars. I bet she's being imprisoned. I bet they're kidnappers."

"They wouldn't be showing people over the house and trying to sell it if they were kidnappers. Not while the kidnapping was actually going on, anyway. No, you can tell –" Fran was explaining away, pulling off the petals. "There wasn't anyone there but me." She looked up at the windows in the stable-block she was passing. They were partly covered with creeper, but one of them stood open and a girl in a tee-shirt was sitting in it, watching Fran.

This time she didn't vanish. Her shiny short hair and white shirt shone out clear. Across her humped-up knees lay a comic. She was very much the present day.

"It's you again," she said.

She was so ordinary that Fran's heart did not begin to thump at all. She thought, "It must be the gardener's daughter. They must live over the stables and she's just been in the house. I'll bet she wasn't meant to. That's why she ducked away."

"I saw you in the house," Fran said. "I thought you were a reflection of me."

"Reflection?"

"In the picture."

The girl looked disdainful. "When you've been in the house as long as I have," she said, "let's hope you'll know a bit more. Oil paintings don't give off reflections. They're not covered in glass."

"We won't be keeping the oil paintings," said Fran grandly. "I'm not interested in things like that."

"I wasn't at first," said the girl. "D'you want to come up?

58

You can climb over the creeper if you like. It's cool up here."

"No thanks. We'll have to go soon. They'll wonder where I am when they see I'm not waiting by the car."

"Car?" said the girl. "Did you come in a car?"

"Of course we came in a car." She felt furious suddenly. The girl was looking at her oddly, maybe as if she wasn't rich enough to have a car. Just because she lived at The Elms. And she was only the gardener's daughter anyway. Who did she think she was?

"Well take care on the turn-out to the road then. It's a dangerous curve. It's much too hot to go driving today."

"I'm not hot," said Fran.

"You ought to be," said the girl in the tee-shirt, "with all that hair and those awful black stockings."

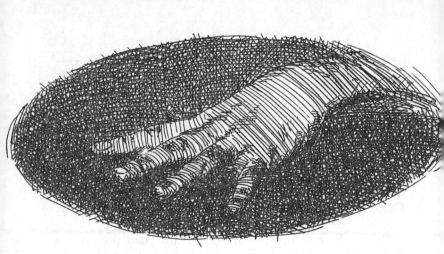

THE COLD HAND

JEROME CARDAN

Jerome Cardan, the famous physician, tells the following anecdote in his De Rerum Varietate. *Jerome only once heard a rapping himself, at the time of the death of a friend at a distance. He was in a terrible fright, and dared not leave his room all day.*

A STORY WHICH my father used often to tell: "I was brought up," he said, "in the house of Joannes Resta, and therein taught Latin to his three sons; when I left them I supported myself on my own means. It chanced that one of these lads, while I was studying medicine, fell deadly sick, he being now a young man grown, and I was called in to be with the youth, partly for my knowledge of medicine, partly for old friendship's sake. The master of the house happened to be absent; the patient slept in an upper chamber, one of his brothers and I in a lower room, the third brother, Isidore, was not at home. Each of the rooms was next to a turret; turrets being common in that city. When we went to bed on the first night of my visit, I heard a constant knocking on the wall of the room.

"'What is that?' I said.

"'Don't be afraid, it is only a familiar spirit,' said my companion. 'They call them *follets*; it is harmless enough, and seldom so troublesome as it is now: I don't know what can be the matter with it.'

"The young fellow went to sleep, but I was kept awake for a while, wondering and observing. After half an hour of stillness I felt a thumb press on my head, and a sense of cold. I kept watching; the forefinger, the middle finger, and the rest of the hand were next laid on, the little finger nearly reaching my forehead. The hand was like that of a boy of ten, to guess by the size, and so cold that it was extremely unpleasant. Meantime I was chuckling over my luck in such an opportunity of witnessing a wonder, and I listened eagerly.

"The hand stole with the ring finger foremost over my face and down my nose, it was slipping into my mouth, and two fingertips had entered, when I threw it off with my right hand, thinking it was uncanny, and not relishing it inside my body. Silence followed and I lay awake, distrusting the spectre more or less. In about half an hour it returned and repeated its former conduct, touching me very lightly, yet very chilly. When it reached my mouth I again drove it away. Though my lips were tightly closed, I felt an extreme icy cold in my teeth. I now got out of bed, thinking this might be a friendly visit from the ghost of the sick lad upstairs, who must have died.

"As I went to the door, the thing passed before me, rapping on the walls. When I was got to the door it knocked outside; when I opened the door, it began to knock on the turret. The moon was shining; I went on to see what would happen, but it beat on the other sides of the tower, and, as it always evaded me, I went up to see how my patient was. He was alive, but very weak.

"As I was speaking to those who stood about his bed, we heard a noise as if the house was falling. In rushed my bedfellow, the brother of the sick lad, half dead with terror.

"'When you got up,' he said, 'I felt a cold hand on my back. I thought it was you who wanted to waken me and take me to see my brother, so I pretended to be asleep and lay quiet, supposing that you would go alone when you found me so sound asleep. But when I did not feel you get up, and the cold hand grew to be more than I could bear, I hit out to push your hand away, and felt your place empty – but warm. Then I remembered the *follet*, and ran upstairs as hard as I could put my feet to the ground: never was I in such a fright!'

"The sick lad died on the following night."

THORNS

MARTIN WILKINSON

ONE OF MY BOOTS trod in snow and came up with a soggy tearing noise. The other sank in a mossy swamp and came out with a sentimental giant's kiss. They were both full of cold water.

It had been raining for the last nine miles, right across the hills. Behind me there were clouds, in front a valley full of mill chimneys and long low workshops, several miles away. The rain tasted of factories.

I came to a wall with no gate in it. I looked at the map and decided I wasn't anywhere at all. I began to climb the wall, then stopped. A stone fell from the top and to the far side. I waited for it to thud on wet grass. It did not. After a long time it hit another rock far down below, and then rattled further. This wall was on top of a crag, with nothing but a cliff-face beyond.

I turned left and plodded on. The wall seemed to go on for ever. I began to be colder and colder. And I began to feel something under the sole of my right foot. At first I thought it was imaginary; then it seemed to be grit; then that my woollen sock was matting up. At last I decided a nail was coming up out of the boot. I sat on a sticking-out piece of wall and took the boot off, wet laces spitting, the boot hard as a stone, the sock like a limpet, not wanting to come off.

I found nothing, no lump, no sharpness, no nail, only the straight stocking stitch, the smooth leather of my walking boots, the horny surface of my sole – no tenderness or blister.

But when I stood up the pain in my foot turned to fire. But at last I was going downhill, into the head of a small valley. My foot hurt all the time. There was snow in the gill and I slid on it, sat on it, rolled in it and scratched my face.

When I got up I came on the house, all at once and hardly believing it. There were four bright windows, and an open door with a warm fire inside – put there to rescue me, I knew.

In a second the welcome faded. This was only the front wall of a house, with gaping windows and door, the last glisten of sunset through those openings fading to drear moorland again.

But there is always a road to a house, and I followed between its walls until I came to a barbed wire fence blocking it. I climbed the wall to one side, and climbed it back again. On the far side of the wire a notice said, PRIVATE, THORNS FARM. It was faded but quite clear. I read it without difficulty.

Below it, in the coils of wire, was another notice a few inches high, a little post with a board on it. I bent to read that too. It was slightly self-luminous, the lettering densely black and distinct against the moony background.

The letters were unknown to me. But I was fascinated. I pulled up the little notice on its post, and stowed it in my pocket. It was the size of a postcard altogether.

A minute later I was on a tarmac road, and two minutes after that a bus came lumbering along, with a dull English word shining on the front. BATWORTH, it read, and Batworth is good enough for any man on a wet night.

When I sat down in the smoky light and bought a ticket, I realized that I had been silly about the notice. After all there are a million children in Yorkshire, and one of them had wrought this little sign for some mysterious purpose of his own.

I stayed at the Crown Inn. On my feet I wore a pair of large slippers belonging to the landlord, and a strip of plaster. I was alone in the dining-room, and no one else was to come, said the landlord, shaking his head at me for being here at all.

After my meal I brought the boot to the fire and began looking for the nail.

"It's a problem, is a real boot," said the landlord, bringing me a tacklifter to pull the nail. "Stands to reason it has to be leather you can nail to. Owt else is too soft."

Then his voice hardened. He had picked up the little notice I had, well, stolen. He examined it as if it were not only rare, but strange as well. "Have you looked at this?" he demanded. "Where did you come by it?"

I had to show him on the map, as well as I could for someone who had been lost at the time. But some mixture of excitement and fear made him unable to read it. "You just take a look," he said, his hands shaking with his feelings. He handed the notice back to me. "Look at it," he repeated.

I looked. The thing was queerer than I had thought. I expected a slip of wood, and another for the little post. But not this sort of wood. The thing was one piece, but woven from raw twigs, the bark removed except for the lettering. The patterning of the small stems was clear to my eyes, and could be felt by my fingers. It was like a compressed miniature forest. It was not only queer, but knew it was; it was not here alone, and someone or something else knew where it was. It was looking at me as much as I was looking at it.

"You could tell this wasn't made by men," said the landlord.

"Children, I thought," I said feebly. But I knew I was wrong before I met his glance of scorn.

"There are things out of human nature," he said. "I'll get the car out. There's other folk want to hear of this."

There was just room in the car for me, because the back seat had been filled with five spare wheels.

We went this way and that, among steep streets, as if we were lost again. "It won't put them off the track," he said, mysteriously. "It's just the best road."

We walked in at the door of an untidy cobbler's shop, no shoes to sell, only shoes to mend, tied in loose pairs, unlabelled. The cobbler himself came out from the back unconcerned.

"Jack," he said, through his ragged moustache, sitting on a stool behind a treadle machine.

"Fast wi' a nail," said the landlord, handing over the boot.

The cobbler felt round inside with a hand. "Not while Tuesday," he said. "There's that much on."

"Best look now," said the landlord. "It's one of them."

The cobbler looked. He held the boot up to a small electric bulb and eyed the inside. "Aye," he said.

"It's thy grandfather," said the landlord. "But this man found it, and summat else, so you'll have to tell."

The cobbler's tale was simple. About a hundred years before, the cobbler's grandfather had taken a hill farm for five years. The first year was well enough, but in the second the grass was short and they were light of hay and cheese, and the wife and new child were sickly. The third year was worse, and during its winter the farmer knew he had trouble. He had neighbours. Someone else was living in the end of the house with the cows.

His cows were part milked before he got to them. His store of oatmeal was being taken. Time and again he heard voices and the sounds of feet going on the flags, or overhead on the balks where the hay stood. He found little cheeses he had never made. His wife laughed at him for trying to make his tales appear true by such tricks.

One day when he was spreading his fields he heard voices over the wall. In a small field beyond stood a group of tiny people, gathered like leaves, but with hands and faces and voices, round a fire. Some were sitting and sewing, some were tending ponies like rabbits, some were leading cows like kittens.

The cloth they were stitching came from his baby's cot. The pot on the fire was a kitchen measure his wife had lost. The tiny saddles were made from red leather bought to cover a stool but mislaid. The cows were led with ropes made from his own market-day socks.

Seeing this, he did the wrong thing. He shouted over the wall, and scolded them, then climbed over and jumped down among them, not thinking what he was doing.

He hurt one or two of them, just by being so clumsy, not with a bad intent. But it made them ugly. They pulled

67

away their injured and scrambled into the wall, but for one red cow that hid under the thistles.

When they were safe, they unslung their bows and fired their arrows at him. There was something on the arrows that blinded him for the time, and made him so daft with dizziness he fell down. After a time he could not move at all.

He felt them walking about on him, going into his pockets, pulling his beard, listening to the slow thump of his heart. He saw nothing, because his eyes could not open.

A pair of them pulled his lids up, and there on his chest were some old ones, one of them the leader.

"We were here first," he said. "You and your kind will pay the rent for ever." The rent was to be one thousand nails, which the farmer would know when he saw, and feel before that. When a thousand nails were gathered, men could have the farm again.

And that was that. His eyes closed once more, and some time towards night he was able to move and go in.

At the end of the fourth year he and his wife moved away, abandoning all they had put into the farm. A hundred years later it stood with three walls fallen. It was, of course, Thorns Farm.

The cobbler operated with a cobbling tool and lifted the nail. It was not a nail but a wooden splinter or spell.

"This is what they meant," he said. "These are the rent." He reached behind him for a leather bag. He drew the mouth open and dropped the nail in. It was a delicate white thing, one end touched with my blood.

"Go through owt, them thorns," said the landlord. "How many is it?"

"Four hundred, three score, and twain," the cobbler said slowly. "A bit to go yet."

"We're cousins," said the landlord, when we were on the way again. "We're all cousins here. A few thorns turn up each year. When we have the thousand we'll get the land back, that's all."

It took us some time to get to our destination, because we had two flat tyres on the way. "Yours is not the only one, sithee," said the landlord. "It's how we get most of them. All the garages know to look out for them."

We had left Batworth for the open countryside again, and in the middle of it we stopped. Far away the glow of town lights was luminous in fog, without giving me anything to see by. I borrowed a box of matches and carried out my errand.

I found the barbed wire across the lane by walking into it. I struck a match and found the name of the farm, and by the glare of the next one the very place I had pulled the notice from.

I stood it in there. The match went out. I turned and walked away, shuffling in the landlord's slippers. Behind me a diminutive hammer tapped the notice into place again.

"Happen we'll say nowt," said the landlord as we drove back.

A LESSON

ELIZABETH GARNER

H E WAS TRYING to teach them Geography – or so he said. He drew on the globe a black dot. It marked a town in Australia.

The town on the other side of the world plunged into darkness. No match would strike. No fire could burn. In terrified blindness they all reached for the modern reassurance of electricity. The switches gave nothing. Together they rushed to their television sets and turned them on.

Blank.

There was nothing; not even a dancing fog of black and white dots. Only a silent, menacing darkness.

They tried to tune their radios to hear some sound other than their own.

Silence.

The speakers hissed at them.

They thought that it was the end of the world.

*

He was trying to teach them Geography – or so he said. He spun the globe faster and faster.

Words which marked time were soon forgotten. Lifetimes dwindled to a passing moment.

Their suffering did not last long. They became accustomed to the dank silence which grew over them. They each held their own dark close.

He stopped the globe.

Time waited for him.

He wiped the black dot clean and placed the globe on the table.

On the other side of the world the sun shone through the town. The radios spewed loud music. Brightly-coloured figures leered at them from their television screens. These sudden noises attacked them all.

They felt it was the end of their world.

He looked up and saw that the classroom was empty. He thought it was some childish prank. He stood up sharply, in his anger knocking over the globe. It fell and shattered into a thousand pieces.

MAGICIANS OF THE WAY

CYRIL BIRCH

A Chinese legend

BUDDHIST PRIESTS shave their heads. But often in a Chinese painting you will see a man, perhaps seated in meditation, whose pious attitude contrasts with his ragged clothes and the mass of unkempt hair on his head. He also will be a holy man, but of the Taoist belief, one who follows the Way or *Tao* of the ancient sage Lao Tzu. Many such men believed that by purifying themselves, or by eating magic herbs or concocting some secret pill or elixir, they could increase their power far beyond the limits of the ordinary human body. Perhaps some of them did so. At any rate, ordinary people heard enough stories about them to believe them the most skilful magicians in the land.

There was the matter of sleep, for instance. A Taoist named Ch'en T'uan, realizing that sleep strengthened both body and mind, set himself to perfect the art. He holds the world record with a sleep of eight hundred years. But he was not always left undisturbed for so long. He lived in seclusion on a mountain called T'ai-hua-shan. One day he was seen to go down the mountain, and although several months passed he did not return. Other holy men who lived on the mountain told themselves that he had gone to live elsewhere, and returned to their meditations.

Winter drew on, and the stocks of firewood that had been made ready against the cold began to dwindle. The day came when one man was nearing the end of the pile in his woodshed. He took hold of a long thin log and pulled – and discovered that he was grasping a human leg! Horrified, he removed the remaining logs from the top. Then he roared with laughter – to see Ch'en T'uan sit up, rub his eyes, stretch himself and begin to brush the shavings from his person.

On another day, much later, a farmer was scything grass for hay on the lower slope of the mountain. He came to a break in the ground where the dried-up gully of a stream ran down, and there in the gully he was saddened to see a corpse lying. "Poor fellow," thought the farmer, and he stooped to take a closer look. Grass and weeds were growing in the soil which had drifted on to the body, and a lark had built its nest between the feet. The farmer was moved to pity. He decided that he would bring a cart to take the corpse away and give it a decent burial. But at this point Ch'en T'uan woke up. Opening wide his eyes he said, "I was just enjoying a most pleasant nap. Who is this that has disturbed me?"

The farmer recognized the great sage of the mountain. He apologized most humbly for having spoilt the master's rest, and then returned to his scything while Ch'en T'uan strolled slowly off to breakfast.

Liu Ken was a man who devoted himself to Taoism on the mountain Sung-shan. There he acquired many marvellous powers. One of his discoveries was the secret of youth. It was said that when he was over a hundred years old he looked like a boy of fifteen.

Nor did he benefit himself alone. Once a plague broke out in the city of Ying-chuan. Not even the family of the Governor himself was spared. But fortunately the

Governor had a high regard for the Way, and when he heard that Liu Ken was in the vicinity he sought his help. Liu Ken at once gave him a piece of paper bearing strangely-written characters. It was a charm, which the Governor must paste on the door of his residence at night. The Governor did so: and when morning came, not one member of his family showed any further trace of the dread disease.

But before long Ying-chuan had a change of Governor. The new man, an official named Chang, was very different from his predecessor. He sneered when his subordinates told him of the deeds of Liu Ken. When they persisted with their stories Chang grew angry. He determined to show up this man of marvels, and sent out runners to arrest him. News of this spread quickly through the city. When the runners left the Governor's residence they found the streets blocked by indignant crowds. They themselves had little heart for their task and turned back. But the Governor, nothing daunted, sent troops to break through the crowd and bring Liu Ken to court for questioning.

At length Liu Ken, barefoot and in rags, stood below the gilded chair of the Governor. The court had been cleared of all but the troops, who looked on impassively, determined not to risk their necks by crossing their stern superior. The Governor leant down and addressed Liu Ken in a voice of thunder.

"Are you a magician?" he roared.

Liu Ken's reply showed neither pride nor deference. Calmly he answered, "Yes."

"Can you bring down the spirits from the Next World?" the Governor continued.

"I can."

The Governor was delighted. This was really too easy. This charlatan had fallen straight into his trap. Louder than ever he roared, "Then let me see some spirits, now in this very court, or you will be punished as an impostor and a swindler."

Liu Ken glanced to one side, where lay the instruments already prepared for his punishment: the boards for squeezing his ankles, the heavy bamboo rod with which he would be beaten. Then he turned back to the Governor, who was amazed to observe a quiet smile on the holy man's face.

"Nothing could be easier," said Liu Ken softly. He asked for brush, ink-slab and paper. When a guard had passed them to him he made a few deft strokes on the paper, which he took over to a brazier and committed to the flames. No sooner had the last corner of the paper blackened than the court was filled with the din of trampling hooves and the clatter of armour. The wall at the far end of the court had swung open, to admit a great troop of riders armed with swords and spears. They crowded, four or five hundred of them, into the hall. Then their ranks parted, to reveal a cart in which knelt the two prisoners they were escorting.

Liu ordered the prisoners to be brought out of the cart and led up to the Governor. One was an old man, the other clearly his wife. The old man raised his head and addressed the Governor in tones of stern reproof:

"To think that you, our son, should have brought such disgrace upon us! Do you think your duty to us ended with our death? Or that you can give offence to a holy man without involving us also in your punishment? How can you dare to look us, your dead parents, in the face?"

Ashen-faced, the Governor hastened down from his seat and fell to his knees, weeping, before Liu Ken. He begged him to have mercy, to release his parents.

Liu Ken gave an order, and the Governor looked up to find the court empty save for the holy man and the guards. The far wall was as solid and substantial as ever it had been. And never again did the Governor Chang venture to doubt the powers of those who follow the Way.

Another magician who came up against the authorities was a Taoist named Tso Tz'u, who played a whole series of tricks on the august Duke of Wei. It all began when Tso Tz'u was walking one day along a highway and saw coming towards him a string of a dozen or so coolies, each one laden with a huge basket. Straw packing covered the top of each basket. Tso Tz'u stopped the little procession.

"What have you got in those baskets?" he asked.

"Oranges for the Duke of Wei," answered the leading porter.

"Oranges!" exclaimed Tso Tz'u. "How nice for the Duke! But what heavy loads for you poor fellows! Let me help you a little of the way." And so saying he took the basket from the leading coolie and hoisted it on to his own back. He carried it for a mile or so, then returned it to the first coolie and took over the load of the second. In this way he went right down the line. Now every porter when he received his load back found it lighter than before, and each wondered whether this was merely because of the rest he had had, or whether the Taoist had worked some magic charm for his benefit. When Tso Tz'u had reached the end of the line he took his leave of them, and in due course they reached the Duke's palace and delivered the oranges into the storehouse.

A day or two later the Duke held a small banquet for some visiting noblemen. When all the rich dishes had been disposed of, servants brought in silver dishes laden with luscious golden fruit, and the Duke turned to his guests, "A rare pleasure, gentlemen! Sweet oranges, freshly brought from the south!"

The mouths of the guests watered as they contemplated the glowing golden fruit. But the first guest to cut one open with the silver knife he was given gaped in dismay – for inside the inviting skin was nothing but empty air. He cast a furtive glance towards the smiling Duke, and wondered fearfully what kind of malice such an insult as this might portend. Then to his surprise he noticed his neighbour looking up in exactly the same way, and then—

"Ancestors bear witness!" roared the Duke in a voice which set all the silver rattling on the tables. "STEWARD!"

The Duke cursed the steward and his ancestors, and the steward cursed the storekeeper and *his* ancestors, and the storekeeper sought out the chief porter and cursed him and *his* ancestors: for every single one of the whole consignment of oranges was nothing but an empty skin.

Well, of course, the chief porter realized that here was the explanation of the lightness of the loads after Tso Tz'u had carried them for a while, and he told the storekeeper who told the steward who told the Duke that it was all Tso Tz'u's doing. And in no time at all the Duke had Tso Tz'u arrested and thrown into a tiny cell in the state prison.

"He has fed enough at my expense," said the Duke. "There is no need to feed him any more."

And so Tso Tz'u was left to languish and die, and the Duke forgot all about him. He was reminded of the incident only after a year had passed, when one of his earlier guests paid a new visit and asked what punishment had befallen the mischievous Taoist.

"To be sure," said the Duke, "it's time his body was taken out and burned." And he gave orders that this should be done.

But when they lifted the bars and opened the door of the cell, what should meet their eyes but the sight of Tso Tz'u, rapt in meditation, but as ruddy-cheeked and firmly fleshed as ever he had been!

They hardly dared to report their finding to the Duke. But he was not a mean-minded man, and he realized that this was no common malefactor he was dealing with. He gave orders for Tso Tz'u's release and invited him to a dinner. At the end of the dinner Tso Tz'u announced that he was going away, and suggested that the Duke and he should drink a parting cup together. He took a cup of wine and asked for a pin. With the pin he drew a line across the middle of the wine. The wine split down the middle into two portions, which remained separate. Tso Tz'u drank off his portion and handed the Duke the cup, one side of which was still full of wine. But the Duke feared some fresh mischief and would not drink. Tso Tz'u then cheerfully drank up the rest of the wine, and threw up the empty goblet. It did not fall at once, but soared and hovered like a bird below the ceiling of the hall. Everyone watched in astonishment: and when they looked down again, no sign of Tso Tz'u was to be seen.

The tale of these wonders began to spread among the people of Wei, and the Duke grew uneasy at the thought of fresh mishaps that might occur. He regretted his leniency in releasing Tso Tz'u, and gave orders for him to be re-arrested. Soldiers scoured the countryside in search of him. At last a party of troops came across him on a hillside. When Tso Tz'u saw them coming he ran off up the hill. Just above him a flock of sheep were grazing. The soldiers watched him run and started in pursuit. But suddenly, there was no old Taoist to be seen.

"Vanished into thin air," said the captain of the soldiers

in disgust. With pursed lips he surveyed the drifting sheep. Then inspiration seized him. He strode over to a rock on which lay, dozing in the sun, the shepherd of the flock. This man scrambled to his feet as the captain addressed him.

"How many sheep are in your flock?"

"Sixty-nine, sir,"

"Are you sure?" asked the captain.

"Sure? Of course I'm sure. There's Bosseye, and Shaggy, and Twirlyhorn, and Flatnose, and ..."

"I don't want to know all the family!" shouted the captain. "But we'll see whether you've still got sixty-nine – or seventy!"

And he ordered his men to count them. Unfortunately the sheep wouldn't stand still or form fours to be counted. There were sixteen men in the party, and the captain was given sixteen totals, between forty-two and ninety-three. In desperation he appealed to the shepherd, who was looking on with a grin like a split watermelon. The shepherd gave one glance at the flock, then started in surprise.

"You're right, Captain," he said. "There's seventy there. Now who's this come along all uninvited?"

"I know very well who it is," said the captain. He turned to address the flock. "Mr Taoist," he said, "I do urge you to come along with me. The Duke, my master, is waiting to welcome you."

There in the middle of the flock, one of the sheep knelt down on the grass and bleated, "Can I really believe that?"

"That's him," said the soldiers. They w 'e just making after him – when every sheep in the flock knelt down and bleated, "Can I really believe that?"

Not wishing to arrest the whole flock, and not at all sure that he would have Tso Tz'u even then, the captain gave up his hopeless task and led his men away.

A HAUNTED TERRACE

WILLIAM MAYNE

WE LIVE IN a good house, but only at the top. There's one thing about a flat: you don't get noticed every time you go out of the front door, because you might be somebody from the other two flats, so I can slip in and say goodnight and then go out again. Roger didn't have to be at home until an hour after me, and then I would go in again very quiet, and be looking asleep when Mum came in to see about the window being open and that awful yellow convent dress being hung up, because it had to last a week, and wasn't made of drip-dry or non-crease, which wouldn't have cost more, but would have been twice as useful.

I ought to say about the house. It's the end one of a very long row, and right at the other end Jennifer lives. She's in the fourth form with me, and about thirty more, but they don't matter for now, though they do at school because of their way of knowing too much and getting above me. Of course, they haven't got Roger to fuss over, which I have when they're swotting, but Roger needs that much looking after, you wouldn't believe, though I only took him out of kindness when he had that purple on his face to cure his skin which he got from his sister, so he calls her his skin and blister, instead, rhyming, which is his way of talking. He comes from London, because his father's with the Admiralty down here, and he hasn't much to do with this I'm telling you, so I won't say anything about him. I'm not really going steady with him, he's only my second, and you don't want a steady until about your fourth.

Jennifer lives the other end of the terrace, but it isn't a straight row. We don't go much for straight rows in Bath, not in the good houses. Ours is good, and you see pictures of it on calendars, for beauty. It was built two hundred years ago, but the rooms are quite big and high, not like cottages. The row goes in a curve, part of a circle, with sixty houses in it, and there aren't any opposite, only the Royal Terrace Gardens. The houses are the Royal Terrace, and the man that built them was called Wood. I remember his name because it's ours too, but he wasn't related to us. I mean, we weren't alive then.

That's the explanation of it, but I'll say what happened. I went in one night, just on nine, but a bit after, and Mum said, "You're late, Margaret."

I wish she'd called me Leigh or Gabrielle, not Margaret, past its sell-by date. "Only just," I said. "I think I've left something downstairs." I really meant I wanted to go down and tell Roger I'd been caught, but Mum knew.

"He can stay down," she said. "And you can stay up."

I said, "If I can stay up, why can't I go out again?"

"I mean you can stay upstairs," said Mum. "Off to bed."

She said she'd hung up that dress, too, which I wouldn't wear outside in case Bonzo heard of me. She's the head of the convent and she wouldn't see me herself, but Mrs White could have, unless I was in my jeans and my hair different. I pretended not to know her once, and she looked at me for lipstick the next day, but I'd got it off, so she thought she was wrong.

This night I went into my bedroom. It's at the front, and I looked out of the window, and Roger was there about an inch high on the road. Mum was still on the landing, so I leaned out of the window to stop her hearing and talked to Roger. I thought the sound wouldn't get back up, because there's a ledge under the window, and I got my chin below it. Roger thought I would fall out, but I didn't. I talked to him for a bit, and he said, "See you tomorrer, ugly horrer," which is what we say, and I said, "After tea, bumble bee," which is what I say, but we made it up, and you aren't supposed to know if you're not us two.

Then Mum began to come in, so I did too, and Roger went away, because he's a bit shy about Mum, because he lives in a square prefab, and our house is better – Regency, he says. He's quite clever in some ways, but I don't always know what he means. I'd rather have a prefab and get out of the window.

In the morning I met that Jennifer, and she said, "After tea, bumble bee," so I gave her one with my satchel, because she must have been listening in the Royal Terrace Gardens. She said she hadn't, and blamed me for talking under her window, so I gave her another for telling a lie, because she must have been in the Gardens. I think she was jealous because her Miles, or whatever his name was, was with a Comprehensive girl in Bathwick, and I don't blame him, but I don't know how she could be jealous of Roger, and he isn't a treat, and such a bother to get tidy before I'll go with him.

But I had to think something different a day or two later. It wasn't quite dark when I went to bed, because of the summer, and I was just looking at the ceiling, when somebody said my name, like Samuel in the temple, which we did in non-Catholic R.I. You would think you were dreaming to hear that. I did, so I thought I would swallow my tongue and choke if I was lying on my back any more and going to sleep. You might. So I turned over and shut my eyes, and somebody said, "Margaret," again, like the

Forsaken Merman, whose wife was called that, only she was human. So am I, of course, so I sat up and said, "Mum, did you call me?"

She said she hadn't, have you hung up that dress? Well, I did that, and put the light out again, because the summer wasn't lasting that long, and said the window was open, and went to bed again, but it wasn't any use, because somebody said, "Margaret," again.

It wasn't Roger, unless his voice had unbroken again. It was very broken just then, and he could sing in two voices if he liked, if you could call it singing. He could do it separately or together, but he couldn't talk except deep, with squeaks.

Anyway, I got the idea it came from the window, so I went to it and listened, without looking out, and whoever it was said it again. It sounded as if it came from just outside in the air, but nobody was there, of course. So I looked out, and the voice said, "Hello."

Nobody was there, even in the Gardens, but I couldn't be certain, they might have been, but the voice didn't sound as if it came from down below at all, it was just by me. I shut the window down and bolted it and drew the curtains and got well into bed, and got as hot as butter and just as sticky. I didn't like it.

Next day I asked Roger if he'd done it, but he said no, cross his horse and cart, which is heart, and slit his pearly, which he says is London for throat, only he says froat. I kept that window closed for another night, but it was too hot the next, and I thought I might have been dreaming, and then I thought of Joan of Arc, and you never know, it might be like Samuel, because it must be true if it's in R.I., even if in non-Catholic. So I thought I ought to listen, in case, except if they wanted me to be a nun I wouldn't because I can't wear black, except the jeans.

Well, it came again, and I got to the window at once. There was nothing to see at all, only the gasworks beyond the road the other side of the Gardens, and even that wasn't easy to see because of the sun setting behind it. It shone into all the terrace. It shone in my room last of all, which made it the hottest of them. The voice came whispering out again. I thought it might be someone in the next window, but it wasn't, they just had high-class music on a catapult or whatever it's called.

"Margaret," said the voice. Then it said, "I am going to haunt you."

"You'd better not," I said, because I didn't want it to, feeling daft talking to all these classical notes pinging out of the window.

"I shall," it said, the voice not the posh music. "My little bumble bee."

There was nobody in sight at all. Not even anyone walking about anywhere. At least, there was one person, and I noticed her by her colour. It was Jennifer, hanging out of her window, but her house is the other end of the terrace, and she was up near the sunset. I knew her by her hair, which is the red sort people are proud of, and don't let you call red, but urban or something, like the city council dust carts, but not in colour because they are green.

I put the window down again and sweated to death under the blankets again. I would rather do that than be haunted.

The next night I thought there must be somebody, so I put Roger in the Gardens when I came in. Mum was pleased to see me so early, but I didn't get undressed, I only waited after I'd put the light out. It sort of needs a light to go to bed by, even if it isn't dark. I told Roger to look out for people, and when the voice came again, just saying, "Margaret," I waved to him, and he began to look. But there was no one there.

I leaned out quickly and told him to look everywhere. But he didn't see anyone; and before I had waved goodbye to him the voice said, "There is no one to be seen, I am a ghost, little bumble bee."

Jennifer was looking out of her window again, so I didn't

want to look a fool standing at my window watching the sunset, so I sat inside, still dressed, because clothes make you braver.

The voice said, "I will haunt you, Margaret," and then it said, "Ow," as if it had got hit, and stopped. Then there was a sort of thump, like my window being closed, and I thought the voice must belong to my room now it was closing the window, and there wasn't any escape. But my window was open, and I didn't dare touch it, or even look at it. But nothing else happened that night when I was awake, or come in a dream when I was asleep.

The next day Jennifer wasn't at school, I noticed, because I was going to ask her whether she had heard the voice too. She might have been at her window listening like me. I thought I might go round after and see whether she had. She might have been haunted ill, I thought, seeing she wasn't there, and I thought it might happen to me. It might have begun.

At dinner time somebody bought a paper, and they brought it to me and showed me a bit, and there was the voice, printed down, Mysterious Haunting of Royal Terrace By Disembodied Voice, which means it wasn't the voice of someone there, like a ghost, and it said numerous residents had heard it and numerous is more than one so I wasn't the only one, and I didn't mind any more.

I got to keep the paper. I showed it to Roger, and he didn't know what disembodied meant either and he sort of thought it might be artificial which was worse than a natural ghost. He doesn't know a thing. He'd been tattooing himself with Quink, and he looked as if he had the purple stuff on him again.

When he had gone I listened again, and when the voice came, this time all along the terrace, people looked out, which I thought was odd, to have such a long voice. It hadn't said more than "Margaret" once, when there was a great noise like a crowd talking, and they began to say, "It's that girl at the end," and the people began to leave the windows and come down into the road; so I got the door open and came down too.

The people were all going to the other end, so I went too. They went right along, and looked up, and there was Jennifer, with that hair, hung out of the window without noticing us down there at all, talking to herself, saying, "Margaret, I will haunt you, my little bumble bee," and stuff like that, until someone in the crowd of us said, "Hey, can't you be quiet, we can hear you all along the row."

Jennifer heard that, and hopped in at once and put the window down. Mr Mortimer, who lives in the middle, with a whole house to himself, went up to their flat, and in a little while he came down and stood on the steps with his hand up for silence, and he told us how voices went round curved buildings, like the Whispering Gallery in St Paul's in London, and it wasn't a haunting but a foolish schoolgirl talking to her friend at the other end of the Terrace. He meant me, at the other end, but I'm not a friend of Jennifer.

Actually, people don't live in churches, they just die there, look at the Abbey, all the tablets on the walls, Roger says, they should have kept on taking their tablets.

I told Jennifer next day she was a foolish schoolgirl, but she was still puffed up at having found out about voices going round curves before anyone else, because she had heard me talking down to Roger, which was how she knew about the bumble bee. Then I got her bang in the breath with my satchel and it's the last I heard.

I asked Roger about Whispering Galleries, but he said he had never been up there because of the apples and pears, which is London for stairs. He's no use at knowing anything. Also he is too inquisitive about Jennifer, and I might give him up.

But I'll be able to hear what they say.

THE WALKING BOUNDARY STONE

SORCHE NIC LEODHAS

A Scottish folktale

THERE ONCE WERE two old crofters named Jamie MacNab and Rab MacRae, whose farms lay alongside of each other. Each of these old fellows had a good flock of sheep, good fields for growing corn and for grazing, and a good sound house. Each of them also had a good wife and a good son, and since they were hard-working and thrifty, they didn't lack for a bit of gold and gear. Neither of them could boast of having more than the other, so neither of them had any reason to wish himself in the other's shoes. For that reason, they were the best of friends.

Where their lands met at the high road there was a huge square stone. Half of the stone was on Rab MacRae's land and the other half on Jamie MacNab's, so the middle of it marked where one farm left off and the other one began. Both the MacNabs and the MacRaes were uncommonly proud of the stone, each family owning half of it, as you might say. It was terribly ancient, having been there since the beginning of time, and it had always belonged to MacNabs and MacRaes. Everybody called it the Boundary Stone.

When the day's work was over, if the weather was fine, the two old crofters liked to walk down to the road in the gloaming and sit on the stone, each on his own side. Maybe they'd talk, or maybe they'd just sit there quiet and peaceful-like, but it gave them great satisfaction.

Well, in time the two old crofters died and were laid away to rest in the churchyard down over the hill. Their two good sons took over, and now they each had the good flock of sheep and the good fields and the good sound house, all of which was left them by their fathers. And each of them had a good wife and a good son, both of which they'd got for themselves.

Their two young lads were called Young Jamie MacNab and Young Rab MacRae, both having been named after their grandsires.

Of course, the two old crofters' sons each had their half of the Boundary Stone. They worked hard and laid a bit by, and they took their rest together of a fine evening on the stone just as their fathers had done before them. They, too, grew old and died and were laid away to rest in the churchyard down over the hill.

Then it was the turn of Young Jamie MacNab and Young Rab MacRae to take over. Both of them were as good lads as you'd hope to find in a long day's journey. They were as hard-working and thrifty as the MacNabs and MacRaes had ever been, and they'd been friends since they were born. With all that, and the example of their fathers and their grandsires to guide them, all should have gone well.

Now 'tis a sure thing that when trouble comes between two friends it is always a third person sets it going, and so it was in this case. The cause of the trouble, strange enough, was the Boundary Stone.

It all started when Young Jamie MacNab met old Sandy MacBean by the stone one morn. Jamie was out looking for a teg that had strayed away from the rest of his sheep when old Sandy hailed him.

Jamie was in a terrible hurry to find the teg, but Sandy

was such an old man that Jamie paid him the courtesy of waiting a bit. After they had passed the time of day and talked of this and that old Sandy said, "A-well, Jamie, I see someone's been shiftin' the old Boundary Stone."

Jamie took a look at the stone. "'Tis as it was, far as I can see," said he.

"Nay, Jamie," old Sandy said stubbornly. "I'm pushin' ninety year, and I'm tellin' ye that stone should be closer to the burn by twenty foot. My memory's as long as my years, and there's little I've forgot. 'Tis so the stone was in your grandsire's day and 'tis so it should be now."

Jamie looked at the stream, and then he took another look at the stone. "Maybe so," he said doubtfully. "Happen 'twould be the road menders moved it. I never gave heed to it." After all, Jamie thought, Sandy MacBean was very likely right. He was a great hand at remembering things everyone else forgot. "I'll get an ox and a chain and shift it back," said Jamie.

Now Sandy MacBean did have a prodigious memory, but what slipped his mind this time was the great storm which swept over Scotland before Young Jamie was ever born. It wasn't the stone that had been shifted, but the stream. The heavy rains had cut a new bed for it beyond the old one and left the stone high and dry and full twenty feet away. Sandy MacBean forgot that entirely. Down there was the burn and up here was the stone, and they ought to be together. That's what old Sandy MacBean said.

Sandy MacBean went off, terribly pleased with the wonderful memory he had, and Jamie fetched the ox and the chain and hauled the stone down the road until it was twenty feet closer to the stream.

That night, when the two friends met by the road, Young Rab MacRae let out a whistle. "Losh!" he cried in surprise. "Who's been shifting the stone then?"

"'Twas me," said Jamie.

"What way would you do so?" asked Rab.

"Sandy MacBean said it was always down there near the

stream," Jamie told him. "The road menders must have shifted it."

"But 'tis over on my land now," Rab protested.

"That it isn't," said Jamie. "'Tis between your land and mine."

"'Tis not!" said Rab. "'Tis on my land and I'll take it kindly if you'll shift it back again!"

"I'll not do it!" shouted Jamie. "Sandy MacBean says ..."

"The de'il take old Sandy MacBean!" Rab shouted right back to him. "I'll shift it back my own self!"

So the two of them turned their backs to each other and walked away. Rab went and got one of his oxen and a chain and shifted the stone up the road to where it was in the first place.

After that, Rab MacRae shifted the stone up the road away from the burn on Mondays, Wednesdays, and

Fridays, and Jamie MacNab shifted it back down the road on Tuesdays, Thursdays, and Saturdays. On Sunday, which was the Lord's Day, when neither of them dared lay hand on the stone to shift it, they sat and glowered at each other in church while the dominie preached at them about loving their neighbour, to which neither of them paid any heed at all.

There was no more sitting on the stone of an evening, side by side.

Jamie and Rab stalked off to the tavern in the village to find company, and when they found each other there, they took great care to pretend they didn't see each other at all.

Things went on that way for quite a while, with the stone travelling up and down regular-like. Then, one night Rab stood up and said he was tired of the whole business and that he'd shift the stone no more. Folk at the tavern had been taking sides and laying bets on who'd win in the end; but Jamie told them no matter what Rab said, they'd better not settle their bets yet. For his part, he was going to wait and see if Rab meant it or not.

He'd hauled the stone down to the burn that day, so the next morning he went down to have a look. He was half hoping the stone would be where he'd put it, because he was tired of the quarrel too, to tell the truth. But the stone had been moved, so what could he do but haul it back to the stream again? If Rab wouldn't give up, no more would he! But, after another week of it, Jamie could stand no more.

He told folk at the tavern that it was queer enough that every time he got the stone by the burn it was back up by the road the next morning. And Rab got mad and said he'd not laid a hand on the stone for the past week, and that, for all he knew, Jamie was amusing himself, hauling it back and forth just to make it look as if Rab was doing it. They almost came to blows and maybe they would have, if just at the moment, something hadn't stopped them. The door flew open and in rushed old Sandy MacBean. There was no doubt about it. Sandy was in a terrible taking, for his white hair stood up on his head and his face was as white as his hair.

"Lads!" he cried in his old cracked voice. "Lads! I come by yon stone of Jamie's and Rab's the noo, and it's *walking*."

Jamie and Rab forgot their fight entirely. Out of the door and up the road they tore, side by side. When they got there, they both stopped in their tracks. They clutched each other, and lucky they did, for neither of them could have stood up alone, they were so taken with fright.

Because the stone *was* walking.

There were two pairs of legs at each corner, shuffling along under the stone.

"Och, I've gone daft," groaned Jamie.

"Me too," moaned Rab.

Just at that moment the stone began to settle down in the place it had stood before old Sandy MacBean had started all the shifting. Out from under the corners of the stone stepped four ghosts. They were the ghosts of Grandsire MacNab and Grandsire MacRae, and their two good sons who were the fathers of Young Jamie and Young Rab. And all of them were terribly cross.

The four of them lined up in a row and looked sternly at Young Jamie and Young Rab, while the two lads stood shaking in their shoes.

"A fine thing it is that a man cannot be left to lie in his grave in peace," said the ghost of Grandsire MacNab.

"We've been lugging that stone up the road full a week," said the ghost of Grandsire MacRae. "All along o' that old gander of a Sandy MacBean. I'm telling you now, Jamie; Rab was right and you were wrong. The stone is where it ought to be, so leave it there!"

"After Rab stopped shifting it we had to do it ourselves," said Jamie's father's ghost.

"And we'll have you know we're not meaning to do so any more. So leave it be, Jamie," commanded the ghost of Rab's father angrily. "'Twas the stream that shifted in the big storm, and not the stone at all."

And two by two and arm in arm the four ghosts turned away and started back to the churchyard.

Halfway down the hill Grandsire MacNab called back to them, "You pass the word to old Sandy MacBean that thinks his memory's so wonderful. Just tell him he'll be with us soon, and when he is, the four of us'll put a flea in his ear about forgetting about that big storm."

So that was the end of the trouble.

Jamie said he had been a dolt to ever listen to old Sandy MacBean in the first place. And Rab said why wouldn't Jamie listen, with old Sandy having such a name for his wonderful memory?

The two lads shook hands with each other over the stone, and after that they were better friends than ever.

Sandy MacBean was the one who suffered most, the poor old bodach! Whenever he said anything about the prodigious memory that he had, someone was sure to ask him how it came about that he forgot the big storm that shifted the burn away from the Boundary Stone.

A KIND OF SWAN SONG

HELEN CRESSWELL

WHEN I SAY that Lisa was someone special, right from the beginning, I expect that you will smile. *All* mothers think their children are special – and so they are, of course. In my case, Lisa was my only child, and so you will think that perhaps it is only natural that I should think her special. And when I tell you that my husband (who was a violinist with a well-known symphony orchestra) died when she was only a few months old, then you will quite understandably suspect me of exaggeration. I don't blame you. This is how it might seem.

But I must insist – Lisa *was* special. And perhaps it is partly because it is important to me that other people should realize this too, that I am now writing her story. It will not take long. She was only eight when she died.

The other reason I feel bound to tell her story is because I want you to know, as certainly as I now do myself, that death is not the end, not a full stop.

"Ah," I hear you say, "but she is *bound* to say that. She had no one in the world but her little daughter, and she died. Now she is trying to convince herself that death is not the end of everything. It's understandable, but she can't expect *us* to believe that!"

To this I simply reply – "Wait. Wait until you have heard my story. Then decide."

At birth, Lisa was special to Peter and myself in exactly the same way as any other baby born to loving parents. In our case, there was an extra dimension to our joy, because we knew already that in Peter's case it was to be short-lived. We knew that he had only a few months, at most, to savour the delights of parenthood. He had had to leave the orchestra several weeks before her birth. And so, for those first few months of Lisa's life Peter was as close to her as any father can be. He would sit with her for hours, studying her tiny, peaceful face as if he wanted to imprint it on his heart forever. In the early days, before he grew too weak, he would bathe her, change her, put her to bed.

And then he would play music to her, for hours on end. Not himself – he had sorrowfully put his violin away before her birth, but on tapes, and records. She would lie there kicking on the rug to the strains of Bach and Mozart, songs of Schubert and grand opera.

Sometimes I would laugh and say that I thought it all rather beyond the grasp of a baby, and that we should be playing her nursery rhymes instead. But he would say, quite seriously, "That baby may not be able to talk, yet, but she can hear. She is listening, the whole time, trying to make a pattern of this strange new world she has entered. If what she hears is joyful, if she hears harmony, then all her life long she will seek out joy and harmony for herself. Believe me, Martha, I know that I am right."

Even at the time I acknowledged that what he said might be true. Now, I know that it was.

I don't want to give the impression by this that we were too serious about things, or that Lisa had a strange start in life. Like any young parents we romped and played with her, looked for ways of making her smile or, better still, laugh. And we sang nursery rhymes as well. But I honestly think that the times she loved best, the times when she seemed happiest, were when she was lying there listening to music – especially songs. There was a special peaceful, wondering look she seemed to wear when she heard a beautiful human voice singing great music.

I don't want to exaggerate this – it is how I remember it, but then perhaps my memory of that time is not very reliable. It is a strange thing for a woman to watch her child blossom and at the same time her husband, the father, fading. Joy and sorrow could hardly be more poignantly interwoven.

Peter refused to let me grieve openly, and himself would show no sign of bitterness that he must soon leave us.

"I want there to be no shadows over her," he said. "Let her be shaped by music, not by sorrow."

Strangely, afterwards, when she was four or five, she would insist that she remembered Peter, though she could not really have done so.

"He was always smiling," she would say. And that was certainly true, so far as she was concerned. If there were times when he allowed his smile to fade, it was never in her presence.

He died when she was just over eight months old – in time to see her crawling, but before she took her first steps.

"Promise you will keep playing her music," he said before he died. And of course I promised. And that was another strange thing.

In those unreal, nightmarish days after he died, Lisa grew pale and quiet. It was as if she, too, were mourning. Then, coming back into the house after the funeral, drained and weary, I was suddenly aware of the great silence and absence. It occurred to me that since Peter died, I had played no music. I went and put on a record – one of his favourites, from Haydn's "Creation". As the pure, triumphant notes swelled about me, I lay back in a chair and surrendered myself to it. Then, beyond that marvellous music, I heard, in a pause, another music, another voice – Lisa's.

I hurried into the next room where she lay, as I thought, sleeping. Instead, she lay there wide-eyed – and round mouthed, too. Her whole tiny being seemed intent on the sounds that she was making with such seriousness, such concentration – Lisa was singing.

Very well – perhaps she was not. Perhaps she was simply cooing, crooning, as babies do. But to me, in my overwrought condition, it seemed that she was singing, herself joining in Haydn's great celebratory hymn. I remember that my tears, all at once released, splashed down on to her face, and that I gathered her up and took her with me, and she lay against me while we listened together.

Some children walk before they talk, some the other way round. Lisa, I swear, sang before she did either. I have the courage to say this, in the light of what came after. I did not merely imagine that Lisa was a child of music. She quite simply, and unarguably, was.

At first it was only I who knew it, and who could hardly believe it when I heard that infant voice playing with scales as other children play with bricks. (She did that, too. She was in every way exactly like all other children of her age. Only this was different – music ran in her veins.)

Then, as she grew older and we went to playgroups, others would remark on the purity and the pitch of her voice, and noticed that she had only to hear a song once to know it off by heart.

"She takes after her father," they all said.

It was true. But only I knew that she was composing music, as well as singing it. She would lie in bed after I had tucked her in for the night, her voice tracing its own melodies in the darkness. Sometimes even I, her own mother, would give a little shiver.

The word "genius" is not an easy one to come to terms

with. Every mother, as I have said, believes her own child to be special. But I do not think that any mother is looking for genius. It is rather a frightening thing, for ordinary people. We admit that it exists – but at a great distance, and in other people (preferably long since dead!)

At two Lisa was picking out tunes on the piano; at three she was playing both piano and violin. But it was the singing that mattered, I knew that. I watched her grow and develop with a delight tinged with sadness. I knew even then that the days of our closeness were numbered. Soon the world would discover her, and then the music would no longer be our shared secret.

When she was only four photographs of her were beginning to appear in the papers, under headlines such as "Child Prodigy wins Premier Award at Festival" and "Little Lisa Triumphs Again".

I don't want you to think that she was in any way strange. She was exactly like every other little girl in most ways. She loved reading, roller-skating and using her computer. When she started school, her marks were average. It was only the music that set her apart.

When she was five all kinds of renowned people – professors and teachers of music – began to visit us. "Soon," I thought, "they will take her away from me."

They wanted me, even then, to send her away to a special school, where her gift could be nurtured.

"It doesn't need nurturing," I told them. "It is natural. It will flower of its own accord."

They went away again, but I knew that it would not be for long. I knew, too, that what I had told them was only partly true. *Any* gift needs the right nourishment, just as a rare and fragile plant.

Lisa herself began to grow away from me. Not in the things that mattered – the things between mother and daughter. In those things we were always close. We teased each other a lot, and sometimes, even then, it would seem as if she were older than I was.

"Dear goose mother!" she would say, if I forgot something, or made a mistake. It became her pet name for me.

At six they tried to take her away again, and again I resisted.

"It's too soon," I said. "She's too young. Leave her with me a little longer, then she can go."

This time, when they had gone, I thought I could sense a sadness in her, a disappointment. I thought perhaps that I was being selfish, over-possessive. And so when they came again, begging me, almost, to send her away, I gave in.

Her delight when she heard the news hurt me, and she must have seen this.

"I'll still be home in the holidays, dear goose mother," she told me. "Don't be sad, or you'll spoil it for me."

So I tried to look glad, for her sake. During those last few months together before she went away, I gathered her music together, to comfort me in her absence. Every song she composed I made her sing into a microphone so that I could record it. I recorded her playing the piano and the violin too, but it was the singing that mattered. We both knew that. When she sang, instrument and music were one, perfect and inviolable.

She was still only seven when she left for her new school. She was radiant. She was like a bride in beret and navy socks.

"No crying, goose mother," she told me. "We'll write to each other."

"And send me tapes," I said. "Please, Lisa. Don't let even a single song you make get away. Put it on tape. That way, we've got it forever."

She smiled then with a curious wisdom.

"It's *making* the song that matters," she said. "*Nothing* gets away – ever."

When she had gone, I *did* cry, as I knew I would, and I kept remembering those words. How could she *know*, I wondered, something that most people never learn in a lifetime?

I took a job – an interesting one, really – in a house belonging to the National Trust, and open to visitors. Even so, that first term dragged. Most evenings I would sit and listen to the tapes we had made that summer. And at weekends I'd go shopping – looking for little things to put in her stocking. Lisa still believed (at least, I think she did) in Father Christmas.

By mid-December she was home. For a day or so we were a little strange together, and then it was as though she had never been away. One evening, we turned on the television to see a programme of carols composed by children. It was a competition, and these were the winning entries. When it was over, Lisa said quietly,

"Next year, goose mother, I shall make a carol!"

That was all. It was so slight a thing that, were it not for what followed, I doubt whether I should have remembered it. Lisa, after all, had been making songs almost all her life.

What was more natural than that she should make a carol?

Christmas and the New Year came and went. This time, when she left for school, the wrench was not so painful. We can become in time accustomed to most things – even to the absence of those we love. It all seemed inevitable, and for me, it was also part of the promise I had made to Peter before he died.

Lisa's letters came every week – badly spelt, and full of the things she was doing, the music she was making. They were full, too, of the ordinary things – requests for clothes that were all the rage, for stamps to swap and posters for her room. That term passed, and the next. In the summer I took a cottage in the Lakes, and we spent most of the time walking and cycling. We were well on the way to establishing a pattern to our lives.

It was sometimes hard to remember that she was still only eight years old. And we never talked about what she would "do" when she was "grown up". Looking back, I think that this was because she was already what she was meant to be. She was all the time in a process of becoming, and this was all that was necessary. She knew it herself.

"It's *making* the song that matters," she had said, over a year ago.

Again I waved her off to the start of a new school year. This time the ache was not so bad. I even registered for evening classes in Italian, and went out occasionally with friends to the theatre, or for a meal. But Lisa still made the tapes, and I still played them, hour upon hour. Now, she was beginning to write her own words to the music. One day I received a cassette with a song called "Goose Mother" and I felt so happy and so honoured that I actually taped it again, on to another cassette, for fear that it might get lost or damaged. Even as I did so, I seemed to hear her saying, "It's *making* the song that matters". I smiled wryly.

"For you, perhaps," I thought. "But for the rest of us, who can only listen, it's the song itself that counts."

In November I was surprised by Lisa calling me on the telephone. This she had done only once before – to inform me that she had chicken pox, but there was no need to worry, and proudly announce the number of spots she had.

"Listen," she said, "I've made a carol!"

"A carol?" I echoed.

"Remember – that competition we saw? And listen – Davey's going home, for the weekend, and I can go with him! So you and I can record it together – on our own piano!"

"Darling, that's wonderful!" I said. "But ..."

"Look – his mother's coming to fetch us in the car. I'll be home Friday, at around six. Can't stop now – bye!"

That was all. It was Tuesday – three days to get used to the wonderful fact that Lisa was coming home. I had quite forgotten (how could I?) that during their first year children at the school were not allowed to go home during termtime, but that this rule was lifted after that.

I spent the interim pleasurably shopping for Lisa's favourite food (not a difficult task, this being mainly a variation on chicken) and bought a new duvet cover for her bedroom. By half past five on the Friday I was fidgeting in the kitchen – opening and re-opening the oven door to check on the degree of brownness of chicken and potatoes, wondering whether I should start thawing the chocolate mousse.

At quarter to six I remembered that I hadn't any fizzy lemonade – her favourite drink, and one not allowed at school. I hesitated.

"I'll write a note," I thought, "and pin it on the door. I'll only be five minutes."

Accordingly I wrote "Back in five minutes" and pinned it on the door and set off. There were no shops nearby. I took the car and made for the nearest late-night supermarket. The traffic was dense, irritatingly slow. I had forgotten what Friday night rush hours were like. At one

105

point, I almost seized the opportunity to turn round and go home without the lemonade. But, I reflected, people rarely arrived on time, especially at the weekends. I carried on.

It was nearly quarter past six when I arrived back. In the space my own car had occupied only half an hour previously, was another. It was a police car. I drew alongside it, oblivious to the hooting behind me. Two figures, a policeman and a policewoman were standing on the steps up to the front door.

I wrenched open the door and got out. I was telling myself to keep calm. My knees were trembling.

"What – what is it?"

They turned. Their faces were young, worried, pitying.

"Mrs Viner?"

I nodded. "Perhaps we can . . .?"

I hardly remember what happened then exactly. Somehow I was inside, somehow I was sitting in my usual chair facing the fire and a voice was talking to me. It was a sympathetic voice, its owner reluctant to give me the news. "Motorway ... wet surface ... central reservation ... lorry ..." The words washed over me. What they were telling me was that Lisa was dead. She had been killed, along with her friend and his mother, on the motorway.

They were very kind. The young woman made me a cup of tea and switched off the oven. Before they left they stood looking at me uncertainly, at a loss. They didn't know what to say.

"Funny thing," said the policeman, "we'd been there on the steps ten minutes before you came."

I said nothing.

"Could've sworn there was someone in here," he went on. "Could hear someone singing – a kid, it sounded like."

"We wondered if the radio had been left on," the girl added.

"And now I come to think of it," he said, "the radio wasn't on. Or the telly. Funny, that ..."

"Yes, funny." I said. "Thank you. Thank you both very much. I think – I think I want to be alone now."

They hesitated.

"Sure you'll be all right?"

"Sure."

They went. The door closed and I was alone. I sat there for I don't know how long. I was seeing Lisa, hearing her, trying to tell myself that I would never see or hear her again. I couldn't cry. I just sat, dry-eyed, remembering.

In the end, after a long dark age, I got up. Mechanically I began turning things off, locking up for the night. The front door, the back, check the oven – still containing the chicken and crisp potatoes – switch off lights, pull out the plug of the TV ...

I stopped. All the lights but one were out. There, glowing in the darkness, were the red and green lights of the stereo deck and cassette recorder. There was a very faint hum. My mind was dense, confused. I had set up the system, that very afternoon, all ready to record the carol. The blank cassette was in place, I had carefully checked the sound levels. *And then I had switched it off.*

I remembered doing it. I had actually thought of the way Peter had always chided me for leaving things on – especially the cassette recorder. He had lectured me about the damage it might do.

I advanced towards the deck. Hesitantly, I pressed the PLAY switch. There came only a faint hissing. Then, hardly knowing why I did so, I pressed REWIND. *The tape rewound.* It stopped with a click.

"But it was a new cassette," I thought. "Brand new."

I stood there for a long time in the dim remaining light. Then I pressed another key – PLAY.

The room filled with sound. A noise – Lisa's voice, pure and sweet, sang:

"On a far midnight,

Long, long ago . . ."

There was no accompaniment, no piano, just that young, miraculous voice, singing of that long-ago miracle that Christmas celebrates.

I stood dazed, listening. Then, when at last the carol ended, I heard – or thought I heard (it certainly was not there on the tape, afterwards) – "There, dear goose mother! I told you – it's *making* the song that matters!"

And I knew that this was her last present to me. It was not for her own sake, but for mine, that the carol was there, locked for all time, on tape.

I sent that tape to the contest. It won. The presenter said, "It is with great sadness that we have to tell you that Lisa, aged eight, died tragically in a car accident, just after she had recorded this carol for our contest. It was to be her swan song."

Only I knew that the carol had been recorded not before, but after the accident. Though perhaps it could, after all, be called a *kind* of swan song.

THE FOUL FORDS

TRADITIONAL

An English folktale

ABOUT 1820 THERE LIVED a farrier of the name of Keane in the village of Longformacus in Lammermoor. He was a rough, passionate man, much addicted to swearing. For many years he was farrier to the Eagle or Spottiswood troop of Yeomanry. One day he went to Greenlaw to attend the funeral of his sister, intending to be home early in the afternoon. His wife and family were surprised when he did not appear as they expected and they sat up watching for him. About two o'clock in the morning a heavy weight was heard to fall against the door of the house, and on opening it to see what was the matter, old Keane was discovered lying in a fainting fit on the threshold. He was put to bed and means used for his recovery, but when he came out of the fit he was raving mad and talked of such frightful things that his family were quite terrified. He continued till next day in the same state, but at length his senses returned and he desired to see the minister alone.

After a long conversation with him he called all his family round his bed, and required from each of his children and his wife a solemn promise that they would none of them ever pass over a particular spot in the moor between Longformacus and Greenlaw, known by the name of "The Foul Fords" (it is the ford over a little water-course just east of Castle Shields). He assigned no reason to them for this demand, but the promise was given and he spoke no more, and died that evening.

About ten years after his death, his eldest son Henry Keane had to go to Greenlaw on business, and in the afternoon he prepared to return home. The last person who saw him as he was leaving the town was the blacksmith of Spottiswood, John Michie. He tried to persuade Michie to accompany him home, which he refused to do as it would take him several miles out of his way. Keane begged him most earnestly to go with him as he said he *must* pass the Foul Fords that night, and he would rather go through hell-fire than do so. Michie asked him why he said he *must* pass the Foul Fords, as by going a few yards on either side of them he might avoid them entirely. He persisted that he *must* pass them and Michie at last left him, a good deal surprised that he should talk of going over the Foul Fords when everyone knew that he and his whole family were bound, by a promise to their dead father, never to go by the place.

Next morning a labouring man from Castle Shields, by name Adam Redpath, was going to his work (digging sheep-drains on the moor), when on the Foul Fords he met Henry Keane lying stone dead and with no mark of violence on his body. His hat, coat, waistcoat, shoes and stockings were lying at about 100 yards distance from him on the Greenlaw side of the Fords, and while his flannel drawers were off and lying with the rest of his clothes, his trousers were on. Mr Ord, the minister of Longformacus, told one or two persons what John Keane (the father) had said to him on his deathbed, and by degrees the story got abroad. It was this. Keane said that he was returning home slowly after his sister's funeral, looking on the ground,

110

when he was suddenly roused by hearing the tramping of horses, and on looking up he saw a large troop of riders coming towards him two and two. What was his horror when he saw that one of the two foremost was the sister whom he had that day seen buried at Greenlaw! On looking further he saw many relations and friends long before dead; but when the two last horses came up to him he saw that one was mounted by a dark man whose face he had never seen before. He led the other horse, which, though saddled and bridled, was riderless, and on this horse the whole company wanted to compel Keane to get. He struggled violently, he said, for some time, and at last got off by promising that one of his family should go instead of him.

There still lives at Longformacus his remaining son Robert; he has the same horror of the Foul Fords that his brother had, and will not speak, nor allow anyone to speak to him on the subject.

Three or four years ago a herd of the name of Burton was found dead within a short distance of the spot, without any apparent cause for his death.

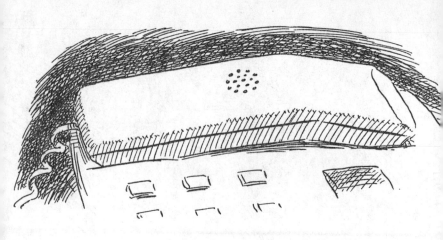

THE CALL

ROBERT WESTALL

I'M ROTA-SECRETARY of our local Samaritans. My job's to see our office is staffed twenty-four hours a day, 365 days a year. It's a load of headaches, I can tell you. And the worst headache for any branch is overnight on Christmas Eve.

Christmas night's easy; plenty have had enough of family junketings by then; nice to go on duty and give your stomach a rest. And New Year's Eve's OK, because we have Methodists and other teetotal types. But Christmas Eve . . .

Except we had Harry Lancaster.

In a way, Harry *was* the branch. Founder-member in 1963. A marvellous director all through the sixties. Available on the phone, day or night. Always the same quiet, unflappable voice, asking the right questions, soothing over-excited volunteers.

But he paid the price.

When he took early retirement from his firm in '73, we were glad. We thought we'd see even more of him. But we didn't. He took a six-month break from Sams. When he came back, he didn't take up the reins again. He took a much lighter job, treasurer. He didn't look ill, but he looked *faded*. Too long as a Sam. director can do that to you. But we were awfully glad just to have him back. No one was gladder than Maureen, the new director. Everybody cried on Maureen's shoulder, and Maureen cried on Harry's when it got rough.

Harry was the kind of guy you wish could go on for ever. But every so often, over the years, we'd realize he wasn't going to. His hair went snow-white; he got thinner and thinner. Gave up the treasurership. From doing a duty once a week, he dropped to once a month. But we still *had* him. His presence was everywhere in the branch. The new directors, leaders, he'd trained them all. They still asked themselves in a tight spot, "What would Harry do?" And what he did do was as good as ever. But his birthday kept on coming round. People would say with horrified disbelief, "Harry'll be *seventy-four* next year!"

And yet, most of the time, we still had in our minds the fifty-year-old Harry, full of life, brimming with new ideas. We couldn't do without that dark-haired ghost.

And the one thing he never gave up was overnight duty on Christmas Eve. Rain, hail or snow, he'd be there. Alone.

Now alone is wrong; the rules say the office must be double-staffed at all times. There are two emergency phones. How could even Harry cope with both at once?

But Christmas Eve is hell to cover. Everyone's got children or grandchildren, or is going away. And Harry had always done it alone. He said it was a quiet shift; hardly anybody ever rang. Harry's empty log-book was there to prove it; never more than a couple of long-term clients who only wanted to talk over old times and wish Harry Merry Christmas.

So I let it go on.

Until, two days before Christmas last year, Harry went down with flu. Bad. He tried dosing himself with all kinds

113

of things; swore he was still coming. Was *desperate* to come. But Mrs Harry got in the doctor; and the doctor was adamant. Harry argued; tried getting out of bed and dressed to prove he was OK. Then he fell and cracked his head on the bedpost, and the doctor gave him a shot meant to put him right out. But Harry, raving by this time, kept trying to get up, saying he must go . . .

But I only heard about that later. As rota-secretary I had my own troubles, finding his replacement. The rule is that if the rota-bloke can't get a replacement, he does the duty himself. In our branch, anyway. But I was already doing the seven-to-ten shift that night, then driving north to my parents.

Eighteen fruitless phone-calls later, I got somebody. Meg and Geoff Charlesworth. Just married; no kids.

When they came in at ten to relieve me, they were happy. Maybe they'd had a couple of drinks in the course of the evening. They were laughing; but they were certainly fit to drive. It is wrong to accuse them, as some did, later, of having had too many. Meg gave me a Christmas kiss. She'd wound a bit of silver tinsel through her hair, as some girls do at Christmas. They'd brought long red candles to light, and mince-pies to heat up in our kitchen and eat at midnight. It was just happiness; and it *was* Christmas Eve.

Then my wife tooted our car-horn outside, and I passed out of the story. The rest is hearsay: from the log they kept, and the reports they wrote, that were still lying in the in-tray the following morning.

They heard the distant bells of the parish church, filtering through the falling snow, announcing midnight. Meg got the mince-pies out of the oven, and Geoff was just kissing her, mouth full of flaky pasty, when the emergency phone went.

Being young and keen, they both grabbed for it. Meg won. Geoff shook his fist at her silently, and dutifully logged the call. Midnight exactly, according to his new watch. He heard Meg say what she'd been carefully coached to say, like Samaritans the world over.

"Samaritans – can I help you?"

She said it just right. Warm, but not gushing. Interested, but not *too* interested. That first phrase is all-important. Say it wrong, the client rings off without speaking.

Meg frowned. She said the phrase again. Geoff crouched close in support, trying to catch what he could from Meg's ear-piece. He said afterwards the line was very bad. Crackly, very crackly. Nothing but crackles, coming and going.

Meg said her phrase the third time. She gestured to Geoff that she wanted a chair. He silently got one, pushed it in behind her knees. She began to wind her fingers into the coiled telephone-cord, like all Samaritans do when they're anxious.

Meg said into the phone, "I'd like to help if I can." It was good to vary the phrase, otherwise clients began to think you were a tape-recording. She added, "My name's Meg. What can I call *you*?" You never ask for their *real* name, at that stage; always what you can call them. Often they start off by giving a false name . . .

A voice spoke through the crackle. A female voice.

"He's going to kill me. I know he's going to kill me. When he comes back." Geoff, who caught it from a distance, said it wasn't the phrases that were so awful. It was the way they were said.

Cold; so cold. And certain. It left no doubt in your mind he *would* come back and kill her. It wasn't a wild voice you could hope to calm down. It wasn't a cunning hysterical voice, trying to upset you. It wasn't the voice of a hoaxer, that to the trained Samaritan ear always has that little wobble in it, that might break down into a giggle at any minute and yet, till it does, must be taken absolutely seriously. Geoff said it was a voice as cold, as real, as hopeless as a tombstone.

"Why do you think he's going to kill you?" Geoff said Meg's voice was shaking, but only a little. Still warm, still interested.

Silence. Crackle.

"Has he threatened you?"

When the voice came again, it wasn't an answer to her question. It was another chunk of lonely hell, being spat out automatically; as if the woman at the other end was really only talking to herself.

"He's gone to let a boat through the lock. When he comes back, he's going to kill me."

Meg's voice tried to go up an octave; she caught it just in time.

"Has he *threatened* you? What is he going to do?"

"He's goin' to push me in the river, so it looks like an accident."

"Can't you swim?"

"There's half an inch of ice on the water. Nobody could live a minute."

"Can't you get away . . . before he comes back?"

"Nobody lives within miles. And I'm lame."

"Can't I . . . you . . . ring the police?"

Geoff heard a click as the line went dead. The dialling tone resumed. Meg put the phone down wearily, and suddenly shivered, though the office was over-warm from the roaring gas-fire.

"Christ, I'm so *cold*!"

Geoff brought her cardigan, and put it round her. "Shall I ring the duty-director, or will you?"

"You. If you heard it all."

Tom Brett came down the line, brisk and cheerful. "I've not gone to bed yet. Been filling the little blighter's Christmas stocking . . ."

Geoff gave him the details. Tom Brett was everything a good duty-director should be. Listened without interrupting; came back solid and reassuring as a house.

"Boats don't go through the locks this time of night.

116

Haven't done for twenty years. The old alkali steamers used to, when the alkali-trade was still going strong. The locks are only manned nine till five nowadays. Pleasure-boats can wait till morning. As if anyone would be moving a pleasure-boat this weather . . ."

"Are you *sure*?" asked Geoff doubtfully.

"Quite sure. Tell you something else – the river's nowhere near freezing over. Runs past my back-fence. Been watching it all day, 'cos I bought the lad a fishing-rod for Christmas, and it's not much fun if he can't try it out. You've been *had*, old son. Some Christmas joker having you on. Goodnight!"

"Hoax call," said Geoff heavily, putting the phone down. "No boats going through locks. No ice on the river. Look!"

He pulled back the curtain from the office window. "It's still quite warm out – the snow's melting, not even lying."

Meg looked at the black wet road, and shivered again. "That was no hoax. Did you think that voice was a hoax?"

"We'll do what the boss-man says. Ours not to reason why . . ."

He was still waiting for the kettle to boil, when the emergency phone went again.

The same voice.

"But he *can't* just push you in the river and get away with it!" said Meg desperately.

"He can. I always take the dog for a walk last thing. And there's places where the bank is crumbling and the fence's rotting. And the fog's coming down. He'll break a bit of fence, then put the leash on the dog, and throw it in after me. Doesn't matter whether the dog drowns or is found wanderin'. Either'll suit *him*. Then he'll ring the police an' say I'm missin' . . ."

"But why should he *want* to? What've you *done*? To deserve it?"

"I'm gettin' old. I've got a bad leg. I'm not much use to him. He's got a new bit o' skirt down the village . . ."

"But can't we . . ."

"All you can do for me, love, is to keep me company till he comes. It's lonely . . . That's not much to ask, is it?"

"Where *are* you?"

Geoff heard the line go dead again. He thought Meg looked like a corpse herself. White as a sheet. Dull dead eyes, full of pain. Ugly, almost. How she would look as an old woman, if life was rough on her. He hovered, helpless, desperate, while the whistling kettle wailed from the warm Samaritan kitchen.

"Ring Tom again, for Christ's sake," said Meg, savagely.

Tom's voice was a little less genial. He'd got into bed and turned the light off . . .

"Same joker, eh? Bloody persistent. But she's getting her facts wrong. No fog where I am. Any where you are?"

"No," said Geoff, pulling back the curtain again, feeling a nitwit.

"There were no fog-warnings on the late-night weather forecast. Not even for low-lying districts . . ."

"No."

"Well, I'll try to get my head down again. But don't hesitate to ring if anything *serious* crops up. As for this other lady . . . if she comes on again, just try to humour her. Don't argue – just try to make a relationship."

In other words, thought Geoff miserably, don't bother me with *her* again.

But he turned back to a Meg still frantic with worry. Who would not be convinced. Even after she'd rung the local British Telecom weather summary, and was told quite clearly the night would be clear all over the Eastern Region.

"I want to know where she *is*. I want to know where she's ringing from . . ."

To placate her, Geoff got out the large-scale Ordnance-Survey maps that some offices carry. It wasn't a great problem. The Ousam was a rarity; the only canalized river with locks for fifty miles around. And there were only eight sets of locks on it.

"These four," said Geoff, "are right in the middle of towns and villages. So it can't be *them*. And there's a whole row of Navigation cottages at Sutton's Lock, and I know they're occupied, so it can't be *there*. And this last one – Ousby Point – is right on the sea and it's all docks and stone quays – there's no river-bank to crumble. So it's either Yaxton Bridge, or Moresby Abbey locks . . ."

The emergency phone rang again. There is a myth among old Samaritans that you can tell the quality of the incoming call by the sound of the phone-bell. Sometimes it's lonely, sometimes cheerful, sometimes downright frantic. Nonsense, of course. A bell is a bell is a bell . . .

But this ringing sounded so cold, so dreary, so dead,

that for a second they both hesitated and looked at each other with dread. Then Meg slowly picked the phone up; like a bather hesitating on the bank of a cold grey river.

It was the voice again.

"The boat's gone through. He's just closing the lock gates. He'll be here in a minute . . ."

"What kind of boat is it?" asked Meg, with a desperate attempt at self-defence.

The voice sounded put out for a second, then said, "Oh, the usual. One of the big steamers. The *Lowestoft*, I think. Aye, the lock-gates are closed. He's coming up the path. Stay with me, love. Stay with me . . ."

Geoff took one look at his wife's grey, frozen, horrified face, and snatched the phone from her hand. He might be a Samaritan; but he was a husband, too. He wasn't sitting and watching his wife being screwed by some vicious hoaxer.

"Now *look*!" he said. "Whoever you are! We want to help. We'd like to help. But stop feeding us lies. I know the *Lowestoft*. I've been aboard her. They gave her to the Sea-scouts, for a headquarters. She hasn't got an engine any more. She's a hulk. She's never moved for years. Now let's cut the cackle . . ."

The line went dead.

"Oh, *Geoff*!" said Meg.

"Sorry. But the moment I called her bluff, she rang off. That *proves* she's a hoaxer. All those old steamers were broken up for scrap, except the *Lowestoft*. She's a *hoaxer*, I tell you!"

"Or an old lady who's living in the past. Some old lady who's muddled and lonely and frightened. And you shouted at her . . ."

He felt like a murderer. It showed in his face. And she made the most of it.

"Go out and find her, Geoff. Drive over and see if you can find her . . ."

"And leave you alone in the office? Tom'd have my guts for garters . . ."

"Harry Lancaster always did it alone. I'll lock the door. I'll be all right. Go on, Geoff. She's lonely. Terrified."

He'd never been so torn in his life. Between being a husband and being a Samaritan. That's why a lot of branches won't let husband and wife do duty together. We won't, now. We had a meeting about it; afterwards.

"Go *on*, Geoff. If she does anything silly, I'll never forgive myself. She might chuck herself in the river . . ."

They both knew. In our parts, the river or the drain is often the favourite way; rather than the usual overdose. The river seems to *call* to the locals, when life gets too much for them.

"Let's ring Tom again . . ."

She gave him a look that withered him and Tom together. In the silence that followed, they realized they were cut off from their duty-director, from *all* the directors,

121

from *all* help. The most fatal thing, for Samaritans. They were poised on the verge of the ultimate sin: going it alone.

He made a despairing noise in his throat; reached for his coat and the car-keys. "I'll do Yaxton Bridge. But I'll not do Moresby Abbey. It's a mile along the towpath in the dark. It'd take me an hour . . ."

He didn't wait for her dissent. He heard her lock the office door behind him. At least she'd be safe behind a locked door . . .

He never thought that telephones got past locked doors.

He made Yaxton Bridge in eight minutes flat, skidding and correcting his skids on the treacherous road. Lucky there wasn't much traffic about.

On his right, the River Ousam beckoned, flat, black, deep and still. A slight steam hung over the water, because it was just a little warmer than the air.

It was getting on for one by the time he reached the lock. But there was still a light in one of the pair of lock-keeper's cottages. And he knew at a glance that this wasn't the place. No ice on the river; no fog. He hovered, unwilling to disturb the occupants. Maybe they were in bed, the light left on to discourage burglars.

But when he crept up the garden path, he heard the sound of the TV, a laugh, coughing. He knocked.

An elderly man's voice called through the door, "Who's there?"

"Samaritans. I'm trying to find somebody's house. I'll push my card through your letter-box."

He scrabbled frantically through his wallet in the dark. The door was opened. He passed through to a snug sitting-room, a roaring fire. The old man turned down the sound of the TV. The wife said he looked perished, and the Samaritans did such good work, turning out at all hours, even at Christmas. Then she went to make a cup of tea.

He asked the old man about ice, and fog, and a lock-keeper who lived alone with a lame wife. The old man

shook his head. "Couple who live next door's got three young kids . . ."

"Wife's not lame, is she?"

"Nay – a fine-lookin' lass wi' two grand legs on her . . ."

His wife, returning with the tea-tray, gave him a *very* old-fashioned look. Then she said, "I've sort of got a memory of a lock-keeper wi' a lame wife – this was years ago, mind. Something not nice . . . but your memory goes, when you get old."

"We worked the lock at Ousby Point on the coast, all our married lives," said the old man apologetically. "They just let us retire here, 'cos the cottage was goin' empty . . ."

Geoff scalded his mouth, drinking their tea, he was so frantic to get back. He did the journey in seven minutes; he was getting used to the skidding, by that time.

*

He parked the car outside the Sam. office, expecting her to hear his return and look out. But she didn't.

He knocked; he shouted to her through the door. No answer. Frantically he groped for his own key in the door, and burst in.

She was sitting at the emergency phone, her face greyer than ever. Her eyes were far away, staring at the blank wall. They didn't swivel to greet him. He bent close to the phone in her hand and heard the same voice, the same cold hopeless tone, going on and on. It was sort of . . . hypnotic. He had to tear himself away, and grab a message pad. On it he scrawled, "WHAT'S HAPPENING? WHERE IS SHE?"

He shoved it under Meg's nose. She didn't respond in any way at all. She seemed frozen, just listening. He pushed her shoulder, half angry, half frantic. But she was wooden, like a statue. Almost as if she was in a trance. In a wave of husbandly terror, he snatched the phone from her.

It immediately went dead.

He put it down, and shook Meg. For a moment she recognized him and smiled, sleepily. Then her face went rigid with fear.

"Her husband was in the house. He was just about to open the door where she was . . ."

"Did you find out where she was?"

"Moresby Abbey lock. She told me in the end. I got her confidence. Then *you* came and ruined it . . ."

She said it as if he was suddenly her enemy. An enemy, a fool, a bully, a murderer. Like all men. Then she said, "I must go to her . . ."

"And leave the office unattended? That's *mad*." He took off his coat with the car-keys, and hung it on the office door. He came back and looked at her again. She still seemed a bit odd, trance-like. But she smiled at him and said, "Make me a quick cup of tea. I must go to the loo, before she rings again."

Glad they were friends again, he went and put the kettle

on. Stood impatiently waiting for it to boil, tapping his fingers on the sink-unit, trying to work out what they should do. He heard Meg's step in the hallway. Heard the toilet flush.

Then he heard a car start up outside.

His car.

He rushed out into the hall. The front door was swinging, letting in the snow. Where his car had been, there were only tyre-marks.

He was terrified now. Not for the woman. For Meg.

He rang Tom Brett, more frightened than any client Tom Brett had ever heard.

He told Tom what he knew.

"Moresby Locks," said Tom. "A lame woman. A murdering husband. Oh, my God. I'll be with you in five."

"The exchange are putting emergency calls through to Jimmy Henry," said Tom, peering through the whirling wet flakes that were clogging his windscreen-wipers. "Do you know what way Meg was getting to Moresby Locks?"

"The only way," said Geoff. "Park at Wylop Bridge and walk a mile up the towpath."

"There's a short cut. Down through the woods by the Abbey, and over the lock-gates. Not a lot of people know about it. I think we'll take that one. I want to get there before she does . . ."

"What the hell do you think's going on?"

"I've got an *idea*. But if I told you, you'd think I was out of my tiny shiny. So I won't. All I want is your Meg safe and dry, back in the Sam. office. And nothing in the log that headquarters might see . . ."

He turned off the by-pass, into a narrow track where hawthorn bushes reached out thorny arms and scraped at the paintwork of the car. After a long while, he grunted with satisfaction, clapped on the brakes and said, "Come on."

They ran across the narrow wooden walkway that sat

precariously on top of the lock-gates. The flakes of snow whirled at them, in the light of Tom's torch. Behind the gates, the water stacked up, black, smooth, slightly steaming because it was warmer than the air. In an evil way, it called to Geoff. So easy to slip in, let the icy arms embrace you, slip away . . .

Then they were over, on the towpath. They looked left, right, listened.

Footsteps, women's footsteps, to the right. They ran that way.

Geoff saw Meg's walking back, in its white raincoat . . .

And beyond Meg, leading Meg, another back, another woman's back. The back of a woman who limped.

A woman with a dog. A little white dog . . .

For some reason, neither of them called out to Meg. Fear of disturbing a Samaritan relationship, perhaps. Fear of breaking up something that neither of them understood. After all, they could afford to be patient now. They had found Meg safe. They were closing up quietly on her, only ten yards away. No danger . . .

Then, in the light of Tom's torch, a break in the white-painted fence on the river side.

And the figure of the limping woman turned through the gap in the fence, and walked out over the still black waters of the river.

And like a sleepwalker, Meg turned to follow . . .

They caught her on the very brink. Each of them caught her violently by one arm, like policemen arresting a criminal. Tom cursed, as one of his feet slipped down the bank and into the water. But he held on to them, as they all swayed on the brink, and he only got one very wet foot.

"What the hell am I doing here?" asked Meg, as if waking from a dream. "She was talking to me. I'd got her confidence . . ."

"Did she tell you her name?"

"Agnes Todd."

"Well," said Tom, "here's where Agnes Todd used to live."

There were only low walls of stone, in the shape of a house. With stretches of concrete and old broken tile in between. There had been a phone, because there was still a telegraph pole, with a broken junction-box from which two black wires flapped like flags in the wind.

"Twenty-one years ago, Reg Todd kept this lock. His lame wife Agnes lived with him. They didn't get on well – people passing the cottage heard them quarrelling. Christmas Eve, 1964, he reported her missing to the police. She'd gone out for a walk with the dog, and not come back. The police searched. There was a bad fog down that night. They found a hole in the railing, just about where we saw one; and a hole in the ice, just glazing over. They found the dog's body next day; but they didn't find her for a month, till the ice on the River Ousam finally broke up.

"The police tried to make a case of it. Reg Todd *had* been carrying on with a girl in the village. But there were no marks of violence. In the end, she could have fallen, she could've been pushed, or she could've jumped. So they let Reg Todd go; and he left the district."

There was a long silence. Then Geoff said, "So you think . . .?"

"I think nowt," said Tom Brett, suddenly very stubborn and solid and Fenman. "I think nowt, and that's all I *know*. Now let's get your missus home."

Nearly a year passed. In the November, after a short illness, Harry Lancaster died peacefully in his sleep. He had an enormous funeral. The church was full. Present Samaritans, past Samaritans from all over the country, more old clients than you could count, and even two of the top brass from Slough.

But it was not till everybody was leaving the house that Tom Brett stopped Geoff and Meg by the gate. More solid and Fenman than ever.

"I had a long chat wi' Harry," he said, "after he knew he was goin'. He told me. About Agnes Todd. She had rung him up on Christmas Eve. Every Christmas Eve for twenty years . . ."

"Did he know she was a . . .?" Geoff still couldn't say it.

"Oh, aye. No flies on Harry. The second year – while he was still director – he persuaded the GPO to get an engineer to trace the number. How he managed to get them to do it on Christmas Eve, God only knows. But he had a way with him, Harry, in his day."

"And . . ."

"The GPO were baffled. It was the old number of the lock-cottage all right. But the lock-cottage was demolished a year after the . . . whatever it was. Nobody would live there, afterwards. All the GPO found was a broken junction-box and wires trailin'. Just like we saw that night."

"So he talked to her all those years . . . knowing?"

"Aye, but he wouldn't let anybody else do Christmas Eve. She was lonely, but he knew she was dangerous. Lonely an' dangerous. She wanted company."

Meg shuddered. "How could he bear it?"

"He was a Samaritan . . ."

"Why didn't he tell anybody?"

"Who'd have believed him?"

There were half a dozen of us in the office this Christmas Eve. Tom Brett, Maureen, Meg and Geoff, me. All waiting for . . .

It never came. Nobody called at all.

"Do you think?" asked Maureen, with an attempt at a smile, her hand to her throat in a nervous gesture, in the weak light of dawn.

"Aye," said Tom Brett. "I think we've heard the last of her. Mebbe Harry took her with him. Or came back for her. Harry was like that. The best Samaritan I ever knew."

His voice went funny on the last two words, and there was a shine on those stolid Fenman eyes. He said, "I'll be off then." And was gone.

FEEL FREE

ALAN GARNER

THE LINE OF SIGHT from Tosh's den to Brian went under the Giant Panda's belly, between the gilded coffin of Bak-en-Mut and the town stocks, through the Taj Mahal and over Lady Henrietta Maria's dyed bodice. The first morning, when Brian had started his drawing, the Taj Mahal had blocked Tosh's view, but when Brian came back from his dinner three doors had been opened to give a clear run through, and whenever he looked Tosh's eye was on him.

Tosh kept to his den, where he brewed tea and filled in his football coupon, unless he was on patrol. He patrolled every hour, on the hour, up one side, across the back and down the other side, which meant that he came upon Brian from behind. He said nothing the first day, but stood at ease, lifting his heels and lowering them: click, click, click; and he sucked his teeth. Then he patrolled back to his den. There were no visitors to the museum all day, all week.

"What are you on?" said Tosh half-way through the second afternoon.

"Eh up," said Brian. "It talks."

"None of your lip," said Tosh. His medal ribbons bristled.

But on the third day Tosh patrolled with a mug of hot brown water thickened with condensed milk. "Cupper tea," he said.

Brian put down his drawing-board. "Thanks, Tosh."

"Yer welcome."

"How's trade?" said Brian.

"Average," said Tosh. "For the season."

"Been pretty quiet here, hasn't it?" said Brian. "Since they built the Holiday Camp, I mean. The old park just can't compete, can it?"

"We have our regulars," said Tosh. "And our aberlutions is second to none."

"It's Open Day up the Camp," said Brian. "Anyone can go, free."

"It's all kidology," said Tosh. "There's nowt free in this world, lad."

"There is today," said Brian. "I'm going, anyroad."

"What are you on here?" said Tosh.

"It's my Project for school," said Brian. "Last term it was Compost: this term it's Pottery."

The next time round Tosh said, "What you got to do with this malarky?"

"I'm trying to draw that Ancient Greek dish from all sides and see if I can copy it."

"What for?"

"Greek pottery's supposed to be the best, so I thought I'd start at the top."

"Fancy it, do you?"

"Yes," said Brian. "It's funny, is that. I seem to be quite knacky with it, though I've only just started. I may go on and do evening classes."

"I'm partial to a bit of art, meself," said Tosh. "Sign-writing: but painting's favourite. Not yon modern stuff, though: more traditional – dogs and flowers and that. It makes you realize how much work they put in, them fellers. Same as him there." Tosh pointed to the Egyptian coffin. "Yon Back-in-a-Minute. The gold leaf and stuff, all them little pictures – that wasn't done on piece-work. Eh? Not on piece-work."

"Nor this dish, neither," said Brian. "That's why I'm having such a sweat over the drawing. Every line's perfect."

"Ah," said Tosh. "They had the time in them days. They had all the time there is. All the time in the world."

The dish stood alone in its case, a typed label on the glass: "Attic Krater, 5th Century BC, Artist Unknown. The scene depicts Charon, ferryman of the dead, conveying a soul across the River Acheron in the Underworld."

At first Brian had thought the design was too wooden and formal. The old boatman Charon crouched with bent knees, and the dead man was as blank as any rush-hour traveller. The waves curled in solid, regular spirals and the rest of the design was geometry – squares, crosses, leaf patterns without life. But as he worked Brian found a balance and a rhythm in the dish. Nothing was there without a reason, and its place in the design was so accurately fixed that to move it was like playing a wrong note. And all this Brian had found in two days from a red-and-black dish in a glass case.

"Have you done, then?" said Tosh an hour later.

Brian sat with this hands in his pockets, glaring at the dish.

"No. Eh, Tosh: let's have the case open. I want to cop hold of that dish."

"Not likely," said Tosh. "It's more than my job's worth. Can't you see all you want from here?"

"Seeing's not enough. That's why these drawings don't work. They're on the flat, and the dish is curved. Pattern and shape are all part of it – you can't have one without the other. My drawing's like sucking sweets with the wrapper on."

"What if you bust it, though?" said Tosh.

"It'd mend. It's been bust before. Come on, Tosh, be a pal."

Tosh went to his den and came back with a key. "I know nowt about this," he said.

Brian moved his fingers along the surfaces of the dish. "That's it," he kept saying. "That's it. Yes. That's it. Eh, Tosh, the man as made this was a blooming marvel. It's perfect. It's like I don't know what, it's like – it's – heck, it's like flying."

"Ay, well, one thing's for sure," said Tosh. "The feller as made yon: his head doesn't ache. How old is it?"

"A good two thousand year," said Brian. "Two thousand year. He sat and worked this out, these curves and lines and colours and patterns, and then he made it. Two thousand year. Heck. And it's come all that way. To me. So as I know what he was thinking. Two thousand—"

"Ay, his head doesn't ache any more, right enough," said Tosh.

Brian turned the cup over to examine the base.

"It'd do for a cake-stand, would that," said Tosh. "For Sundays."

"Tosh! Look!" Brian nearly dropped the dish. On the base was a clear thumb-print fired hard as the rest of the clay.

"There he is," whispered Brian.

The change from the case to the outside air had put a mist on the surface of the dish, and Brian set his own fingers against the other hand.

"Two thousand year, Tosh. That's nothing. Who was he?"

"No, he'll not have a headache."

Brian stared at his own print and the fossilled clay. "Tosh," he said, "they're the same. That thumb-print and mine. What do you make of it?"

"They're not," said Tosh. "No two people ever has the same tabs."

"These are."

"They can't be," said Tosh. "I went on courses down London when I was a constable."

"These are the same."

"You might think so, but you'd be wrong. It's been proved as how every man, woman and child is born with different fingerprints from anyone else."

"How's it been proved?" said Brian.

"Because the same prints have never turned up twice. Why, men have been hanged on the strength of that, and where would be the sense if it wasn't true?"

"Look for yourself," said Brian.

Tosh put on his glasses. For a while he said nothing, then, "Ah. Very good. Very close, I'll allow, but see at yon line across the other feller's thumb. That's a scar. You haven't got one."

"But a scar's something that happens," said Brian. "It's nothing to do with what you're born like. If he hadn't gashed his thumb, they'd be the same."

"But they're not, are they?" said Tosh. "And it was a long time ago, so what's the odds?"

Brian finished his drawings early. He was taking Sandra to the Open Day at the Camp, and he wanted to have a shave. They met at the bus stop.

"There's that Beryl Fletcher," said Sandra.

"What about her?" said Brian.

"She only left school last week and she's cracking on she's dead sophisticated."

"Give over," said Brian. "You're jealous."

Two buses came and went.

"Do you like me dress?" said Sandra.

"Yes."

"Just 'yes'?"

"It's all right," said Brian. "Smashing."

"You never noticed," said Sandra.

"I did. It's nice – better than Beryl Fletcher's."

Sandra laughed. "You'd never notice, you great cloth-head. What's up? You've not had two words to say for yourself."

"Sorry," said Brian. "I was thinking about that dish I've

135

been working on all week at the museum."

"What's her name?"

"I don't know her name, but she's very mature."

"How old is she?" said Sandra.

"Two-and-a-bit thousand year."

A bus came and they got on.

"You know Tosh, the head Parky, him as looks after the museum?" said Brian.

"Yes. He's our kid's wife's uncle."

"Was he ever a bobby?"

"He used to be a sergeant," said Sandra.

Three stops later Sandra said, "You're quiet."

"Am I? Sorry."

"What's to do, love? What's wrong?"

"Have you ever hidden something to chance it being found again years and years later – perhaps long after you're dead?"

"No," said Sandra.

"I have," said Brian. "I was a great one for filling screw-top bottles with junk and then burying them. I put notes inside, and pieces out of the newspaper. You're talking to somebody you'll never meet, never know: but if they find the bottle they'll know you. There's bits of you in the bottle, waiting all this time, see, in the dark, and as soon as the bottle's opened – time's nothing – and – and – "

"Eh up," said Sandra, "people are looking. You do get some ideas, Brian Walton!"

"It's that dish at the museum," said Brian. "I thought it was a crummy old pot, but when I started to sort it out I found what was inside it."

"What? A message?" said Sandra.

"No. Better than that. This fellow as made it over two thousand year ago – he knew nothing about me, but he worked out how to fit the picture and the shape together. When you look at it you don't see how clever he was, but when you touch it, and try to copy it, you're suddenly with him – same as if you're watching over his shoulder and he's talking to you, showing you. So when I do a pot next, he'll be helping. It'll be his pot. And he's been dead two thousand year! What about that, eh?"

"Fancy," said Sandra.

The bus had arrived at the Camp. Sandra was about to step down from the platform when she tipped forward at the waist. Her eyes widened and she clutched at the rail.

"What's the matter?" said Brian.

"It's me shoe!" she hissed. "It's fast!" The stiletto heel had jammed between the ridges of the platform, and Sandra had to take off her shoe to get it free. "Oh, it's scratched!" she said. "First time out, and all."

"Come on," said Brian. "If you will be sophisticated – "

"Hello! Hello! Hello!" said the loudspeakers. "This is Open Day, friends, and it's free, free, free! Walk in! Have fun!"

"Where do you want to start?" said Brian.

"I don't know," said Sandra. "Let's see what there is."

"Hello! Hello! Hello! This is Your Day, and Your Camp. The Camp With A Difference, friends and neighbours. Where Only You Matter. This is The Camp With Only One Rule – Feel Free! Feel free, friends!"

Brian and Sandra danced to two of the five resident tape-recordings, drove a motor-boat on the Marine Lake, spun their own candy floss—

"Hello! Hello! Hello! Feel free, friends! This is the Lay-Say-Fair Holiday Camp, a totally new concept in family Camping, adding a new dimension to leisure, where folk come to stay, play, make hay, or relax in the laze-away-days that you find only at the Lay-Say-Fair Holiday Camp. Yes! And it's all free, friends. Thanks to the All-in L.S.F. Tarrif, which you pay when you reserve your chalet. There are no hidden extras: this once-and-for-all payment is your passport to delight. Yes! Remember! L.S.F. saves L.S.D! Now!"

"Me feet are killing me," said Sandra.

They sat on a bench in the Willow Pattern Garden. Brian

stroked the head of a Chinese bronze dragon, from which the Camp's music tinkled. The sun was low, the day at its best after the heat.

"Isn't it dreamy?" said Sandra. "Better than the old park. These banks and banks of flowers and rock-gardens: and the bees buzzing."

"It's hard luck on the bees," said Brian. "They'll be dead by morning."

"You're proper cheerful today, you are," said Sandra. "Why will they be dead?"

"Selective weedkiller," said Brian. "You couldn't keep the soil as clean as that, else. They spray it on, and nobody bothers to tell the bees."

"How do you know?"

"I read quite a lot about it last term," said Brian, "when I was doing Compost. There's a lot in soil; you may not think it, but there is."

"We're off," said Sandra.

"No, look," said Brian, and leant backwards to gather a

handful of earth from a rockery flower-bed. "Soil isn't muck, it's – well, I'll be – Sandra! This here soil's plastic!"

Smooth, clean granules rolled between his fingers.

"The whole blooming lot's plastic – grass, flowers, and all!"

"Now that's what I call sensible. It helps to keep the cost down," said Sandra. "And it doesn't kill bees."

"Ay," said Brian. "Bees. Surely they're not that daft."

He climbed up the rockery, and he soon found the bees. They were each mounted on a quivering hair spring, the buzzer plugged in to a time-switch.

"Hello! Hello! Hello!" said the bronze dragon. "Lay-Say-Fair. The Camp With A Difference. Have you visited the Pleasureteria yet, friends? The L.S.F. Pleasureteria is the only Do-It-Yourself Fun-Drome in existence: all the fun of the fair for free! Free! Now!"

"We'll have a stab at that, shall we?" said Brian.

They rode on the Big Wheel, the Dodgems, the Roller Coaster, the Dive Bomber, the Octopus. The equipment was automatically controlled. Lights winked, recorded voices gave instructions, bells rang.

In the Pally-Palais Sandra battled with sudden air jets from the floor, and clung to Brian on the Cake Walk. It was late dusk when they came out of the Palais. They laughed a lot.

"Well, something's made you buck up at last," said Sandra. "I thought I was landed with pottery and compost for the night."

"What shall we go on now?" said Brian.

"There's the Tunnel of Love, if you're feeling romantic," said Sandra.

"You never know till you try, do you?" said Brian.

They walked on to the stage by the water channel. There was a gate across the channel with a notice saying: "Passengers wait here. Pull handle for boat. Do not board boat until boat has stopped. Do not stand up in boat. Passengers must be seated when bell rings. No smoking."

"'Feel free, friends'," said Brian.

Beyond the gate was a grotto of plaster stalactites and stalagmites, and the channel rushed among them to a black tunnel.

"Queer green there, isn't it?" said Sandra. "Ever so eerie."

"Special paint," said Brian. "It shows up luminous in ultra-violet light. Remember that Bottom of the Sea Spectacular in 'Goldilocks on Ice' at the Opera House last year? Same thing in this grotto."

Brian pulled the lever and a boat came out of the darkness up-stream. Its prow was shaped to fit in a recess in the gate, which kept it firm.

"Passengers board now," said a recorded voice. "Take your seats immediately. Passengers board now. Take your seats immediately. Do not stand."

Brian climbed into the boat and turned to help Sandra. She put one foot on the seat, then twisted awkwardly.

"Hurry up," said Brian.

"It's me heel again. It's caught in something. On the stage."

They began to laugh. Brian tried to lift Sandra into the boat but had nothing to brace himself against.

"Kick your shoe off."

"I can't."

They pushed and pulled. A bell rang. "All passengers sit. Stand clear. Do not try to board. Stand clear."

The bell rang again, and the gate flew open.

Sandra was still laughing, but Brian felt the water take the boat, and he knew he could not hold it. Already he was being dragged off balance.

"Get back," he said. "You'll fall in. Get back."

"I can't. I'm stuck."

"I'm going to shove you," said Brian. "Shove you. Ready? On three. One. Two. Three – !"

He pushed Sandra as hard as he could, and she fell back on to the stage. He lurched in the boat and grabbed at the stern to save himself. For a moment the boat hung level with Sandra, who was three feet away, but dry, as she scrambled up, still laughing.

"Enjoy yourself!" she shouted. The boat bobbed away on the race, and Brian stood watching. Now he was in the grotto, and Sandra was distant in another light.

"Sit down, Brian! Coo-ee! Have a nice trip, love, and if you can't be good be careful! Shall I see you next time round? Coo-ee!"

She was swinging away from him, a tiny figure lost among stalactites. He stood, looking, looking, and slowly lifted his hand off the nail that had worked loose at the edge of the stern. He had not felt its sharpness, but now the gash throbbed across the ball of his thumb. The boat danced towards the tunnel.

MIRIAM

TRUMAN CAPOTE

FOR SEVERAL YEARS, Mrs H. T. Miller had lived alone in a pleasant apartment (two rooms with kitchenette) in a remodelled brownstone near the East River. She was a widow: Mr H. T. Miller had left her a reasonable amount of insurance. Her interests were narrow, she had no friends to speak of, and she rarely journeyed farther than the corner grocery. The other people in the house never seemed to notice her: her clothes were matter-of-fact, her hair iron-grey, clipped and casually waved; she did not use cosmetics, her features were plain and inconspicuous, and on her last birthday she was sixty-one. Her activities were seldom spontaneous; she kept the two rooms immaculate, smoked an occasional cigarette, prepared her own meals and tended a canary.

Then she met Miriam. It was snowing that night. Mrs Miller had finished drying the supper dishes and was thumbing through an afternoon paper when she saw an advertizement of a picture playing at a neighbourhood theatre. The title sounded good, so she struggled into her beaver coat, laced her galoshes and left the apartment, leaving one light burning in the foyer: she found nothing more disturbing than a sensation of darkness.

The snow was fine, falling gently, not yet making an impression on the pavement. The wind from the river cut only at street crossings. Mrs Miller hurried, her head bowed, oblivious as a mole burrowing a blind path. She stopped at a drugstore and bought a package of peppermints.

A long line stretched in front of the box office; she took her place at the end. There would be (a tired voice groaned) a short wait for all seats. Mrs Miller rummaged in her leather handbag till she collected exactly the correct change for admission. The line seemed to be taking its own time and, looking around for some distraction, she suddenly became conscious of a little girl standing under the edge of the marquee.

Her hair was the longest and strangest Mrs Miller had ever seen: absolutely silver-white, like an albino's. It flowed waist-length in smooth, loose lines. She was thin and fragilely constructed. There was a simple, special elegance in the way she stood with her thumbs in the pockets of a tailored plum-velvet coat.

Mrs Miller felt oddly excited, and when the little girl glanced towards her, she smiled warmly. The little girl walked over and said, "Would you care to do me a favour?"

"I'd be glad to, if I can," said Mrs Miller.

"Oh, it's quite easy. I merely want you to buy a ticket for me; they won't let me in otherwise. Here, I have the money." And gracefully she handed Mrs Miller two dimes and a nickel.

They went into the theatre together. An usherette directed them to a lounge; in twenty minutes the picture would be over.

"I feel just like a genuine criminal," said Mrs Miller gaily, as she sat down. "I mean that sort of thing's against the

143

law, isn't it? I do hope I haven't done the wrong thing. Your mother knows where you are, dear? I mean she does, doesn't she?"

The little girl said nothing. She unbuttoned her coat and folded it across her lap. Her dress underneath was prim and dark blue. A gold chain dangled about her neck, and her fingers, sensitive and musical-looking, toyed with it. Examining her more attentively, Mrs Miller decided the truly distinctive feature was not her hair, but her eyes; they were hazel, steady, lacking any childlike quality whatsoever and, because of their size, seemed to consume her small face.

Mrs Miller offered a peppermint. "What's your name, dear?"

"Miriam," she said, as though, in some curious way, it were information already familiar.

"Why, isn't that funny – my name's Miriam, too. And it's not a terribly common name either. Now don't tell me your last name's Miller!"

"Just Miriam."

"But isn't that funny?"

"Moderately," said Miriam, and rolled the peppermint on her tongue.

Mrs Miller flushed and shifted uncomfortably. "You have such a large vocabulary for such a little girl."

"Do I?"

"Well, yes," said Mrs Miller, hastily changing the topic to: "Do you like the movies?"

"I really wouldn't know," said Miriam. "I've never been before."

Women began filling the lounge; the rumble of the newsreel bombs exploded in the distance. Mrs Miller rose, tucking her purse under her arm. "I guess I'd better be running now if I want to get a seat," she said. "It was nice to have met you."

Miriam nodded ever so slightly.

It snowed all week. Wheels and footsteps moved soundlessly on the street, as if the business of living continued secretly behind a pale but impenetrable curtain. In the falling quiet there was no sky or earth, only snow lifting in the wind, frosting the window glass, chilling the rooms, deadening and hushing the city. At all hours it was necessary to keep a lamp lighted and Mrs Miller lost track of the days; Friday was no different from Saturday and on Sunday she went to the grocery; closed, of course.

That evening she scrambled eggs and fixed a bowl of tomato soup. Then, after putting on a flannel robe and cold-creaming her face, she propped herself up in bed with a hot-water bottle under her feet. She was reading the *Times* when the doorbell rang. At first she thought it must be a mistake and whoever it was would go away. But it rang and rang and settled to a persistent buzz. She looked at the clock; a little after eleven; it did not seem possible, she was always asleep by ten.

Climbing out of bed, she trotted barefoot across the living-room. "I'm coming, please be patient." The latch was caught; she turned it this way and that way and the bell never paused an instant. "Stop it," she cried. The bolt gave way and she opened the door an inch. "What in heaven's name?"

"Hello," said Miriam.

"Oh . . . why, hello," said Mrs Miller, stepping hesitantly into the hall. "You're that little girl."

"I thought you'd never answer, but I kept my finger on the button; I knew you were home. Aren't you glad to see me?"

Mrs Miller did not know what to say. Miriam, she saw, wore the same plum-velvet coat and now she had also a

beret to match; her white hair was braided in two shining plaits and looped at the ends with enormous white ribbons.

"Since I've waited so long, you could at least let me in," she said.

"It's awfully late . . ."

Miriam regarded her blankly. "What difference does that make? Let me in. It's cold out here and I have on a silk dress." Then, with a gentle gesture, she urged Mrs Miller aside and passed into the apartment.

She dropped her coat and beret on a chair. She was indeed wearing a silk dress. White silk. White silk in February. The skirt was beautifully pleated and the sleeves long. It made a faint rustle as she strolled about the room. "I like your place," she said, "I like the rug, blue's my favourite colour." She touched a paper rose in a vase on the coffee table. "Imitation," she commented wanly. "How sad. Aren't imitations sad?" She seated herself on the sofa, daintily spreading her skirt.

"What do you want?" asked Mrs Miller.

"Sit down," said Miriam. "It makes me nervous to see people stand."

Mrs Miller sank to a hassock. "What do you want?" she repeated.

"You know, I don't think you're glad I came."

For a second time Mrs Miller was without an answer; her hand motioned vaguely. Miriam giggled and pressed back on a mound of chintz pillows. Mrs Miller observed that the girl was less pale than she remembered; her cheeks were flushed.

"How did you know where I lived?"

Miriam frowned. "That's no question at all. What's your name? What's mine?"

"But I'm not listed in the phone book."

"Oh, let's talk about something else."

Mrs Miller said, "Your mother must be insane to let a child like you wander around at all hours of the night –

147

and in such ridiculous clothes. She must be out of her mind."

Miriam got up and moved to a corner where a covered bird cage hung from a ceiling chain. She peeked beneath the cover. "It's a canary," she said. "Would you mind if I woke him? I'd like to hear him sing."

"Leave Tommy alone," said Mrs Miller anxiously. "Don't you dare wake him."

"Certainly," said Miriam. "But I don't see why I can't hear him sing." And then, "Have you anything to eat? I'm starving! Even milk and a jam sandwich would be fine."

"Look," said Mrs Miller, rising from the hassock, "look – if I make some nice sandwiches will you be a good child and run along home? It's past midnight, I'm sure."

"It's snowing," reproached Miriam. "And cold and dark."

"Well, you shouldn't have come here to begin with," said Mrs Miller, struggling to control her voice. "I can't help the weather. If you want anything to eat you'll have to promise to leave."

Miriam brushed a braid against her cheek. Her eyes were thoughtful, as if weighing the proposition. She turned towards the bird cage. "Very well," she said, "I promise."

How old is she? Ten? Eleven? Mrs Miller, in the kitchen, unsealed a jar of strawberry preserves and cut four slices of bread. She poured a glass of milk and paused to light a cigarette. And why had she come? Her hand shook as she held the match, fascinated, till it burned her finger. The canary was singing; singing as he did in the morning and at no other time. "Miriam," she called, "Miriam, I told you not to disturb Tommy." There was no answer. She called again; all she heard was the canary. She inhaled a cigarette and discovered she had lighted the cork-tip end and – oh, really, she mustn't lose her temper.

She carried the food in on a tray and set it on the coffee table. She saw first the bird cage still wore its night cover.

And Tommy was singing. It gave her a queer sensation. And no one was in the room. Mrs Miller went through an alcove leading to her bedroom; at the door she caught her breath.

"What are you doing?" she asked.

Miriam glanced up and in her eyes there was a look that was not ordinary. She was standing by the bureau, a jewel case opened before her. For a few minutes she studied Mrs Miller, forcing their eyes to meet, and she smiled. "There's nothing good here," she said. "But I like this." Her hand held a cameo brooch. "It's charming."

"Suppose – perhaps you'd better put it back," said Mrs Miller, feeling suddenly the need of some support. She leaned against the door frame; her head was unbearably heavy; a pressure weighted the rhythm of her heartbeat. The light seemed to flutter defectively. "Please, child – a gift from my husband . . ."

"But it's beautiful and I want it," said Miriam. "Give it to me."

As she stood, striving to shape a sentence which would somehow save the brooch, it came to Mrs Miller there was no one to whom she might turn; she was alone; a fact that had not been among her thoughts for a long time. Its sheer emphasis was stunning. But here in her own room in the hushed snow-city were evidences she could not ignore or, she knew with startling clarity, resist.

Miriam ate ravenously, and when the sandwiches and milk were gone, her fingers made cobweb movements over the plate, gathering crumbs. The cameo gleamed on her blouse, the blond profile like a trick reflection of its wearer. "That was very nice," she sighed, "though now an almond cake or a cherry would be ideal. Sweets are lovely, don't you think?"

Mrs Miller was perched precariously on the hassock, smoking a cigarette. Her hair net had slipped lopsided and loose strands straggled down her face. Her eyes were stupidly concentrated on nothing and her cheeks were mottled in red patches, as though a fierce slap had left permanent marks.

"Is there a candy – a cake?"

Mrs Miller tapped ash on the rug. Her head swayed slightly as she tried to focus her eyes. "You promised to leave if I made the sandwiches," she said.

"Dear me, did I?"

"It was a promise and I'm tired and I don't feel well at all."

"Mustn't fret," said Miriam. "I'm only teasing."

She picked up her coat, slung it over her arm, and arranged her beret in front of a mirror. Presently she bent close to Mrs Miller and whispered, "Kiss me goodnight."

"Please – I'd rather not," said Mrs Miller.

Miriam lifted a shoulder, arched an eyebrow. "As you like," she said, and went directly to the coffee table, seized the vase containing the paper roses, carried it to where the hard surface of the floor lay bare, and hurled it downward. Glass sprayed in all directions and she stamped her foot on the bouquet.

Then slowly she walked to the door, but before closing it she looked back at Mrs Miller with a slyly innocent curiosity.

Mrs Miller spent the next day in bed, rising once to feed the canary and drink a cup of tea; she took her temperature and had none, yet her dreams were feverishly agitated; their unbalanced mood lingered even as she lay staring wide-eyed at the ceiling. One dream threaded through the others like an elusively mysterious theme in a complicated symphony, and the scenes it depicted were sharply outlined, as though sketched by a hand of gifted intensity; a small girl wearing a bridal gown and a wreath of leaves, led a grey procession down a mountain path, and among them there was unusual silence till a woman at the rear asked, "Where is she taking us?" "No one knows," said an old man marching in front. "But isn't she pretty?"

volunteered a third voice. "Isn't she like a frost flower . . . so shining and white?"

Tuesday morning she woke up feeling better; harsh slats of sunlight, slanting through Venetian blinds, shed a disrupting light on her unwholesome fancies. She opened the window to discover a thawed, mild-as-spring day; a sweep of clean new clouds crumpled against a vastly blue, out-of-season sky; and across the low line of rooftops she could see the river and smoke curving from the tugboat stacks in a warm wind. A great silver truck ploughed the snow-banked street, its machine sound humming in the air.

After straightening the apartment, she went to the grocer's, cashed a cheque and continued to Schrafft's where she ate breakfast and chatted happily with the waitress. Oh, it was a wonderful day – more like a holiday – and it would be foolish to go home.

She boarded a Lexington Avenue bus and rode up to Eighty-sixth Street; it was here that she had decided to do a little shopping.

She had no idea what she wanted or needed, but she idled along, intent only upon the passers-by, brisk and preoccupied, who gave her a disturbing sense of separateness.

It was while waiting at the corner of Third Avenue that she saw the man; an old man, bow-legged and stooped under an armload of bulging packages; he wore a shabby brown coat and a chequered cap. Suddenly she realized they were exchanging a smile: there was nothing friendly about this smile, it was two cold flickers of recognition. But she was certain she had never seen him before. He was standing next to an El pillar, and as she crossed the street he turned and followed. He kept quite close; from the corner of her eye she watched his reflection wavering on the shop windows.

Then in the middle of the block she stopped and faced him. He stopped also and cocked his head, grinning. But

what could she say? Do? Here, in broad daylight, on Eighty-sixth Street? It was useless and, despising her own helplessness, she quickened her steps.

Now, Second Avenue is a dismal street, made from scraps and ends; part cobblestone, part asphalt, part cement; and its atmosphere of desertion is permanent. Mrs Miller walked five blocks without meeting anyone, and all the while the steady crunch of his footfalls in the snow stayed near. And when she came to a florist's shop, the sound was still with her. She hurried inside and watched through the glass door as the old man passed; he kept his eyes straight ahead and didn't slow his pace, but he did one strange, telling thing; he tipped his cap.

"Six white ones, did you say?" asked the florist. "Yes," she told him, "white roses." From there she went to a glassware store and selected a vase, presumably a replacement for the one Miriam had broken, thought the price was intolerable and the vase itself (she thought) grotesquely vulgar. But a series of unaccountable purchases had begun, as if by prearranged plan: a plan of which she had not the least knowledge or control.

She bought a bag of glazed cherries, and at a place called the Knickerbocker Bakery she paid forty cents for six almond cakes.

Within the last hour the weather had turned cold again; like blurred lenses, winter clouds cast a shade over the sun, and the skeleton of an early dusk coloured the sky; a damp mist mixed with the wind and the voices of a few children who romped high on mountains of gutter snow, seemed lonely and cheerless. Soon the first flake fell, and when Mrs Miller reached the brownstone house, snow was falling in a swift screen and foot tracks vanished as they were printed.

The white roses were arranged decoratively in the vase. The glazed cherries shone on a ceramic plate. The almond cakes, dusted with sugar, awaited a hand. The canary fluttered on its swing and picked at a bar of seed.

At precisely five the doorbell rang. Mrs Miller knew who it was. The hem of her housecoat trailed as she crossed the floor. "Is that you?" she called.

"Naturally," said Miriam, the word resounding shrilly from the hall. "Open this door."

"Go away," said Mrs Miller.

"Please hurry . . . I have a heavy package."

"Go away," said Mrs Miller. She returned to the living-room, lighted a cigarette, sat down and calmly listened to the buzzer; on and on and on. "You might as well leave. I have no intention of letting you in."

Shortly, the bell stopped. For possibly ten minutes Mrs Miller did not move. Then, hearing no sound, she concluded Miriam had gone. She tiptoed to the door and opened it a sliver; Miriam was half-reclining atop a cardboard box with a beautiful French doll cradled in her arms.

"Really, I thought you were never coming," she said peevishly. "Here, help me get this in, it's awfully heavy."

It was not spell-like compulsion that Mrs Miller felt, but rather a curious passivity; she brought in the box, Miriam the doll. Miriam curled up on the sofa, not troubling to remove her coat or beret, and watched disinterestedly as Mrs Miller dropped the box and stood trembling, trying to catch her breath.

"Thank you," she said. In the daylight she looked pinched and drawn, her hair less luminous. The French doll she was loving wore an exquisite powdered wig and its idiot glass eyes sought solace in Miriam's. "I have a surprise," she continued. "Look into my box."

Kneeling, Mrs Miller parted the flaps and lifted out another doll; then a blue dress which she recalled as the one Miriam had worn that first night at the theatre; and of the remainder she said, "It's all clothes. Why?"

"Because I've come to live with you," said Miriam, twisting a cherry stem. "Wasn't it nice of you to buy me the cherries . . .?"

"But you can't! For God's sake go away – go away and leave me alone!"

". . . and the roses and the almond cakes? How really wonderfully generous. You know, these cherries are delicious. The last place I lived was with an old man; he was terribly poor and we never had good things to eat. But I think I'll be happy here." She paused to snuggle her doll closer. "Now, if you'll just show me where to put my things . . ."

Mrs Miller's face dissolved into a mask of ugly red lines; she began to cry, and it was an unnatural, tearless sort of weeping, as though, not having wept for a long time, she had forgotten how. Carefully she edged backward till she touched the door.

She fumbled through the hall and down the stairs to a landing below. She pounded frantically on the door of the first apartment she came to; a short red-headed man answered and she pushed past him. "Say, what the hell is

this?" he said. "Anything wrong, lover?" asked a young woman who appeared from the kitchen, drying her hands. And it was to her that Mrs Miller turned.

"Listen," she cried, "I'm ashamed behaving this way but – well, I'm Mrs H. T. Miller and I live upstairs and . . ." She pressed her hands over her face. "It sounds so absurd . . ."

The woman guided her to a chair, while the man excitedly rattled pocket change. "Yeah?"

"I live upstairs and there's a little girl visiting me, and I suppose that I'm afraid of her. She won't leave and I can't make her and – she's going to do something terrible. She's already stolen my cameo, but she's about to do something worse – something terrible!"

The man asked, "Is she a relative, huh?"

Mrs Miller shook her head. "I don't know who she is. Her name's Miriam, but I don't know for certain who she is."

"You gotta calm down, honey," said the woman, stroking Mrs Miller's arm. "Harry here'll tend to this kid. Go on, lover." And Mrs Miller said, "The door's open – 5A."

After the man left, the woman brought a towel and bathed Mrs Miller's face. "You're very kind," Mrs Miller said. "I'm sorry to act such a fool, only this wicked child . . ."

"Sure, honey," consoled the woman. "Now, you better take it easy."

Mrs Miller rested her head in the crook of her arm; she was quiet enough to be asleep. The woman turned a radio dial; a piano and a husky voice filled the silence, and the woman, tapping her foot, kept excellent time. "Maybe we oughta go up too," she said.

"I don't want to see her again. I don't want to be anywhere near her."

"Uh-huh, but what you shoulda done, you shoulda called a cop."

Presently they heard the man on the stairs. He strode into the room frowning and scratching the back of his neck, "Nobody there," he said, honestly embarrassed. "She musta beat it."

"Harry, you're a jerk," announced the woman. "We been sitting here the whole time and we woulda seen . . ." She stopped abruptly, for the man's glance was sharp.

"I looked all over," he said, "and there just ain't nobody there. Nobody, understand?"

"Tell me," said Mrs Miller, rising, "tell me, did you see a large box? Or a doll?"

"No, maam, I didn't."

And the woman, as if delivering a verdict, said, "Well, for cryin' out loud . . ."

Mrs Miller entered her apartment softly; she walked to the centre of the room and stood quite still. No, in a sense it had not changed; the roses, the cakes, and the cherries were in place. But this was an empty room, emptier than if the furnishings and familiars were not present, lifeless and petrified as in a funeral parlour. The sofa loomed before her with a new strangeness; its vacancy had a meaning that would have been less penetrating and terrible had Miriam been curled on it. She gazed fixedly at the space where she remembered setting the box, and, for a moment, the hassock spun desperately. And she looked through the window; surely the river was real, surely snow was falling – but then, one could not be certain witness to anything: Miriam, so vividly there – and yet, where was she? Where, where?

As though moving in a dream, she sank to a chair. The room was losing shape; it was dark and getting darker and there was nothing to be done about it; she could not lift her hand to light a lamp.

Suddenly, closing her eyes, she felt an upward surge, like a diver emerging from some deeper, greener depth. In times of terror or immense distress, there are moments when the mind waits as though for a revelation, while a skein of calm is woven over thought; it is like a sleep, or a supernatural trance; and during this lull one is aware of a force of quiet reasoning: well, what if she had never really known a girl named Miriam? That she had been foolishly frightened on the street? In the end, like everything else, it was of no importance. For the only thing she had lost to Miriam was her identity, but now she knew she had found again the person who lived in this room, who cooked her own meals, who owned a canary, who was someone she could trust and believe in: Mrs H. T. Miller.

Listening in contentment, she became aware of a double sound: a bureau drawer opening and closing; she seemed to hear it long after completion – opening and closing. Then gradually the harshness of it was replaced by the murmur of a silk dress and this, delicately faint, was moving nearer and swelling in intensity till the walls trembled with the vibration and the room was caving under a wave of whispers. Mrs Miller stiffened her eyes to a dull, direct stare.

"Hello," said Miriam.

THE OPEN WINDOW

SAKI (H. H. MUNRO)

"**M**Y AUNT WILL BE down presently, Mr Nuttel," said a very self-possessed young lady of fifteen; "in the meantime you must try to put up with me."

Framton Nuttel endeavoured to say the correct something which should duly flatter the niece of the moment without unduly discounting the aunt that was to come. Privately he doubted more than ever whether these formal visits on a succession of total strangers would do much towards helping the nerve cure which he was supposed to be undergoing.

"I know how it will be," his sister had said when he was preparing to migrate to his rural retreat; "you will bury yourself down there and not speak to a living soul, and your nerves will be worse than ever from moping. I shall just give you letters of introduction to all the people I know there. Some of them, as far as I can remember, were quite nice."

Framton wondered whether Mrs Sappleton, the lady to whom he was presenting one of the letters of introduction, came into the nice division.

"Do you know many of the people round here?" asked the niece, when she judged that they had had sufficient silent communion.

"Hardly a soul," said Framton. "My sister was staying

here, at the rectory, you know, some four years ago, and she gave me letters of introduction to some of the people here."

He made the last statement in a tone of distinct regret.

"Then you know practically nothing about my aunt?" pursued the self-possessed young lady.

"Only her name and address," admitted the caller. He was wondering whether Mrs Sappleton was in the married or widowed state. An undefinable something about the room seemed to suggest masculine habitation.

"Her great tragedy happened just three years ago," said the child; "that would be since your sister's time."

"Her tragedy?" asked Framton; somehow in this restful country spot tragedies seemed out of place.

"You may wonder why we keep that window wide open on an October afternoon," said the niece, indicating a large French window that opened on to a lawn.

"It is quite warm for the time of the year," said Framton; "but has that window got anything to do with the tragedy?"

"Out through that window, three years ago to a day, her husband and her two young brothers went off for their day's shooting. They never came back. In crossing the moor to their favourite snipe-shooting ground they were all three engulfed in a treacherous piece of bog. It had been that dreadful wet summer, you know, and places that were safe in other years gave way suddenly without warning. Their bodies were never recovered. That was the dreadful part of it." Here the child's voice lost its self-possessed note and became falteringly human. "Poor aunt always thinks that they will come back some day, they and the little brown spaniel that was lost with them, and walk in at that window just as they used to do. This is why the window is kept open every evening till it is quite dusk. Poor dear aunt, she has often told me how they went out, her husband with his white waterproof coat over his arm, and Ronnie, her youngest brother, singing, 'Bertie, why do you bound?' as he always did to tease her, because she said it got on her nerves. Do you know, sometimes on still, quiet evenings like this, I almost get a creepy feeling that they will all walk in through that window—"

She broke off with a little shudder. It was a relief to Framton when the aunt bustled into the room with a whirl of apologies for being late in making her appearance.

"I hope Vera has been amusing you?" she said.

"She has been very interesting," said Framton.

"I hope you don't mind the open window," said Mrs Sappleton briskly; "my husband and brothers will be home directly from shooting, and they always come in this way. They've been out for snipe in the marshes today, so they'll make a fine mess over my poor carpets. So like you men-folk, isn't it?"

She rattled on cheerfully about the shooting and the scarcity of birds, and the prospects for duck in the winter. To Framton it was all purely horrible. He made a desperate but only partially successful effort to turn the talk on to a less ghastly topic; he was conscious that his hostess was giving him only a fragment of her attention, and her eyes were constantly straying past him to the open window and the lawn beyond. It was certainly an unfortunate coincidence that he should have paid his visit on this tragic anniversary.

"The doctors agree in ordering me complete rest, an absence of mental excitement, and avoidance of anything in the nature of violent physical exercise," announced Framton, who laboured under the tolerably widespread delusion that total strangers and chance acquaintances are hungry for the least detail of one's ailments and infirmities, their cause and cure. "On the matter of diet they are not so much in agreement," he continued.

"No?" said Mrs Sappleton, in a voice which only replaced a yawn at the last moment. Then she suddenly brightened into alert attention – but not to what Framton was saying.

"Here they are at last!" she cried. "Just in time for tea, and don't they look as if they were muddy up to the eyes!"

Framton shivered slightly and turned towards the niece with a look intended to convey sympathetic comprehension. The child was staring out through the open window with dazed horror in her eyes. In a chill shock of nameless fear Framton swung round in his seat and looked in the same direction.

In the deepening twilight three figures were walking across the lawn towards the window; they all carried guns under their arms, and one of them was additionally burdened with a white coat hung over his shoulders. A tired brown spaniel kept close at their heels. Noiselessly they neared the house, and then a hoarse young voice chanted out of the dusk: "I said, Bertie, why do you bound?"

Framton grabbed wildly at his stick and hat; the hall-door, the gravel drive, and the front gate were dimly-noted stages in his headlong retreat. A cyclist coming along the road had to run into the hedge to avoid imminent collision.

"Here we are, my dear," said the bearer of the white mackintosh, coming in through the window; "fairly muddy, but most of it's dry. Who was that who bolted out as we came up?"

"A most extraordinary man, a Mr Nuttel," said Mrs Sappleton; "could only talk about his illnesses, and dashed off without a word of goodbye or apology when you arrived. One would think he had seen a ghost."

"I expect it was the spaniel," said the niece calmly; "he told me he had a horror of dogs. He was once hunted into a cemetery somewhere on the banks of the Ganges by a pack of pariah dogs, and had to spend the night in a newly dug grave with the creatures snarling and grinning and foaming just above him. Enough to make anyone lose their nerve."

Romance at short notice was her speciality.

THE STORY OF GLAM

WILLIAM MAYNE

Edited from an Icelandic account of 1853

I N THE NORTH of Iceland, about the year 1000, a man
named Thorhall lived at Thorhall-stead in Waterdale.
He was fairly wealthy, and no one round about had so
much livestock as he had.

His part of Waterdale was greatly haunted, so that he
could scarcely get a shepherd to stay with him, and with
Grettir, a very strong no-nonsense lad, being away at the
time, he could find no one to help or advise him. So one
summer at the Althing, or yearly assembly of the people,
Thorhall went to the booth of Skafti, the lawyer, who
received him in a friendly way and asked him what news
he had.

"Ill news," said Thorhall. "I need advice from you. I
would go to Grettir, though he is only eighteen years of
age; but no one speaks of him."

"He has been sent abroad for three years as an outlaw,"
said Skafti. "The youth has done shameful deeds, so he
cannot help. But what is the matter? What is your ill
news?"

"It is this," said Thorhall, "I have had very bad luck with my shepherds for these last few years. Some of them get injured, and others do not serve out their time; and now none of them will take the position at all."

"Waterdale is a wild place," said Skafti. "There must be some evil spirit there, but it is a long time before Grettir can return and sort things out. However, I can get a shepherd for you. His name is Glam, and he came from Sweden last summer. He is big and strong, but moody and not well liked by most people."

Thorhall said that his shepherd would be out on the fell looking after the sheep, with no one to like him or not; and in any case there was no hope of another man doing it.

"Glam is strong and stout-hearted," said Skafti. "You will find him somewhere along Armann's Fell."

Thorhall's road home led him south along Armann's Fell. He saw a tall man coming down from the mountain, leading a horse laden with bundles of brushwood. His eyes were blue and staring, and his hair wolf-grey in colour. Thorhall was certain that this was the man he had been told about. They met, and Thorhall asked his name.

The man said, "I am Glam, from Sweden."

"Skafti told me of you, and that I should meet you here," said Thorhall. "I am looking for a shepherd for the winter."

"On condition, you must understand," said Glam, "that I have my own free will. I know the work and what to do, and do not take orders from day to day. I must be my own master."

"That will do very well," said Thorhall.

"But I wonder why you ask *me* to do the work," said Glam; "is there some trouble at your place? I imagine there is."

"It is supposed to be haunted," said Thorhall.

"I am not afraid of ghosts," said Glam, "I will have a merry time with them."

They parted, and the summer passed, and at the time appointed Glam came to Thorhall-stead.

He began his work among the sheep with little trouble, for the flock all ran together when he shouted in his loud, hoarse voice.

There was a church at Thorhall-stead, but Glam would never go to it nor join in the service. He was surly, and difficult to deal with, just as he promised, and no one liked him and his rough ways.

On Christmas Eve morning Glam rose early and called for food, which he expected as usual.

The goodwife answered: "It is not the custom of Christian people to eat today, because tomorrow is the first day of Christmas, and today we fast."

Glam replied: "You have foolish fashions that I see no good in. It was far better when men were heathens. Now I want my food, and no nonsense."

The goodwife answered: "You will come to sorrow today if you act so wickedly."

"Food," said Glam. "Now, or it will be the worse for you."

She brought him cold crusts, which did not please him. After he had eaten he left in a great rage. It was dark and gloomy all round; the weather was very bad; snowflakes were driving; loud noises filled the air and grew worse as the day wore on.

Those at the stead heard the shepherd's voice during the forenoon, but less of him as the day passed. Snow began to drift, and by evening there was a violent storm. People came to the service in church, but still Glam did not come home. There was talk of going to look for him, but no search was made because of the storm and darkness.

In the morning men went to look for him. They found sheep scattered in the fens, beaten down by the storm, or up on the hills. They came to a place in the valley where the snow was greatly trampled, as if there had been a dreadful struggle there, with stones and frozen earth torn up all round about.

They found Glam lying a little distance off, quite dead.

He was black in colour, and swollen up as big as an ox. They were horrified, fell silent, and shuddered in their hearts at such a sight on Christmas Day.

All the same, they tried to carry him to the church, but could get him no further than to the edge of a gill, a little lower down.

They left him there and went home to tell Thorhall what had happened. They said that they had traced footprints in the snow as large as the bottom of a barrel, leading from the trampled place up to the cliffs at the head of the valley, and that all along the track there were huge bloodstains.

From this Thorhall guessed that an evil spirit which lived there must have killed Glam, but had received so many wounds itself that it had died. Certainly nothing was ever seen of it afterwards.

The second day of Christmas, they tried again to bring Glam to the church. They yoked horses to him, but after they had come down the slope and reached level ground they could drag him no further. He had to be left there.

On the third day, a priest went with them, but Glam was not to be found, although they searched all day. The priest refused to go a second time, and then Glam was found at once. He did not want to be at church, they realized, and they buried him on the spot under a mound of stones.

In the following days they became aware that Glam was not lying quiet, and that great damage was being done by him, for those that saw him on the hillside fainted and lost their reason for a time. After Yule men believed that he was about the farm itself, and many of them ran away.

Then Glam began to ride on the house-top by night, and nearly shook it to pieces; and he walked about night and day. Men hardly dared to go up into the valley, even though they had urgent business there. Everyone in the district blamed Thorhall for hiring him.

In spring Thorhall hired new men, and started the farm again, while Glam's walkings began to grow less frequent as the days grew longer.

That summer a ship from Norway came into the creek of Waterdale, bringing a man called Thorgaut. He was foreign by birth, very big, and as strong as two men. He was looking for work. Thorhall rode to the ship, and asked him whether he would enter his service. Thorgaut answered that he might well do so, and that he did not care much what work he did.

"You might care at last, however," said Thorhall, "Thorhall-stead is no place for any faint-hearted man, on account of the hauntings. I do not wish to deceive you in any way, so I tell you at once they have been bad."

"Ghosts!" said Thorgaut. "When I come it is the ghosts who will take up their packs and leave. You will see."

The summer went past, and Thorgaut began shepherding when the winter nights came, and was well liked by everyone.

Glam began to ride again on the house-top. Thorgaut laughed at that, saying that the thing would have to come much closer before he would be afraid of it.

Thorhall said, "It will be better for you if you do not meet at all."

"It will be better for him," said Thorgaut; "and I am not going to fall dead at such talk."

Christmas came round again, and on Christmas Eve the shepherd went out to his sheep.

"God send," said the goodwife, "that things will not go as they did a year since."

"I have no fear of that, goodwife," said Thorgaut; "there will be something worth talking about if I don't come back."

Thorgaut was in the habit of coming home when it was half-dark, but on this occasion he did not return at his usual time. The weather was cold again, and a heavy drift blew. People came to church, and began to say that things were to happen as they had before. Thorhall wished to search for the shepherd, but the church-goers shook their heads, and would not risk meeting evil demons by night.

But after their morning meal on Christmas Day they went out to look for the shepherd, first going to Glam's cairn, guessing that he was the cause of the man's disappearance.

There they found the shepherd with his neck broken and every bone in his body smashed in pieces. They carried him to the church, as they had never managed to do with Glam's body. Thorgaut's poor body did no harm to any man at all, and they gave it a Christian burial.

But Glam began his mischief again, and so much of it that everyone fled from Thorhall-stead, except Thorhall himself and his goodwife; and his chief cattleman, who had been there for a long time, did not want to go away either, saying that everything his master had would go to rack and ruin if there was no one to look after it.

One morning after the middle of winter the goodwife went out to the byre to milk the cows. It was broad daylight, since she wouldn't venture outside earlier than that. She heard a great noise and a fearful bellowing in the byre, and ran back into the house shouting out that some awful thing was going on there.

Thorhall went out to the cattle and found them goring each other with their horns. He went through into the barn, and saw the cattleman lying on his back with his head in one stall and his feet in another, his back broken over the upright stone between the stalls.

Thorhall thought it was time to leave the farm with all that he could remove. All the livestock he left behind was killed by Glam, who then went through the whole dale and laid waste all the farms up to the mountains. Thorhall spent the rest of the winter with various friends. No one could go into the dale with horse or dog, for these were killed at once; but when spring came again and the days began to lengthen, Glam's walkings grew less frequent.

Thorhall returned to Thorhall-stead. He had difficulty in getting servants, but managed to set up his home again. Things went just as before. When autumn came, the hauntings began, and now it was Thorhall's daughter who was most attacked, hearing and seeing what no other person saw. By the end of the winter she died of fright.

It seemed as if the whole dale would be laid waste.

At this time, as Skafti had said, it was safe for Grettir to return home, and he landed in autumn. When the winter nights were well advanced, he rode north to Waterdale to visit his uncle Jokull. He stayed there for three nights, and there was much talk about Glam's walkings.

Grettir inquired closely about what had happened, and Jokull told him the stories reported no more than had indeed taken place.

"But are you intending to go there?" he asked.

"Indeed I am," said Grettir.

"It is unwise," said Jokull. "It is a dangerous undertaking, and there is a great risk of you losing your life and your friends losing you. Ill will come of ill where Glam is. It is better to seek honour among mortal men than with evil spirits. Good luck and good heart are not the same."

Grettir said, "I did ill deeds when I was a lad. I have paid with being outlawed, but that was far from the sight of men. Now I shall seek this danger and pay that past part of my debt in the sight of them. But I see no good coming of it."

"Both of us see some way into the future," said Jokull; "yet neither of us can do anything to prevent it."

Grettir rode to Thorhall-stead and said that he wished to stay there if Thorhall would allow him. "I have heard how matters stand," said Grettir, "and that they must be put right."

Thorhall said that he would be very glad if he would stay; "but I shall be very unwilling for you to come to harm on my account. Even if you yourself escape safe and sound, you will lose your horse, for no man that comes here can keep his mount uninjured."

Grettir said that there were horses enough to be got, whatever might happen to this one. Thorhall then gave him a hearty welcome.

The horse was locked and barred in a stable, and the men went to sleep at the hearth in the house. That night passed without Glam appearing.

"Your coming here," said Thorhall, "has made a change. Until now Glam was in the habit of riding the house every night."

"I shall stay for another night, and see how things go," said Grettir. "He knows my strength."

After this they went to look at Grettir's horse, and found that he had not been meddled with, so they thought that everything was going on well. Grettir stayed another night, and still Glam did not come about them. But when Thorhall went to look to Grettir's horse he found the stable broken up, the horse dragged outside, and every bone of it broken. Grettir saw what had happened, and said, "The least I can do for my horse is to see the thing that has done this."

Thorhall said that it would do him no good to see Glam, who was now unlike anything in human shape.

"But I shall stay," said Grettir. "I came to see and fight."

"Glam is sure to ride the rigging of the roof tonight," said Thorhall. "Hear him and go."

At bedtime Grettir lay down on the floor against Thorhall's bed-closet. He put a thick cloak above himself, buttoning one end beneath his feet, and doubling the other under his head, and he looked out at the hole for the neck. There was a strong plank in front of the floored space, and against this he pressed his feet.

The fittings had long broken off from the outer door by Glam, but here was a hurdle set up instead, tightly lashed. The wainscot that had once stretched across the hall was broken down, both above and below the cross-beam. The beds were pulled out of their places, and everything was in confusion.

A light was left burning in the hall. When the third part of the night was past Grettir heard loud noises outside. Something went up on top of the house, and rode a long time above the hall, beating the roof with its heels till every beam cracked. Then it came down off the house and went to the door and thrust in its head, of ghastly size, huge of feature.

Glam bent to come in slowly, and stood up when he was inside the doorway, high against the roof. He turned his face down the hall, laid his arms on the cross-beam, and glared all over the place.

Thorhall did not dare move, thinking it bad enough to hear what was going on outside.

Grettir lay inside the cloak, watched, and never moved. Glam saw that there was a bundle lying on the floor, and went to pick it up.

Inside the bundle was Grettir. Grettir placed his feet against the plank, and held himself back. Glam tugged a second time, much harder than before, but still the bundle did not move. A third time Glam pulled with both his hands, so strongly that he raised Grettir up from the floor, hold on as he might; and they rived the cloak apart between them.

Glam stood staring at the piece which he held in his hands, wondering what it was and who could have pulled so hard against him.

At that moment Grettir sprang in under the monster's hands, and threw his arms around his waist, intending to make him fall backwards. Glam, however, was so strong that Grettir gave way before him. He was pushed through the hall benches, but these gave way with him, and next the table, and then the meal-kists; and the fire was scattered.

Glam wanted to get him outside. Although Grettir set his feet against everything that he could, Glam dragged him out into the porch. There they had a fierce struggle, for Glam meant to have him out of doors, and Grettir saw that it would be worse outside, and struggled not to be carried out.

Glam used all his strength, and pulled Grettir close to him. Grettir changed his plan, and threw himself as hard as he could against the monster's breast, setting both his feet against an earth-fast stone that lay in the doorway. Glam was pulling Grettir towards him and was not prepared for this, and went crashing out through the door, his shoulders catching the lintel as he fell.

The roof of the porch was wrenched in two, rafters and frozen thatch alike, and he went backwards out of the house with Grettir above him.

There was bright moonlight and broken clouds, sometimes drifting over the moon and sometimes leaving it clear. As Glam fell a cloud passed off the moon, and he cast up his eyes sharply towards it. Grettir himself said that this was the only sight he ever saw that terrified him, those eyes rolling and glaring.

Grettir grew so helpless, with weariness and at seeing Glam roll his eyes so horribly, that he was unable to draw his dagger, and lay limply between life and death.

"You have great strength, Grettir," said Glam. "But you have now received only half of the strength and vigour that was destined for you if you had not come to fight against me. I cannot now take from you the strength you have already gained, but you will never be stronger than you are now, and yet you will think it hard to be alone, at any time; and that will bring you to your death."

When Glam had said this, Grettir saw that the victory was his all the same, drew his dagger, cut off Glam's head, and laid it beside his thigh.

Thorhall then came out, into the quiet after the battle, having put on his clothes while Glam was talking, but never venturing to come near until he had fallen.

They set to work, and burned Glam to ashes, which they placed in a sack, and buried where cattle were least likely to pasture or men to walk.

Thorhall sent to the next farm for the men there, and told them what had happened. After that it was the common talk of Iceland there was no man like Grettir for strength and courage and all kinds of bodily feats. Thorhall gave him a good horse when he went away, as well as a fine suit of clothes, for the ones he had been wearing were all torn to pieces. The two then parted with the utmost friendship.

Grettir rode to his own farmstead. When he was asked how he now was, Grettir answered that his temper was not improved; he was more easily roused than ever, and less able to bear opposition. But worst, he had become so much afraid of the dark that he dared not go anywhere alone after night began to fall, because he saw phantoms and monsters of every kind, and if he did not see them, he fancied he might. This evil gift is called glam-sight.

Such fear, and a horror of being alone brought Grettir, at last, to his end.

THE HIGHBOY

ALISON LURIE

EVEN BEFORE I knew more about that piece of furniture I wouldn't have wanted it in my house. For a valuable antique, it wasn't particularly attractive. With that tall stack of dark mahogany drawers, and those long spindly bowed legs, it looked not only heavy but top-heavy. But then Clark and I have never cared much for Chippendale; we prefer simple lines and light woods. The carved bonnet-top of the highboy was too elaborate for my taste, and the surface had been polished till it glistened a deep blackish brown, exactly the colour of canned prunes.

Still, I could understand why the piece meant so much to Clark's sister-in-law, Buffy Stockwell. It mattered to her that she had what she called "really good things": that her antiques were genuine and her china was Spode. She never made a point of how superior her "things" were to most people's, but one was aware of it. And besides, the highboy was an heirloom; it had been in her family for years. I could see why she was disappointed and cross when her aunt left it to Buffy's brother.

"I don't want to sound ungrateful, Janet, honestly," Buffy told me over lunch at the country club. "I realize Jack's carrying on the family name and I'm not. And of course I was glad to have Aunt Betsy's Tiffany coffee service. I suppose it's worth as much as the highboy actually, but it just doesn't have any past. It's got no personality, if you know what I mean."

Buffy giggled. My sister-in-law was given to anthropomorphizing her possessions, speaking of them as if they had human traits: "A dear little Paul Revere sugar-spoon." "It's lively, even kind of aggressive, for a plant-stand – but I think it'll be really happy on the sunporch." Whenever their washer or sit-down mower or VCR wasn't working properly she'd say it was "ill". I'd found the habit endearing once, but it had begun to bore me.

"I don't understand it really," Buffy said, digging her dessert fork into the lemon cream tart that she always ordered at the club after declaring that she shouldn't. "After all, I'm the one who was named for Aunt Betsy, and she knew how interested I was in family history. I always thought I was her favourite. Well, live and learn." She giggled again and took another bite, leaving a fleck of whipped cream on her short, lifted upper lip.

You mustn't get me wrong. Buffy and her husband Bobby, Clark's brother, were both dears, and as affectionate and reliable and nice as anyone could possibly be. But even Clark had to admit that they'd never quite grown up. Bobby was sixty-one and a vice-president of his company, but his life still centred around golf and tennis.

Buffy, who was nearly his age, didn't play any more because of her heart. But she still favoured yellow and shocking-pink sportswear, and kept her hair in blond all-over curls and maintained her girlish manner. Then of course she had these bouts of childlike whimsicality: she attributed opinions to their pets, and named their automobiles. She insisted that their poodle Suzy disliked the mailman because he was a Democrat, and for years she'd driven a series of Plymouth Valiant wagons called Prince.

*

The next time the subject of the highboy came up was at a dinner-party at our house about a month later, after Buffy'd been to see her brother in Connecticut. "It wasn't all that successful a visit," she reported, "You know my Aunt Betsy left Jack her Newport highboy, that I was hoping would come to me. I think I told you."

I agreed that she had.

"Well, it's in his house in Stonington now. But it's completely out of place among all that pickled-walnut imitation French provincial furniture that Jack's new wife chose. It looked so uncomfortable." Buffy sighed and helped herself to roast potatoes as they went round.

"It really makes me sad," she went on. "I could tell right away that Jack and his wife don't appreciate Aunt Betsy's highboy, the way they've shoved it slap up into the corner behind the patio door. Jack claims it's because he can't get it to stand steady, and the drawers always stick."

"Well, perhaps they do," I said. "After all, the piece must be over two hundred years old."

But Buffy wouldn't agree. Aunt Betsy had almost never had that sort of trouble, though she admitted once to Buffy that the highboy was temperamental. Usually the drawers would slide open as smoothly as butter, but now and then they seized up.

It probably had something to do with the humidity, I suggested. But according to Buffy her Aunt Betsy, who seems to have had the same sort of imagination as her niece, used to say that the highboy was sulking; someone had been rough with it, she would suggest, or it hadn't been polished lately.

"I'm sure Jack's wife doesn't know how to take proper care of good furniture either," Buffy went on during the salad course. "She's too busy with her high-powered executive job."

"Honestly, Janet, it's true," she added. "When I was there last week the finish was already beginning to look dull, almost soapy. Aunt Betsy always used to polish it

177

once a week with beeswax, to keep the patina. I mentioned that twice, but I could see Jack's wife wasn't paying any attention. Not that she ever pays any attention to me." Buffy gave a little short nervous giggle like a hiccup. Her brother's wife wasn't the only one of the family who thought of her as a lightweight, and she wasn't too silly to know it.

"What I suspect is, Janet, I suspect she's letting her cleaning-lady spray it with that awful synthetic no-rub polish they make now," Buffy went on, frowning across the glazed damask. "I found a can of the stuff under her sink. Full of nasty chemicals you can't pronounce. Anyhow, I'm sure the climate in Stonington can't be good for old furniture; not with all that salt and damp in the air."

There was a lull in the conversation then, and at the other end of the table Buffy's husband heard her and gave a kind of guffaw. "Say, Clark," he called to my husband. "I wish you'd tell Buffy to forget about that old highboy."

Well naturally Clark was not going to do anything of the sort. But he leant towards us and listened to Buffy's story, and then he suggested that she ask her brother if he'd be willing to exchange the highboy for her aunt's coffee service.

I thought this was a good idea, and so did Buffy. She wrote off to her brother, and a few days later Jack phoned to say that was fine by him. He was sick of the highboy; no matter how he tried to prop up the legs it still wobbled.

Besides, the day before he'd gone to get out some maps for a trip they were planning and the whole thing just kind of seized up. He'd stopped trying to free the top drawer with a screwdriver, and was working on one of the lower ones, when he got a hell of a crack on the head. He must have loosened something somehow, he told Buffy, so that when he pulled on the lower drawer the upper one slid out noiselessly above him. And when he stood up, bingo.

It was Saturday, and their doctor was off call, so Jack's

wife had to drive him ten miles to the Westerly emergency room; he was too dizzy and confused to drive himself. There wasn't any concussion, according to the X-rays, but he had a lump on his head the size of a plum and a headache the size of a football. He'd be happy to ship that goddamned piece of furniture to her as soon as it was convenient, he told Buffy, and she could take her time about sending along the coffee service.

Two weeks later when I went over to Buffy's for tea her aunt's highboy had arrived. She was so pleased that I bore with her when she started talking about how it appreciated the care she was taking of it. "When I rub in the beeswax I can almost feel it purring under my hand like a big cat," she insisted. I glanced at the highboy again. I thought I'd never seen a less agreeable-looking piece of furniture. Its pretentious high-arched bonnet top resembled a clumsy mahogany Napoleon hat, and the ball-and-claw feet made the thing look as if it were up on tiptoe. If it was a big cat, it was a cat with bird's legs – a sort of gryphon.

"I know it's grateful to be here," Buffy told me. "The other day I couldn't find my reading-glasses anywhere; but then, when I was standing in the sitting-room, at my wits' end, I heard a little creak, or maybe it was more sort of a pop. I looked round and one of the top drawers of the highboy was out about an inch. Well, I went to shut it, and there were my glasses! Now what do you make of that?"

I made nothing of it, but humoured her. "Quite a coincidence."

"Oh, more than that." Buffy gave a rippling giggle. "And it's completely steady now. Try and see."

I put one hand on the highboy and gave the thing a little push, and she was perfectly right. It stood solid and heavy against the cream Colonial Willliamsburg wallpaper, as if it had been in Buffy's house for centuries. The prune-dark mahogany was waxy to the touch and colder than I would have expected.

"And the drawers don't stick the least little bit." Buffy slid them open and shut to demonstrate. "I know it's going to be happy here."

It was early spring when the highboy arrived and whether or not it was happy, it gave no trouble until that summer. Then in July we had a week of drenching thunderstorms and the drawers began to jam. I saw it happen one Sunday when Clark and I were over and Bobby tried to get out the slides of their recent trip to Quebec. He started shaking the thing and swearing, and Buffy got up and hurried over to him.

"There's nothing at all wrong with the highboy," she whispered to me afterwards. "Bobby just doesn't understand how to treat it. You mustn't force the drawers open like that; you have to be gentle."

After we'd sat through the slides, Bobby went to put them away.

"Careful, darling," Buffy warned him.

"Okay, okay," Bobby said; but it was clear he wasn't

listening seriously. He yanked the drawer open without much trouble; but when he slammed it shut he let out a frightful howl: he'd shut his right thumb inside.

"Christ, will you look at that!" he shouted, holding out his broad red hand to show us a deep dented gash below the knuckle. "I think the damn thing's broken."

Well, Bobby's thumb wasn't broken; but it was bruised rather badly, as it turned out. His hand was swollen for over a week, so that he couldn't play in the golf tournament at the club, which meant a lot to him.

Buffy and I were sitting on the clubhouse terrace that day, and Bobby was moseying about by the first tee in a baby-blue golf shirt, with his hand still wadded up in bandages.

"Poor darling, he's so cross," Buffy said.

"Cross?" I asked; in fact Bobby didn't look cross, only foolish and disconsolate.

"He's furious at Aunt Betsy's highboy, Janet," she said. "And what I've decided is, there's no point any longer in trying to persuade him to treat it right. After what happened last week, I realized it would be better to keep them apart. So I've simply moved all his things out of the drawers, and now I'm using them for my writing-paper and tapestry wools."

This time, perhaps because it was such a sticky hot day and there were too many flies on the terrace, I felt more than usually impatient with Buffy's whimsy. "Really, dear, you mustn't let your imagination run away with you," I said, squeezing more lemon into my iced tea. "Your aunt's highboy doesn't have any quarrel with Bobby. It isn't a human being, it's a piece of furniture."

"But that's just it," Buffy insisted. "That's why it matters so much. I mean, you and I, and everybody else." She waved her plump freckled hand at the other people under their pink and white umbrellas, and the golfers scattered over the rolling green plush of the course. "We all know we've got to die sooner or later, no matter how careful we are. Isn't that so?"

"Well, yes," I admitted.

"But furniture and things can be practically immortal, if they're lucky. An heirloom piece like Aunt Betsy's highboy – I really feel I've got an obligation to preserve it."

"For the children and grandchildren, you mean."

"Oh, that too, certainly. But they're just temporary themselves, you know." Buffy exhaled a sigh of hot summer air. "You see, from our point of view we own our things. But really, as far as they're concerned we're only looking after them for a while. We're just caretakers, like poor old Billy here at the club."

"He's retiring this year, I heard," I said, hoping to change the subject.

"Yes. But they'll hire someone else, you know, and if he's competent it won't make any difference to the place. Well, it's the same with our things, Janet. Naturally they want to do whatever they can to preserve themselves, and to find the best possible caretakers. They don't ask much: just to be polished regularly, and not to have their drawers wrenched open and slammed shut. And of course they don't want to get cold or wet or dirty, or have lighted cigarettes put down on them, or drinks or houseplants."

"It sounds like quite a lot to ask," I said.

"But Janet, it's so important for them!" Buffy cried. "Of course it was naughty of the highboy to give Bobby such a bad pinch, but I think it was understandable. He was being awfully rough and it got frightened."

"Now, Buffy," I said, stirring my iced tea so that the cubes clinked impatiently. "You can't possibly believe that we're all in danger of being injured by our possessions."

"Oh no." She gave another little rippling giggle. "Most of them don't have the strength to do any serious damage. But I'm not worried anyhow. I have a lovely relationship with all my nice things: they know I have their best interests at heart."

*

I didn't scold Buffy any more; it was too hot, and I realized there wasn't any point. My sister-in-law was fifty-six years old, and if she hadn't grown up by then she probably never would. Anyhow, I heard no more about the highboy until about a month later, when Buffy's grandchildren were staying with her. One hazy wet afternoon in August I drove over to the house with a basket of surplus tomatoes and zucchini. The children were building with blocks and Buffy was working on a *gros-point* cushion-cover design from the Metropolitan Museum. After a while she needed more pink wool and she asked her grandson, who was about six, to run over to the highboy and fetch it.

He got up and went at once – he's really a very nice little boy. But when he pulled on the bottom drawer it wouldn't come out and he gave the bird leg a kick. It was nothing serious, but Buffy screamed and leapt up as if she had been stung, spilling her canvas and coloured wools.

"Jamie!" Really, she was almost shrieking. "You must never, never do that!" And she grabbed the child by the arm and dragged him away roughly.

Well naturally Jamie was shocked and upset; he cast a terrified look at Buffy and burst into tears. That brought her to her senses. She hugged him and explained that Grandma wasn't angry; but he must be very, very careful of the highboy, because it was so old and valuable.

I thought Buffy had over-reacted terribly, and when she went out to the kitchen to fix two gin-and-tonics, and milk and peanut-butter cookies for the children, "to settle us all down", I followed her in and told her so. Surely, I said, she cared more for her grandchildren than she did for her furniture.

Buffy gave me an odd look; then she pushed the swing door shut.

"You don't understand, Janet," she said in a low voice, as if someone might overhear. "Jamie really mustn't annoy the highboy. It's been rather difficult lately, you see." She tried to open a bottle of tonic, but couldn't – I had to take it from her.

"Oh, thank you," she said distractedly. "It's just – Well, for instance. The other day Betsy Lee was playing house under the highboy: she'd made a kind of nest for herself with the sofa pillows, and she had some of her dolls in there. I don't know what happened exactly, but one of the claw feet gave her that nasty-looking scratch you noticed on her leg." Buffy looked over her shoulder apprehensively and spoke even lower. "And there've been other incidents – Oh, never mind." She sighed, then giggled. "I know you think it's all perfect nonsense, Janet. Would you like lime or lemon?"

I was disturbed by this conversation, and that evening I told Clark so; but he made light of it. "Darling, I wouldn't worry. It's just the way Buffy always goes on."

"Well, but this time she was carrying the joke too far," I said. "She frightened those children. Even if she was fooling, I think she cares far too much about her old furniture. Really, it made me cross."

"I think you should feel sorry for Buffy," Clark remarked. "You know what we've said so often: now that she's had to give up sports, she doesn't have enough to do. I expect she's just trying to add a little interest to her life."

I said that perhaps he was right. And then I had an idea: I'd get Buffy elected secretary of the Historical Society, to fill out the term of the woman who'd just resigned. I knew it wouldn't be easy, because she had no experience and a lot of people thought she was flighty. But I was sure she could do it; she'd always run that big house perfectly, and she knew lots about local history and genealogy and antiques.

First I had to convince the Historical Society board that they wanted her, and then I had to convince Buffy of the same thing; but I managed. I was quite proud of myself. And I was even prouder as time went on and she not only did the job beautifully, she also seemed to have forgotten all that nonsense about the highboy. That whole fall and winter she didn't mention it once.

It wasn't until early the following spring that Buffy phoned one morning, in what was obviously rather a state, and asked me to come over. I found her waiting for me in the front hall, wearing her white quilted parka. Her fine blond-tinted curls were all over the place, her eyes unnaturally round and bright, and the tip of her snub nose pink; she looked like a distracted rabbit.

"Don't take off your coat yet, Janet," she told me breathlessly. "Come out into the garden; I must show you something."

I was surprised, because it was a cold blowy day in March. Apart from a few snowdrops and frozen-looking white crocuses scattered over the lawn, there was nothing to see. But it wasn't the garden Buffy had on her mind.

"You know that woman from New York, that Abigail

Jones, who spoke on 'Decorating with Antiques' yesterday at the Society?" she asked as we stood between two beds of spaded earth and sodden compost.

"Mm."

"Well, I was talking to her after the lecture, and I invited her to come for brunch this morning and see the house."

"Mm? And how did that go?"

"It was awful, Janet. I don't mean—" Buffy hunched her shoulders and swallowed as if she were about to sob. "I mean, Mrs Jones was very pleasant. She admired my Hepplewhite table and chairs; and she was very nice about the canopy bed in the blue room too, though I felt I had to tell her that one of the posts wasn't original. But what she liked best was Aunt Betsy's highboy."

"Oh yes?"

"She thought it was a really fine piece. I told her we'd always believed it was made in Newport, but Mrs Jones thought Salem was more likely. Well that naturally made me uneasy."

"What? I mean, why?"

"Because of the witches, you know." Buffy gave her nervous giggle. "Then Mrs Jones said she hoped I was taking good care of the highboy. So of course I told her I was. Mrs Jones said she could see that, but what I should realize was that my piece was unique, with the carved feathering of the legs, and what looked like all the original hardware. It really ought to be in a museum, she said. I tried to stop her, because I could tell the highboy was getting upset."

"Upset?" I laughed, because I still assumed that it was a joke. "Why should it be upset? I should think it would be pleased to be admired by an expert."

"But don't you see, Janet?" Buffy almost wailed. "It didn't know about museums before. It didn't realize that there were places where it could be well taken care of and perfectly safe for, well, almost forever. It wouldn't know about them, you see, because when pieces of furniture go

to a museum they don't come back to tell the others. It's like our going to heaven, I suppose. Only now the highboy knows, that's what it will want."

"But a piece of furniture can't force you to send it to a museum," I protested, thinking how crazy this conversation would sound to anyone who didn't know Buffy.

"Oh, can't it?" She brushed some wispy curls out of her face. "You don't know what it can do, Janet. None of us does. There've been things I didn't tell you about – But never mind that. Only in fairness I must say I'm beginning to have a different idea of why Aunt Betsy didn't leave the highboy to me in the first place. I don't think it was because of the family name at all. I think she was trying to protect me." She giggled with a sound like ice cracking.

"Really, Buffy—" Wearily, warily, I played along. "If it's as clever as you say, the highboy must know Mrs Jones was just being polite. She didn't really mean—"

"But she did, you see. She said that if I ever thought of donating the piece to a museum, where it could be really well cared for, she hoped I would let her know. I tried to change the subject, but I couldn't. She went on telling me how there was always the danger of fire or theft in a private home. She said home instead of house, that's the kind of woman she is." Buffy giggled miserably. "Then she started to talk about tax deductions, and said she knew of several places that would be interested. I didn't know what to do. I told her that if I did ever decide to part with the highboy I'd probably give it to our Historical Society."

"Well, of course you could," I suggested. "If you felt—"

"But it doesn't matter now," Buffy interrupted, putting a small cold hand on my wrist. "I was weak for a moment, but I'm not going to let it push me around. I've worked out what to do to protect myself: I'm changing my will. I called Toni Stevenson already, and I'm going straight over to her office after you leave."

"You're willing the highboy to the Historical Society?" I asked.

"Well, maybe eventually, if I have to. Not outright; heavens, no. That would be fatal. For the moment I'm going to leave it to Bobby's nephew Fred. But only in case of my accidental death." Behind her distracted wisps of hair, Buffy gave a peculiar little smile.

"Death!" I swallowed. "You don't really think—"

"I think that highboy is capable of absolutely anything. It has no feelings, no gratitude at all. I suppose that's because from its point of view I'm going to die so soon anyway."

"But, Buffy—" The hard wind whisked away the rest of my words, but I doubt if she would have heard them.

"Anyhow, what I'd like you to do now, Janet, is come in with me and be a witness when I tell it what I've planned."

I was almost sure then that Buffy had gone a bit mad; but of course I went back indoors with her.

"Oh, I wanted to tell you, Janet," she said in an unnaturally loud, clear voice when we reached the sitting-room. "Now that I know how valuable Aunt Betsy's highboy is, I've decided to leave it to the Historical Society. I put it in my will today. That's if I die of natural causes, of course. But if it's an accidental death, then I'm giving it to my husband's nephew, Fred Turner." She paused and took a loud breath.

"Really," I said, feeling as if I were in some sort of absurdist play.

"I realize the highboy may feel a little out of place in Fred's house," Buffy went on relentlessly, "because he and his wife have all that weird modern canvas and chrome furniture. But I don't really mind about that. And of course Fred's a little careless sometimes. Once when he was here he left a cigarette burning on the cherry pie table in the study; that's how it got that ugly scorch mark, you know. And he's rather thoughtless about wet glasses and coffee cups too." Though Buffy was still facing me, she kept glancing over my shoulder towards the highboy.

I turned to follow her gaze, and suddenly for a moment I shared her delusion. The highboy had not moved; but now it looked heavy and sullen, and seemed to have developed a kind of vestigial face. The brass pulls of the two top drawers formed the half-shut eyes of this face, and the fluted column between them was its long thin nose; the ornamental brass keyhole of the full-length drawer below supplied a pursed, tight mouth. Under its curved mahogany tricorne hat, it had a mean, calculating expression, like some hypocritical New England Colonial merchant.

"I know exactly what you're thinking," Buffy said, abandoning the pretence of speaking to me. "And if you don't behave yourself, I might give you to Fred and Roo right now. They have children too. Very active children, not nice quiet ones like Jamie and Mary Lee." Her giggle had a chilling fragmented sound now; ice shivering into shreds.

"None of that was true about Bobby's nephew, you know," Buffy confided as she walked me to my car. "They're not really careless, and neither of them smokes. I just wanted to frighten it".

"You rather frightened me," I told her.

Which was no lie, as I said to Clark that evening. It wasn't just the strength of Buffy's delusion, but the way I'd been infected by it. He laughed and said he'd never known she could be so convincing. Also he asked if I was sure she hadn't been teasing me.

Well, I had to admit I wasn't. But I was still worried. Didn't he think we should do something?

"Do what?" Clark said. And he pointed out that even if Buffy hadn't been teasing, he didn't imagine I'd have much luck trying to get her to a therapist; she thought psychologists were completely bogus. He said we should just wait and see what happened.

All the same, the next time I saw Buffy I couldn't help inquiring about the highboy. "Oh, everything's fine now," she said. "Right after I saw you I signed the codicil. I put a copy in one of the drawers to remind it, and it's been as good as gold ever since."

Several months passed, and Buffy never mentioned the subject again. When I finally asked how the highboy was, she said, "What? Oh, fine, thanks," in an uninterested way that suggested she'd forgotten her obsession – or tired of her joke.

The irritating thing was that now I'd seen the unpleasant face of the highboy, it was there every time I went to the house. I would look from it to Buffy's round pink face, and wonder if she had been laughing at me all along.

Finally, though, I began to forget the whole thing. Then one day late that summer Clark and Bobby's nephew's wife, Roo, was at our house. She's a professional photographer, quite a successful one, and she'd come to take a picture of me.

Like many photographers, Roo always kept up a more or less mindless conversation with her subjects as she worked; trying to prevent them from getting stiff and self-conscious, I suppose.

"I like your house, you know, Janet," she said. "You have such simple, great-looking things. Could you turn slowly to the right a little? . . . Good. Hold it . . . Now over

at Uncle Bobby's – Hold it . . . Their garden's great of course, but I don't care much for their furniture. Lower your chin a little, please . . . You know that big dark old chest of drawers that Buffy's left to Fred."

"The highboy," I said.

"Right. Let's move those roses a bit. That's better . . . It's supposed to be so valuable, but I think it's hideous. I told Fred I didn't want it around. Hold it . . . Okay."

"And what did he say?" I asked.

"Huh? Oh, Fred feels the same as I do. He said that if he did inherit the thing he was going to give it to a museum."

"A museum?" I have to admit that my voice rose. "Where was Fred when he told you this?"

"Don't move, please. Okay . . . What? . . . I think we were in Buffy's sitting-room – she wasn't there, of course. You don't have to worry, Janet. Fred wouldn't say anything like that in front of his aunt; he knows it would sound awfully ungrateful."

Well, my first impulse was to pick up the phone and warn my sister-in-law as soon as Roo left. But then I thought that would sound ridiculous. It was crazy to imagine that Buffy was in danger from a chest of drawers. Especially so long after she'd gotten over the idea herself, if she'd ever really had it in the first place.

Buffy might even laugh at me, I thought; she wasn't anywhere near as whimsical as she had been. She'd become more and more involved in the Historical Society,

191

and it looked as if she'd be re-elected automatically next year. Besides, if by any chance she hadn't been kidding and I reminded her of her old delusion and seemed to share it, the delusion might come back and it would be my fault.

So I didn't do anything. I didn't even mention the incident to Clark.

Two days later, while I was writing letters in the study, Clark burst in. I knew something awful had happened as soon as I saw his face.

Bobby had just called from the hospital, he told me. Buffy was in intensive care and the prognosis was bad. She had a broken hip and a concussion, but the real problem was the shock to her weak heart. Apparently, he said, some big piece of furniture had fallen on her.

I didn't ask what piece of furniture that was. I drove straight to the hospital with him, but by the time we got there Buffy was in a coma.

Though she was nearer plump than slim, Buffy seemed horribly small in that room, on that high flat bed – like a kind of faded child. Her head was in bandages, and there were tubes and wires all over her like mechanical snakes; her little freckled hands lay in weak fists on the white hospital sheet. You could see right away that it was all over with her, though in fact they managed to keep her alive, if you can use that word, for nearly three days more.

Fred Turner, just as he had promised, gave the highboy to a New York museum. I went to see it there recently. Behind its maroon velvet rope it looked exactly the same: tall, glossy, top-heavy, bird-legged and claw-footed.

"You wicked, selfish, ungrateful thing," I told it. "I hope you get termites. I hope some madman comes in here and attacks you with an axe."

The highboy did not answer me, of course. But under its mahogany Napoleon hat it seemed to wear a little self-satisfied smile.

THE HUNTER IN THE HAUNTED FOREST

ROBERT D. SAN SOUCI

A Native American legend

ONCE A YOUNG HUNTER of the Teton tribe went seeking game in a forest that was supposed to be haunted. His relatives and friends tried to discourage him from going there. But he said, "I have a wife and two children to feed. Winter is coming, and luck has been against me. We have very little to eat. If I don't bring back game, my family will starve."

"We will share what we have with you," promised his relatives.

"No," he said, "if the winter lingers, and my family eats too much of your food, we will all starve. I have heard there is much game in those woods because no one goes there."

"That is because ghosts roam its paths at night," said his friends. "Anyone who goes there does not come back."

But the young man's mind was made up. He took a small quantity of *wasna*, which is grease mixed with pounded buffalo meat and wild cherry. His father gave him some tobacco to take with him, also.

Then he set out. After two days he reached the edge of

the haunted forest. Just as he entered its shadows, the Thunder Beings raised a great storm, so he was forced to seek shelter from the pounding rain. Hurrying along the path, he came to a clearing. In the centre was a small tepee made of deer hide.

Just as the hunter was about to lift the flap and go inside, he heard two persons talking.

One voice said, "Hush! There is someone outside. Let us invite him in. We will offer him food and invite him to stay the night here. Then, when he is asleep, we will kill him and follow his ghost along the spirits' road" – which is what the Teton people call the Milky Way.

"Yes, yes," the other voice agreed eagerly.

Then the hunter fled, because he knew they were ghosts inside the tepee. And he knew from their talk that they had not found their way out of this world, but walked a dark trail – probably because they had been wicked when they were alive.

So he ran until he thought his lungs and heart would burst. For a time he was sure he heard the ghosts following him; but when he could run no more, he looked back and realized the sound was only the rain dripping from tree branches onto the leaves spread over the forest floor.

As sunset approached, the rain stopped and the sky cleared. The hunter found what shelter he could under a fallen tree. He tried to sleep, but voices gathered around him and whistled, "*Hyu! hyu! hyu!*" though he could see no one. When the moon rose, the voices scattered like leaves in the wind and left only silence behind. He pulled his blanket over his head and tried again to sleep.

When the hunter awoke the next morning, he decided to go deeper into the woods. But though he found plentiful signs of game all around, he was unable to see a single deer or elk. Disappointed, when night came he found a small clearing and built a fire to warm himself. He ate a bit of *wasna*, then leaned back against a tree trunk to smoke some of the tobacco his father had given him.

He had only taken a puff or two when an old man, wrapped in a red robe, appeared at the edge of the clearing, making the sign of peace. The hunter invited him to sit, and the old man settled down on the other side of the clearing.

The young man, happy to have human company, offered the other some *wasna*. The old man refused, but he asked eagerly for some of his tobacco. The hunter held his pipe out to the other; but when the old man took it and held it by the stem, the younger man saw in the firelight that his fingers were nothing but bones.

Then the stranger let his robe slip back from his shoulders, and all his fleshless ribs were visible. The ghost (for the hunter knew this is what the old man was) did not open his lips when he pulled on the pipe; the smoke came pouring out through his ribs.

When he had finished smoking, the ghost said, "Ho! Now we must wrestle. If I throw you, you will go home empty-handed, to face cold death this winter. If you can throw me, you will catch more game than you can carry, and your family will stay well fed and healthy until the spring."

Since there was nothing else he could do, the young man agreed. But first he threw an armful of brush on the fire; then he put even more brush near the flames.

The ghost rushed at the hunter. He seized him with his bony hands, which hurt the young man painfully, though he did not cry out. Then he tried to push off the ghost, but the skeleton's legs were very powerful, and were locked around the hunter's own.

With great effort, the hunter was able to twist nearer the fire. When the ghost came near it, he grew weak. But when he was able to pull the young man back toward the darkness, he became strong again.

As the fire burned low, the ghost's strength grew. The man began to get weary, but the thought of his family slowly starving to death gave him added vigour. He was able to force the ghost near the fire again. Then, with a last effort, the hunter yanked one foot free and pushed the pile of brush into the fire. It blazed instantly, lighting the whole clearing. The ghost let out an ear-piercing scream, and then his skeletal frame began to crumble, until it was nothing more than a pile of ashes.

But the ghost had spoken the truth. The next day the young man caught all the game he needed – more than enough to provide his family for the long, cold winter ahead.

THE HAIR

A. J. ALAN

I'M GOING TO GIVE you an account of certain occurrences.
I shan't attempt to explain them because they're quite
beyond me. When you've heard all the facts, some of
you may be able to offer suggestions. You must forgive me
for going into a certain amount of detail. When you don't
understand what you're talking about it's so difficult to
know what to leave out.

This business began in the dark ages, before there was
any broadcasting. In fact, in 1921.

I'd been staying the weekend with a friend of mine who
lives about fifteen miles out of Bristol.

There was another man stopping there, too, who lived at
Dawlish. Well, on the Monday morning our host drove us
into Bristol in time for the Dawlish man to catch his train,
which left a good deal earlier than the London one. Of
course, if old Einstein had done his job properly, we could
both have gone by the same train. As it was, I had over
half an hour to wait. Talking of Einstein, wouldn't it be
almost worthwhile dying young so as to hear what Euclid
says to him when they meet – wherever it is?

There was a funny little old sort of curiosity shop in one of the streets I went down, and I stopped to look in the window. Right at the back, on a shelf, was a round brass box, not unlike a powder-box in shape, and it rather took my fancy. I don't know why – perhaps it was because I'd never seen anything quite like it before. That must be why some women buy some hats.

Anyway, the shop window was so dirty that you could hardly see through it, so I went inside to have a closer look. An incredibly old man came out of the back regions and told me all he knew about the box, which wasn't very much. It was fairly heavy, made of brass, round, four inches high, and about three inches in diameter. There was something inside it, which we could hear when we shook it, but no one had ever been able to get the lid off. He'd bought it from a sailor some years before, but couldn't say in the least what part of the world it came from.

"What about fifteen bob?"

I offered him ten, and he took it very quickly, and then I had to sprint back to the station to catch my train. When I got home I took the box up into my workshop and had a proper look at it. It was extremely primitive as regards work, and had evidently been made by hand, and not on a lathe. Also, there had been something engraved on the lid, but it had been taken off with a file. Next job was to get the lid off without doing any damage to it. It was a good deal more than hand tight, and no ordinary methods were any good. I stood it lid downwards for a week in a dish of glycerine as a start, and then made two brass collars, one for the box and one for the lid. At the end of the week I bolted the collars on, fixed the box in the vice and tried tapping the lid round with a hammer – but it wouldn't start. Then, I tried it the other way and it went at once. That explained why no one had ever been able to unscrew it – it had a left-handed thread on it. Rather a dirty trick – especially to go and do it all those years before.

Well, here it was, unscrewing very sweetly, and I began

to feel quite like Howard Carter, wondering what I was going to find. It might go off bang, or jump out and hit me in the face. However, nothing exciting happened when the lid came off. In fact, the box only seemed to be half-full of dust, but at the bottom was a curled-up plait of hair. When straightened out, it was about nine inches long and nearly as thick as a pencil. I unplaited a short length, and found it consisted of some hundreds of very fine hairs, but in such a filthy state (I shoved them under the microscope) that there was nothing much to be seen. So I thought I'd clean them. You may as well know the process – first of all a bath of dilute hydrochloric acid to get the grease off, then a solution of washing soda to remove the acid. Then a washing in distilled water, then a bath of alcohol to get rid of any traces of water, and a final rinsing in ether to top off with.

Just as I took it out of the ether they called me down to the telephone, so I shoved it down on the first clean thing which came handy, namely, a piece of white cardboard, and went downstairs. When I examined the plait later on, the only thing of interest that came to light was the fact that the hairs had all apparently belonged to several different women. The colours ranged from jet-black, through brown, red, and gold, right up to pure white. None of the hair was dyed, which proved how very old it was. I showed it to one or two people, but they didn't seem very enthusiastic, so I put it, and its box, in a little corner cupboard we have, and forgot all about it.

Then the first strange coincidence happened.

About ten days later a pal of mine called Matthews came into the club with a bandage across his forehead. People naturally asked him what was the matter, and he said he didn't know, and what's more his doctor didn't know. He'd suddenly flopped down on his drawing-room floor, in the middle of tea, and lain like a log. His wife was in a fearful stew, of course, and telephoned for the doctor. However, Matthews came round at the end of about five

minutes, and sat up and asked what had hit him. When the doctor blew in a few minutes later he was pretty well all right again except for a good deal of pain in his forehead. The doctor couldn't find anything the matter except a red mark which was beginning to show on the skin just where the pain was.

Well, this mark got clearer and clearer, until it looked just like a blow from a stick. Next day it was about the same, except that a big bruise had come up all round the mark. After that it got gradually better. Matthews took the bandage off and showed it me at the club, and there was nothing much more than a bruise with a curved red line down the middle of it, like the track of a red-hot worm.

They'd decided that he'd had an attack of giddiness and must somehow have bumped his head in falling. And that was that.

About a month later, my wife said to me: "We really must tidy your workshop!" And I said: "Must we?" And she said: "Yes, it's a disgrace." So up we went.

Tidying my workshop consists of putting the tools back in their racks, and of my wife wanting to throw away things she finds on the floor, and me saying: "Oh, no, I could use that for so and so."

The first thing we came across was the piece of white cardboard I'd used to put the plait of hair on while I'd run down to the telephone that day.

When we came to look at the other side we found it was a flash-light photograph of a dinner I'd been at. You know what happens. Just before the speeches a lot of blighters come in with a camera and some poles with tin trays on the top, and someone says: "Will the chairman please stand?" and he's helped to his feet. Then there's a blinding flash and the room's full of smoke, and the blighters go out again. Later on a man comes round with proofs, and if you are very weak – or near the chairman – you order one print.

Well, this dinner had been the worshipful company of skate-fasteners or something, and I'd gone as the guest of the same bloke Matthews I've already been telling you about, and we'd sat "side by each", as the saying is. My wife was looking at the photograph, and she said: "What's that mark on Mr Matthews's forehead?" And I looked – and there, sure enough, was the exact mark that he'd come into the club with a month before. The curious part being, of course, that the photograph had been taken at least six months before he'd had the funny attack which caused the mark. Now, then – on the back of the photograph, when we examined it, was a faint brown line. This was evidently left by the plait of hair when I'd pinned it out to dry, and it had soaked through and caused the mark on Matthews's face. I checked it by shoving a needle right through the cardboard. Of course, this looked like a very strange coincidence, on the face of it. I don't know what your experience of coincidences is – but mine is that they usually aren't. Anyway, I took the trouble to trace out the times, and I finally established, beyond a shadow of doubt, that I had pinned the hair out on the photograph between four and a quarter-past on a particular day, and that Matthews had had his funny attack on the same day at about a quarter past four. That was something *like* a coincidence. Next, the idea came to me to try it again. Not on poor old Matthews, obviously – he'd already had some – and, besides, he was a friend of mine. I know perfectly well that we are told to be kind to our enemies, and so on – in fact I do quite a lot of that – but when it comes to trying an experiment of this kind – even if the chances are a million to one against it being a success, I mean having any result – one naturally chooses an enemy rather than a friend. So I looked round for a suitable – victim – someone who wouldn't be missed much, in case there happened to be another coincidence. The individual on whom my choice fell was the nurse next door.

We can see into their garden from our bathroom window – and we'd often noticed the rotten way she treated the child she had charge of when she thought no one was looking. Nothing one could definitely complain about – you know what a thankless job it is to butt into your neighbour's affairs – but she was systematically unkind, and we hated the sight of her. Another thing – when she first came she used to lean over the garden wall and sneak our roses – at least, she didn't even do that – she used to pull them off their stalks and let them drop – I soon stopped that. I fitted up some little arrangements of fish-hooks round some of the most accessible roses and anchored them to the ground with wires. There was Hell-and-Tommy the next morning, and she had her hand done up in bandages for a week.

Altogether she was just the person for my experiment. The first thing was to get a photograph of her, so the next sunny morning, when she was in the garden, I made a noise like an aeroplane out of the bathroom window to make her look up, and got her nicely. As soon as the first print was dry, about eleven o'clock the same night, I fastened the plait of hair across the forehead with two pins – feeling extremely foolish, as one would, of course, doing an idiotic thing like that – and put it away in a drawer in my workshop. The evening of the next day, when I got home, my wife met me and said: "What do you think – the nurse next door was found dead in bed this morning." And she went on to say that the people were quite upset about it, and there was going to be an inquest, and all the rest of it. I tell you, you could have knocked me down with a brick. I said: "No, not really; what did she die of?" You must understand that my lady wife didn't know anything about the experiment. She'd never have let me try it. She's rather superstitious – in spite of living with me. As soon as I could, I sneaked up to the workshop drawer and got out

the photograph, and – I know you won't believe me, but it doesn't make any difference – when I unpinned the plait of hair and took it off there was a clearly-marked brown stain right across the nurse's forehead. I tell you, that *did* make me sit up, if you like – because that made twice – first Matthews and now – now.

It was rather disturbing, and I know it sounds silly, but I couldn't help feeling to blame in some vague way.

Well, the next thing was the inquest – I attended that, naturally, to know what the poor unfortunate woman had died of. Of course, they brought it in as "death from natural causes," namely, several burst blood-vessels in the brain; but what puzzled the doctors was what had caused the "natural causes" – also, she had the same sort of mark on her forehead as Matthews had had. They had gone very thoroughly into the theory that she might have been exposed to X-rays – it *did* look a bit like that – but it was more or less proved that she couldn't have been, so they frankly gave it up. Of course, it was all very interesting and entertaining, and I quite enjoyed it, as far as one can enjoy an inquest, but they hadn't cleared up the vexed question – did she fall or was she pu – well, had she suffered it on account of the plait of hair, or had she not? Obviously the matter couldn't be allowed to rest there – it was much too thrilling. So I looked about for someone else to try it on, and decided that a man who lived in the house opposite would do beautifully. He wasn't as bad as the nurse because he wasn't cruel – at least, not intentionally – he played the fiddle – so I decided not to kill him more than I could help.

The photograph was rather a bother because he didn't go out much. You've no idea how difficult it is to get a decent full-face photograph of a man who knows you by sight without him knowing. However, I managed to get one after a fortnight or so. It was rather small and I had to enlarge it, but it wasn't bad considering. He used to spend most of his evenings up in a top room practising, double stopping and what-not – so after dinner I went up to my workshop window, which overlooks his, and waited for him to begin. Then, when he'd really warmed up to his job, I just touched the plait across the photograph – not hard, but – well, like you do when you are testing a bit of twin flex to find out which wire is which, you touch the ends across an accumulator or an H.T. battery. Quite indefensible in theory, but invariably done in practice. (Personally, I always the use the electric light mains – the required information is so instantly forthcoming.) Well, that's how I touched the photograph with the plait. The first time I did it my bloke played a wrong note. That was nothing, of course, so I did it again more slowly. This time there was no doubt about it. He hastily put down his fiddle and hung out of the window, gasping like a fish for about five minutes. I tell you, I was so surprised that I felt like doing the same.

However, I pulled myself together, and wondered whether one ought to burn the da-er-plait or not. But there seemed too many possibilities in it for that – so I decided to learn how to use it instead. It would take too long to tell you all about my experiments. They lasted for several months, and I reduced the thing to such an exact science that I could do anything from giving a gnat a headache to killing a man. All this, mind you, at the cost of one man, one woman, lots of wood-lice, and a conscientious objector. You must admit that that's pretty moderate, considering what fun one *could* have had with a discovery of that kind.

Well, it seemed to me that, now the control of my absent treatment had been brought to such a degree of accuracy, it would be rather a pity not to employ it in some practical way. In other words, to make a fortune quickly without undue loss of life.

One could, of course, work steadily through the people one disliked, but it wouldn't bring in anything for some time.

I mean, even if you insure them first you've got to wait a year before they die, or the company won't pay, and in any case it begins to look fishy after you've done it a few times. Then I had my great idea: Why shouldn't my process be applied to horse-racing? All one had to do was to pick some outsider in a race – back it for all you were worth at about 100 to 1, and then see that it didn't get beaten.

The actual operation would be quite simple. One would only have to have a piece of cardboard with photographs of all the runners stuck on it – except the one that was to win, of course – and then take up a position giving a good view of the race.

I wasn't proposing to hurt any of the horses in the least. They were only going to get the lightest of touches, just enough to give them a tired feeling, soon after the start. Then, if my horse didn't seem to have the race well in hand near the finish, I could give one more light treatment to any horse which still looked dangerous.

It stood to reason that great care would have to be taken not to upset the running too much. For instance, if all the horses except one fell down, or even stopped and began to graze, there would be a chance of the race being declared void.

So I had two or three rehearsals. They worked perfectly. The last one hardly was a rehearsal because I had a tenner on at 33 to 1, just for luck – and, of course, it came off.

However, it wasn't as lucky as it sounds. Just outside the entrance to the grandstand there was rather a squash and, as I came away I got surrounded by four or five men who seemed to be pushing me about a bit, but it didn't strike me what the game was until one of them got his hand into the breast-pocket of my coat.

Then I naturally made a grab at him and got him just above the elbow with both hands, and drove his hand still further into my pocket. That naturally pushed the pocket, with his hand inside it, under my right arm, and I squeezed it against my ribs for all I was worth.

Now, there was nothing in that pocket but the test tube with the plait of hair in it, and the moment I started squeezing it went with a crunch. I'm a bit hazy about the next minute because my light-fingered friend tried to get free, and two of his pals helped him by bashing me over the head. They were quite rough. In fact, they entered so heartily into the spirit of the thing that they went on doing it until the police came up and collared them.

You should have seen that hand when it did come out of my pocket. Cut to pieces, and bits of broken glass sticking out all over it – like a crimson tipsy cake. He was so bad that we made a call at a doctor's on the way to the police station for him to have a small artery tied up. There was a cut on the back of my head that wanted a bit of attention, too. Quite a nice chap, the doctor, but he was my undoing. He was, without doubt, the baldest doctor I've ever seen, though I once saw a balder alderman.

When he'd painted me with iodine, I retrieved the rest of the broken glass and the hair from the bottom of my pocket and asked him if he could give me an empty bottle to put it in. He said: "Certainly," and produced one, and we corked the hair up in it. When I got home, eventually, I looked in the bottle, but apart from a little muddy substance at the bottom it was empty – the plait of hair had melted away. Then I looked at the label on the bottle, and found the name of a much-advertized hair restorer.

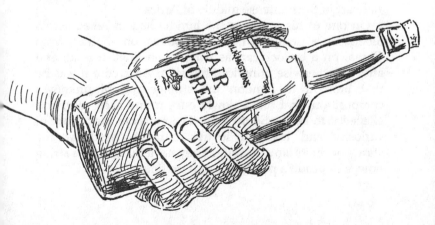

COUSIN EDWARD'S CAT

CLARE WEYMAN

MY COUSIN EDWARD'S CAT, a ginger beast that would leap on your lap suddenly and sit there like a small mountain, was the first to find out the truth.

Edward's wife Elizabeth had a brother who wandered about the world. Now and then he would come back to England with some amazing bundle that was last strapped to a camel crossing an illimitable desert, made fast to a raft on some reeking river, or balanced on the head of a jungle stalwart in the immense middle of Africa.

On one of his journeys the bundle had travelled across Siberia on a sledge of mastodon bones; on another, from China, on a bullock cart as wide as an English road; and after an otherwise unnoticed transit of Antarctica it was he that brought to London the strange rod of unknown composition, that turns slowly once round each year, and alleged it to be the South Pole. The museum took it out of curiosity and fastened it up, until it overthrew the showcase in its slow turning. They have hung it on a string now, a Foucault's pendulum of pure time.

The wanderer comes and goes, thin and silent, now into the northern sun, now into the southern snow. His sister, Elizabeth, Edward's wife, is not like him at all. Content to stay at home, hardly does she leave the place where she and Edward live. Edward himself goes up to London each day and does something in the biggest bank, a sort of meddling with the pound, an alternative to adventure. It was he who once explained that five pounds in sixpences once weighed the same as five pounds in half crowns, an academic jest now, capped only by the fact that neither weighed five pounds. Elizabeth had thought it so sweet of him that she said yes.

But it was the cat, Joey, that understood another thing first. One night, years ago now, when a tanner was legal tender, Edward and Elizabeth were sitting by the fire. Elizabeth finished the last darn of Edward's sock, and put away the wool and the needle.

"The cat likes it," she said.

"It's the fire he likes," said Edward. "He doesn't like your lap when you've a needle in your hand."

"Poor Joey," said Elizabeth. "Did we stitch his ear into a sock one day?"

Joey said nothing, possibly not understanding, possibly unwilling to recall the painful event.

"And I won't have him when I'm reading," said Edward. "It's the floor for you, Joey." When you have been tweaking sterling all day such converse is optimal for the evening.

"I hope he won't moult all over the rug," said Elizabeth, seeing that what she was talking about had not penetrated to Edward, and it was the rug she meant.

"Worse if he moults over me," said Edward, looking to see whether his blue pinstripe was sprinkled with the bullion of Joey's fur. He looked too, over the top of his lunettes, to see whether the blue and red flowers of the rug had ginger hair on them.

The rug was new to the house. The brother had brought

it only the day before, something out of a load he had paddled across the channel in a dug-out canoe, the last stage of a journey from New Guinea.

"Not a cat's whisker in sight," said Edward. Then he saw the clock. "Look at the time," he said. "I suppose we must rouse ourselves and go to bed. I shan't catch the train if I get up late. I'll put the cat out. Come on, Joey."

Joey understood about that, and went to sleep so soundly that to wake him would be cruel.

Those who ride the pound are heartless. Edward leaned down from his chair and put both hands round and under Joey. "Come on, old fellow," he said encouragingly, as he coaxed all day softening currencies trying to firm themselves.

The chair seemed to tip itself over, to uproot itself, and threw him on to the floor in front of the fire, where Joey and the hearth-rug should have been. But when Edward landed there cat and rug had gone. Before he had time to draw a breath, or do the comparable automatic thing with him, moisten a finger preparatory to counting bank notes (he had begun in the City in humble capacity), the rug had come down on top of him. Elizabeth had to lift it from him before he could get up sensibly.

"Chair tipped," he said, or hoped he did, considering that he must have had a stroke, or parity with the dollar. "Look, fallen right over."

"I should think it did," said Elizabeth. "Have you hurt yourself, dear; and where's the cat?"

"Damn the cat," said Edward, as if he were writing off farthings in a bankerly way.

The odd thing is, that Joey was now outside in the garden, pawing at the window, wanting to be in again.

"I don't see how he could have done it," said Edward, casting about in his mind for a system Joey could have used to embezzle event and activity to his own advantage. Then he thought he would think of it no more, because nothing of the sort could have occurred; or the door was open a little and let in a draught. For one able to total five columns at a time the existence of a sequence with no sum was something he must disregard.

He thought of it more factually when Elizabeth one day told him what Joey must have done while she was out shopping. She thought he had dragged the new hearth-rug, tooth and claw, out of the drawing room all the way to the kitchen, then gone to sleep on it under the scrubbed deal table, next to his dinner bowl.

Elizabeth dragged it back to its place. Joey, being that sort of cat, stayed on it for the ride.

Later on Edward came home at the usual time on the usual train, leaving New York, Chicago, Tokyo, to balance any discrepant sterling he had left.

He was interested to see Joey on the roof of the house: cats are capable of such ascents, after all; but Joey was stout and set in his ways; and even in youth had not climbed so high. He was now asleep on something blue.

Indoors Elizabeth was worried and distracted, unable to find the cat or the hearth-rug.

"He's hidden it somewhere," she said. "He gets these strange fancies."

"They go together, after all," said Edward. "But they haven't gone very far."

On the face of it, however, it was not possible for Joey to be on the roof. No window looked out on any tile of it; no ladder gave access; nothing overlooked it; no tree overhung. But there they were. The cat sat on the mat. The mat sat on the roof.

Edward refused, more stoutly than Joey ever was, to ascend any ladder whatever to retrieve either piece of property. The cat, he said, was written down by now so far as to be off the books altogether; and the hearth-rug had cost him and Elizabeth nothing.

Joey came down at his dinner time. He achieved the descent quite comfortably, neither climbing, jumping, or falling. Or moving a muscle. He was conveyed down by what he slept on, the hearth-rug, expeditiously but gently.

He landed at Edward's feet in the garden, opened his eyes, rolled on his ginger back, and pulled at Edward's shoe laces. Written off, maybe, but not played out.

"He's merely too lazy to do his own walking," said Elizabeth, in her factual way, watching the last few feet of the re-entry from the kitchen.

"So he may be," said Edward. "But how on earth, what on earth, where on earth, who on earth?"

"My brother," said Elizabeth, "gets hold of some odd things at times. I've often heard of magic carpets."

"In my experience," said Edward, "you have heard of a great many things for which there is no evidence, however factually you perceive them."

"Facts are my speciality," said Elizabeth. "I saw."

"I thought I still looked pretty smart," said Edward, mishearing the last two words. "A little above par, and the FT index still snappy."

"I saw Joey coming down from the roof on a flying carpet," said Elizabeth. "Such a mechanism is beyond present science, therefore it is magic. However, I have not heard that cats can use them, so let us see whether it will bring him to his supper."

It brought him in, at the sound of the usual call. Elizabeth, with a certain self-consciousness, produced the coaxing message, "Joey din-din," and Joey produced the result.

The hearth-rug rose a little into the air from the grass, humped itself over the contours of the rose bed, the cordillera of the antirrhinums, angled itself over a herbaceous col, and made a sulcus of itself to pass through the open back door.

The traverse of the kitchen door was not observed. But Joey was on the mat, under the table, eating, when Edward and Elizabeth opened that door and went into the room.

"It went through a closed door," said Elizabeth.

"Before my dinner I shall have a stiff Axminster from the roll on the sideboard," said Edward. "You no doubt would prefer a few fingers of broadloom?"

"Anything but shag," said Elizabeth. "I'm getting one of my headaches."

"Afterwards I shall experiment," said Edward. "Why should I cram myself into a train each day? When Joey can drive me to the bank in comfort."

The first experiments were not a success. There is some sequence of events that causes a magic carpet to fly at the flier's behest, traditionally a magic word, but in Joey's case something of another sort. Edward could not hit on it.

He thought he might manage better with Joey off the rug, and put outside, as a cat ought to be.

Joey was a sitting tenant on the rug now, like a rider on a horse, his steed obedient, but to what? To some element of the cat mind? To some tensing of the cat sinews? Joey was a smug and sitting tenant.

The first attempt to unseat him, where he lay under the kitchen table nursing the last fragments of his meal, ended in his being almost at once at the far end of the hall, by the radiator.

Edward essayed an eviction, standing on the rug himself.

"Careful," said Elizabeth. "That's not the best place for a rug, on the slippery parquet."

The rug pulled itself out from under Edward's feet, and left him like an overturned tiger-skin on the polished wood, his small change dancing from his pocket, his shoulders smarting, elbows ringing.

"I told you so," said Elizabeth.

"Go to . . ." Edward began, without breath to finish.

The rug had gone. At what point it went is not clear. At one moment it either was or was not, crumpled under Edward's feet, and the next it was there again.

Or perhaps not. Edward thinks it disappeared for some low percentile of a moment. Then it was back, without seeming to be so. It appeared not to have appeared. The rug itself, with its design of formalized flowers, was a distinctive object, and its eject, or continuing-to-be in the imaging mind, still had flowers, but what came back was black.

In much the same manner, Joey, its passenger, was ginger in recollection. What came back was black.

And there was an awful stink, quite easy to describe. We've all dropped a flaming coal on the hearth-rug and experienced the scorched wool and the gassy fume of the coal itself. That was the stink in the hall by the radiator, at Edward's fallen feet, but the sulphur content was more pronounced, more pungent, more actual. It hung about for days, and its eject for ever.

There was smoke, and a loud cry, withal.

Elizabeth hurried to Edward, thinking he had called, Edward sat himself up. The black image of Joey burst, as it were, and became a lightly scorched cat, subjected to

indignity but unharmed. It was the next day that he got his head stuck through the banisters, having lost his width-gauge whiskers.

Today, though, Edward was intent on rolling a burning cat in a burning rug, without respect for the feelings of either, in order to save his house.

Joey, affronted by something, had other ideas.

"It was quite simple," said Edward, later. "Very simple, once I knew what was happening. Of course I can't have a total body reaction quite so quick as a cat's. To all intents and purposes they move instantly, and my nerves are longer. That's my physical limitation: you can't drop me from five feet and have me land on my toes, because it takes too long to transmit the messages to my muscles. Drop me from fifty feet and I have time to adjust, but the fall kills me. It's the same for my brain. Since it can't work so quickly as a cat's, being many times the size, it has to work in a different way. When you consider it, the more active and large a creature gets the more allusively its brain has to work. And the big allusion I can make, and that

Elizabeth sometimes can, is to the future. I reckon that the cat's allusiveness to the future is very small: unconsciously an hour or two, consciously about two minutes. All its other thoughts are directed soley by the past. But I can plan for next weekend: I can project a whole year, a lifetime, even."

"Not, however," said Elizabeth, "based factually on the past."

"Indeed not," said Edward. "But there was the difference between me and the cat, and the cat did not know that a process was involved. It would think, 'Ah, lying in the kitchen beside my bowl of food would be good, or appropriate,' and the rug conveyed it there. But when I consigned wife, house, rug and feline to the nether regions, those capable of obeying the injunction went – rug and cat. But when they got there the cat knew it would be better off where it had been just before, and came back, done rare."

"I thought they were all dead," said Elizabeth.

"There was no time to explain," said Edward. "I saw what was happening, and the fight began to get the cat off the mat there and then, before it decided to leave home with what seemed to me to be a most valuable article."

"I thought they were all mad," said Elizabeth, later. "Quite plainly they were. I thought all three of them had an inflammatory form of rabies. Edward was pirouetting, yes Edward, you were, round and round on one leg, clutching Joey by the waist, and Joey was howling and spitting, and the rug was flapping round both of you, cinders falling off, smoke going up, and a dreadful smell."

"It was an epic fight," said Edward. "There was a lot at stake." But when he was asked about mankind in general he always said that did not enter into it, only that catkind was not going to abstract all the benefits.

"I won," he said. "I had tight hold of the cat, and the rug had tight hold too, trying to take it where it thought it wanted to go. It wasn't until the cat thought of letting go

and slashing my wrists for me, that I won. I grabbed the rug and dropped the cat."

"You didn't," said Elizabeth. "You threw it at me."

"Cats have a different view of gravity," said Edward. "It was downwards to him. But I won. I rolled up the rug."

"And?" one asks.

"It was a giant step for mankind," said Edward. "Or it would have been if mankind weighed as little as a cat: the rug's carrying capacity is about thirteen pounds on a dry day, and in damp weather rather less. And it isn't any use. You have to have so much intention to send it anywhere that you end with a headache, and it does not always go where you meant it to arrive. Elizabeth once sent me a cup of coffee down the garden, but that was our only success."

"The next time," Elizabeth said, "the rug landed at the church hall, which slipped into my mind at the same time

217

because I was hurrying there for the dress-making class. I found it when I arrived, and drank the coffee."

"Joey used it until he grew too fat," said Edward. "Then we put it in the attic, where we lost it."

"Tidying up," said Elizabeth. "I put a box on it with old rolls of wallpaper standing in it, telling Edward they were for the tip, and him agreeing."

"All of a sudden the box, the wallpaper, the rug, had gone," said Edward. "We ran for the car, to get there first, and then we found neither of us had any idea what we meant by 'the tip', apart from its being a place where rubbish was disposed of."

"I had thought vaguely of a hole in the ground, in a sort of indistinct way," said Elizabeth. "Nowhere in particular, but deep."

"And I," said Edward, "had a precise picture of a place with no known location, where old bank notes are destroyed. In my trade that might be Hell again."

"So we sat in the car for an hour, arguing, then got out and finished tidying the attic," said Elizabeth.

It was all some time ago. By now they both have a feeling they saw it on television. And Joey, having glimpsed the everlasting fires, has gone to the happy hunting grounds.

The wandering brother was last recorded blocking the mouth of the Red Sea with a piece of Ross Shelf, destined for Arabia, amid arguments about whether it was a liquid or wasting asset, a property, cabin baggage, or a territory.

THE DOG FANTI

TRADITIONAL

A Scottish folktale

MRS OGILVIE of Drumquaigh had a poodle named Fanti. Her family, or at least those who lived with her, were her son, the laird, and three daughters. Of these the two younger, at a certain recent date, were paying a short visit to a neighbouring country house. Mrs Ogilvie was accustomed to breakfast in her bedroom, not being in the best of health. One morning Miss Ogilvie came down to breakfast and said to her brother, "I had an odd dream; I dreamed Fanti went mad."

"Well, that *is* odd," said her brother. "So did I. We had better not tell mother; it might make her nervous."

Miss Ogilvie went up after breakfast to see the elder lady, who said, "Do turn out Fanti; I dreamed last night that he went mad and bit."

In the afternoon the two younger sisters came home.

"How did you enjoy yourselves?" one of the others asked.

"We didn't sleep well. I was dreaming that Fanti went mad when Mary wakened me, and said she had dreamed Fanti went mad, and turned into a cat, and we threw him into the fire."

Thus, as several people may see the same ghost at once, several people may dream the same dream at once. As a matter of fact, Fanti lived, sane and harmless, "all the length of all his years".

SPACE INVADERS

MARGARET MAHY

from Aliens In the Family

GLIDING SLOWLY DOWN the street, Bond looked so bright and energetic that some people smiled to see him go by while others frowned, mistrusting his roller skates on a busy city footpath, or puzzled by his suit of many pockets. Pockets of orange, green and gold, all differently shaped, were sewn down the legs of his blue jeans, and there were others like bright windows on his brown shirt. He was still dazed by his surroundings, for although he had been given what the Galgonqua called "false" or "induced" memories which enabled him to recognize and understand the uses of things he had never seen before, it did not altogether take the surprise out of those things. *That's a bicycle!* thought Bond, amazed, for it seemed to him that the pedalling motion of the rider was winding up invisible thread from the road behind him.

As he skated, weaving along the street, Bond was performing two functions – both part of his test. He was receiving all sorts of signals, but was trying to untangle one in particular – the faint, unconscious trace emitted by the "missing" Companion. It was also part of the talent of the Galgonqua that they should record. So Bond looked at things differently from anyone else in the street – for he looked at everything twice. His first glance was the surprised one, and his second was the remembering one. He chose to remember the most ordinary things: empty Coca-Cola cans in the gutter, the ill-shaven old man selling lottery tickets and horse-racing news, people's cars, shoes, shorts, shirts, the chains around their necks, the rings on their fingers. Their faces interested him too but he didn't dare look at them long, in case they noticed his curiosity and studied him too closely.

He skated along, smiling as he went. Sometimes he would see something not included in his false memory file and then he would blink as if his mind was taking a photograph. Later, if he was successful, these details would be read off by the School and recorded in the gigantic Inventory of Galgonqua which was eventually intended to hold all the information, feelings, memories, sensations, ideas, jokes, riddles, mysteries, answers and explanations in the entire universe. They had already been buiding it up for thousands of years but sometimes it seemed as if they had barely begun.

Though Bond drifted through the crowds without any apparent purpose, he was in fact following his clue. The faint impulse from the Companion was a thread he could follow, running through his head, a constant drone like the humming of a tiny fly, and growing more distinct when he turned his face to it – a thrill which he alone in the busy street could pick out of the air. Earlier in the day this sensation had been interrupted by distance, by his own confusion, by pneumatic drills, by the radios of taxis calling to each other across the city like animals separated from their herd, and even by the electronic presence of microwave ovens in restaurants and coffee bars. He had patiently picked his way through all this, untangling that one thread from all the threads the city offered him. But now it was constant. He had trapped it inside him and even began to feel his old confidence returning.

It's not a difficult test after all, he thought, *or perhaps it is –*

for others. He had always been very clever at detecting and unravelling the signals by which the Galgonqua kept in touch with one another. He was a tireless and deft unraveller. So at last, by following this impulse and recording as he went, he came to a particular shop and stood outside it, hesitant and uncertain.

Peering in at the door as a cautious animal might inspect a trap, Bond saw racks of old cardigans and dresses, somehow more sinister than new ones, as if ghosts had been trapped and strung up on coathangers. Even from the door it seemed to Bond that the brown jersey on the front of the rack still carried the shape of the woman who had once worn it. He went in at last, feeling his skates, so quick and clever out on the footpath, grow clumsy and heavy on the worn, green matting. A woman sat knitting behind the counter.

"Can I help you, dear," she asked.

"Just looking," replied Bond, and he *did* look with great curiosity at vases, china ornaments and old cups and saucers set on a shelf. On other shelves behind the woman were the more valuable things, including a black box studded with buttons and little dials. Bond knew at once that this was no ordinary transistor radio. This was what he was searching for – the Companion emitting its constant location call but giving no information about what had happened or quite how he was to get it. He supposed it must be for sale and he had been issued with money – but had he been given enough? He felt frightened at the sight of the box, so square and dark in the shop full of ghosts. It seemed so open, so obvious, yet he was sure there must be a catch. All the time he hesitated he was aware that in that black square, under those studs and dials was unbelievably tiny and intricate machinery, and that set in a maze of pinpoint circuits was the voice, the reasoning and some of the powers of his older sister Solita. She had been sent down in this form to be part of his test, and also to record for the Inventory in a different and more complicated way than a young, untested student such as Bond could manage. The Solita in the box had been set in a state of unconsciousness but the School had told him that her brother's voice was one that might interrupt whatever strange mechanical dreams she was dreaming. He was to reclaim her, awaken her and bring her home.

At that moment the woman behind the counter spoke to him once more. "Can I help you, dear?" she asked with the identical words and expression she had used a moment ago.

"How much is the transistor?" Bond enquired casually. His blood chilled as the woman calmly pulled the knitting off her needles and rose, pointing them at his heart like twin swords. They were steel and very sharp.

"You must be the one," she said in a high, cold voice. Simultaneously, the curtains around the changing booth behind Bond were swept aside and a dark figure appeared – a man with white hair erupting around his forehead and chin as though he were more goat than man. His bumpy forehead even looked as though it might be growing horns, and his yellow eyes bluged.

"You!" the man snorted. "Did you not think there might be a trap for anyone the School sent down? Your people are not all-powerful, you know."

"Who are you?" Bond asked, appalled at being recognized, but even as he spoke, the answer – incredible and terrifying – came into his mind. Under the skin of his wrist throbbed a mechanism called "the pulse" which enabled the School to trace his progress even though he could not contact the School. Contact until the proper time was strictly forbidden. He touched the pulse with his thumb.

"You're Wirdegen!" he cried. "You're trying to find a way into our Inventory!"

"Knowledge is the greatest treasure of all," said the man. "The woman there – she's nothing. She's under our control, as you will be in a minute."

Bond quickly turned and shouted across the counter to the Companion, "Wake up Solita! Wake up!"

"You can't wake a Companion out of a Zahn trance by shouting to it," said the man contemptuously. "Even a Delta function student should know that!" He threw himself at Bond who, still shouting Solita's name, leapt over the counter to brave the steel needles, hoping they were more to frighten him than to kill him. He felt one of them stab his arm as he fell behind the counter taking the bell, invoice book and skeins of wool with him.

"Solita!" he shouted again. The light changed. The box lit up as if a little fire blazed in it.

"Bond? Is that you, Bond? Is it rescue?" asked a girl's voice. The man appeared astounded and stood as if the steel needles had pinned him into the air in some way.

"Audio defence!" commanded Bond desperately, trying to recall all he could about this Wirdegen enemy who had appeared out of nowhere and who now tried to grab him and to set a small disc against his forehead.

"Bond, is that you?" asked Solita again.

"Audio defence!" screamed Bond. "Yes, this is Bond – *Bond*. I wouldn't deceive you. Read my bio-phase! Audio defence! This is override instruction." He shouted a series of numbers, thrashing his head backwards and forwards as he cried out. The disc placed against his temple slid down, scraped the side of his face and struck his ear as he managed to knee the man in the side. The woman toppled like a heavy doll across his legs, trapping him. But even as it seemed as if he might be caught, a thin, keening sound made itself heard, rapidly rising and swooping up into the range of inaudibility.

Several things then happened at once. A fine shiver ran through the shop. There was shocking uproar, not from the transistor but from a little dog tied to a parking meter howling dismally and tugging at its leash. Several car horns sounded in the street outside and could not be turned off, and glasses shattered on nearby tables, exploding into glittering daggers of glass. The woman on top of Bond clasped her hands over her head and tried to crawl towards the door. The bearded figure hanging over Bond suddenly collapsed. One minute it was suspended above him, powerful and menacing, the next it was collapsing with a slow, billowing grace. The pale, goatish face shining between the upper and lower nests of hair, and the live yellow eyes, vanished as if they had been sucked back into darkness. The woman did not vanish in the same way but fell to one side in an apparent faint. Bond pushed his way out from under empty clothes and, shuddering, seized the Companion and clumped out of the shop.

Once back on the pavement he grew as swift and as graceful as a bird, sliding in and out between passers-by, clasping the black box to his chest as if he was warming it back to life. No one followed him.

THE DUKE'S REAPPEARANCE

THOMAS HARDY

A CCORDING TO THE KINSMAN who told me the story, Christopher Swetman's house, on the outskirts of King's-Hintock village, was in those days larger and better kept than when, many years later, it was sold to the lord of the manor adjoining; after having been in the Swetman family, as one may say, since the Conquest.

Some people would have it to be that the thing happened at the house opposite, belonging to one Childs, with whose family the Swetmans afterwards intermarried. But that it was at the original homestead of the Swetmans can be shown in various ways; chiefly by the unbroken traditions of the family, and indirectly by the evidence of the walls themselves, which are the only ones thereabout with windows mullioned in the Elizabethan manner, and plainly of a date anterior to the event; while those of the other house might well have been erected fifty or eighty years later, and probably were; since the choice of Swetman's house by the fugitive was doubtless dictated by no other circumstance than its then suitable loneliness.

It was a cloudy July morning just before dawn, the hour of two having been struck by Swetman's one-handed clock on the stairs, that is still preserved in the family. Christopher heard the strokes from his chamber, immediately at the top of the staircase, and overlooking the front of the house. He did not wonder that he was sleepless. The rumours and excitements which had latterly stirred the neighbourhood, to the effect that the rightful King of England had landed from Holland, at a port only eighteen miles to the south-west of Swetman's house, were enough to make wakeful and anxious even a contented yeoman like him. Some of the villagers, intoxicated by the news, had thrown down their scythes, and rushed to the ranks of the invader. Christopher Swetman had weighed both sides of the question, and had remained at home.

Now as he lay thinking of these and other things he fancied that he could hear the footfall of a man on the road leading up to his house – a by-way, which led scarce anywhere else; and therefore a tread was at any time more apt to startle the inmates of the homestead than if it had stood in a thoroughfare. The footfall came opposite the gate, and stopped there. One minute, two minutes passed, and the pedestrian did not proceed. Christopher Swetman got out of bed and opened the casement. "Hoi! Who's there?" cries he.

"A friend," came from the darkness.

"And what mid ye want at this time o'night?" says Swetman.

"Shelter. I've lost my way."

"What's thy name?"

There came no answer.

"Be ye one of King Monmouth's men?"

"He that asks no questions will hear no lies from me. I am a stranger; and I am spent and hungered. Can you let me lie with you tonight?"

Swetman was generous to people in trouble, and his house was roomy. "Wait a bit," he said, "and I'll come down and have a look at thee, anyhow."

He struck a light, put on his clothes, and descended,

taking his horn-lantern from a nail in the passage, and lighting it before opening the door. The rays fell on the form of a tall, dark man in cavalry accoutrements and wearing a sword. He was pale with fatigue and covered with mud, though the weather was dry.

"Prithee take no heed of my appearance," said the stranger. "But let me in."

That his visitor was in sore distress admitted of no doubt, and the yeoman's natural humanity assisted the other's sad importunity and gentle voice. Swetman took him in, not without a suspicion that this man represented in some way Monmouth's cause, to which he was not unfriendly in his secret heart. At his earnest request the newcomer was given a suit of the yeoman's old clothes in exchange for his own, which with his sword were hidden in a closet in Swetman's chamber; food was then put before him and a lodging provided for him in a room at the back.

Here he slept till quite late in the morning, which was Sunday, the sixth of July, and when he came down in the garments that he had borrowed he met the household with a melancholy smile. Besides Swetman himself, there were only his two daughters, Grace and Leonard (the latter was, oddly enough, a woman's name here), and both had been enjoined to secrecy. They asked no questions and received no information; though the stranger regarded their fair countenances with an interest almost too deep. Having partaken of their usual breakfast of ham and cider he professed weariness and retired to the chamber whence he had come.

In a couple of hours or thereabout he came down again, the two young women having now gone off to morning service. Seeing Christopher bustling about the house without assistance, he asked if he could do anything to aid his host.

As he seemed anxious to hide all differences and appear as one of themselves, Swetman set him to get the vegetables from the garden and fetch water from Buttock's

Spring in the dip near the house (though the spring was not called by that name till years after, by the way).

"And what can I do next?" says the stranger when these services had been performed.

His meekness and docility struck Christopher much, and won upon him. "Since you be minded to," says the latter, "you can take down the dishes and spread the table for dinner. Take a pewter plate for thyself, but the trenchers will do for we."

But the other would not, and took a trencher likewise, in doing which he spoke of the two girls and remarked how comely they were.

This quietude was put an end to by a stir out of doors, which was sufficient to draw Swetman's attention to it, and he went out. Farm hands who had gone off and joined the Duke on his arrival had begun to come in with news that a midnight battle had been fought on the moors to the north, the Duke's men, who had attacked, being entirely worsted; the Duke himself, with one or two lords and other friends, had fled, no one knew whither.

"There has been a battle," says Swetman, on coming indoors after these tidings, and looking earnestly at the stranger.

"May the victory be to the rightful in the end, whatever the issue now," says the other, with a sorrowful sigh.

"Dost really know nothing about it?" said Christopher. "I could have sworn you was one from that very battle!"

"I was here before three o' the clock this morning; and these men have only arrived now."

"True," said the yeoman. "But still, I think—"

"Do not press your question," the stranger urged. "I am in a strait, and can refuse a helper nothing; such inquiry is, therefore, unfair."

"True again," said Swetman, and held his tongue.

The daughters of the house returned from church, where the service had been hurried by reason of the excitement. To their father's questioning if they had spoken of him who sojourned there they replied that they had said never a word; which, indeed, was true, as events proved.

He bade them serve the dinner; and as the visitor had withdrawn since the news of the battle, prepared to take a platter to him upstairs. But he preferred to come down and dine with the family.

During the afternoon more fugitives passed through the village, but Christopher Swetman, his visitor, and his family kept indoors. In the evening, however, Swetman came out from his gate, and, hearkening in silence to these tidings and more, wondered what might be in store for him for his last night's work.

He returned homeward by a path across the mead that skirted his own orchard. Passing here, he heard the voice of his daughter Leonard expostulating inside the hedge, her words being:

"Don't ye, sir; don't! I prithee let me go!"

"Why, sweetheart?"

"Because I've a-promised another!"

Peeping through, as he could not help doing, he saw the girl struggling in the arms of the stranger, who was attempting to kiss her; but finding her resistance to be genuine, and her distress unfeigned, he reluctantly let her go.

Swetman's face grew dark, for his girls were more to him than himself. He hastened on, meditating moodily all the way. He entered the gate, and made straight for the orchard. When he reached it his daughter had disappeared, but the stranger was still standing there.

"Sir!" said the yeoman, his anger having in no wise abated, "I've seen what has happened! I have taken 'ee into my house, at some jeopardy to myself; and, whoever you may be, the least I expected of 'ee was to treat the maidens with a seemly respect. You have not done it, and I no longer trust you. I am the more watchful over them in that they are motherless; and I must ask 'ee to go after dark this night!"

The stranger seemed dazed at discovering what his impulse had brought down upon his head, and his pale face grew paler. He did not reply for a time. When he did speak his soft voice was thick with feeling.

"Sir," says he, "I own that I am in the wrong, if you take the matter gravely. We do not what we would but what we must. Though I have not injured your daughter as a woman, I have been treacherous to her as a hostess and friend in need. I'll go, as you say; I can do no less. I shall doubtless find a refuge elsewhere."

They walked towards the house in silence, where Swetman insisted that his guest should have supper before departing. By the time this was eaten it was dusk and the stranger announced that he was ready.

They went upstairs to where the garments and sword lay hidden, till the departing one said that on further thought he would ask another favour: that he should be allowed to retain the clothes he wore, and that his host would keep the others and the sword till he, the speaker, should come or send for them.

"As you will," said Swetman. "The gain is on my side;

for those clouts were but kept to dress a scarecrow next fall."

"They suit my case," said the stranger sadly. "However much they may misfit me, they do not misfit my sorry fortune now!"

"Nay, then," said Christopher, relenting, "I was too hasty. Sh'lt bide!"

But the other would not, saying that it was better that things should take their course. Notwithstanding that Swetman importuned him, he only added, "If I never come again, do with my belongings as you list. In the pocket you will find a gold snuff-box, and in the snuff-box fifty gold pieces."

"But keep 'em for thy use, man!" said the yeoman.

"No," says the parting guest: "they are foreign pieces and would harm me if I were taken. Do as I bid thee. Put away these things again and take especial charge of the sword. It belonged to my father's father and I value it much. But something more common becomes me now."

Saying which, he took, as he went downstairs, one of the ash sticks used by Swetman himself for walking with. The yeoman lighted him out to the garden hatch, where he disappeared through Clammers Gate by the road that crosses King's-Hintock Park to Evershead.

Christopher returned to the upstairs chamber, and sat down on his bed reflecting. Then he examined the things left behind, and surely enough in one of the pockets the gold snuff-box was revealed, containing the fifty gold pieces as stated by the fugitive. The yeoman next looked at the sword which its owner had stated to have belonged to his grandfather. It was two-edged, so that he almost feared to handle it. On the blade were inscribed the words "ANDREA FERARA", and among the many fine chasings were a rose and crown, the plume of the Prince of Wales, and two portraits; portraits of a man and a woman, the man's having the face of the first King Charles, and the woman's, apparently, that of his Queen.

Swetman, much awed and surprised, returned the articles to the closet, and went downstairs pondering. Of his surmise he said nothing to his daughters, merely declaring to them that the gentleman was gone; and never revealing that he had been an eye-witness of the unpleasant scene in the orchard that was the immediate cause of the departure.

Nothing occurred in Hintock during the week that followed, beyond the fitful arrival of more decided tidings concerning the utter defeat of the Duke's army and his own disappearance at an early stage of the battle. Then it was told that Monmouth was taken, not in his own clothes but in the guise of a countryman. He had been sent to London, and was confined in the Tower.

The possibility that his guest had been no other than the Duke made Swetman unspeakably sorry now; his heart smote him at the thought that, acting so harshly for such a small breach of good faith, he might have been the means of forwarding the unhappy fugitive's capture. On the girls coming up to him he said, "Get away with ye, wenches: I fear you have been the ruin of an unfortunate man!"

On the Thursday night following, when the yeoman was sleeping as usual in his chamber, he was, he said, conscious of the entry of someone. Opening his eyes, he beheld by the light of the moon, which shone upon the front of his house, the figure of a man who seemed to be the stranger moving from the door towards the closet. He was dressed somewhat differently now, but the face was quite that of his late guest in its tragical pensiveness, as was also the tallness of his figure. He neared the closet; and, feeling his visitor to be within his rights, Christopher refrained from stirring. The personage turned his large haggard eyes upon the bed where Swetman lay, and then withdrew from their hiding the articles that belonged to him, again giving a hard gaze at Christopher as he went noiselessly out of the chamber with his properties on his arm. His retreat down the stairs was just audible, and also

his departure by the side-door, through which entrance or exit was easy to those who knew the place.

Nothing further happened, and towards morning Swetman slept. To avoid all risk he said not a word to the girls of the visit of the night, and certainly not to anyone outside the house; for it was dangerous at that time to avow anything.

Among the killed in opposing the recent rising had been a younger brother of the lord of the manor, who lived at King's-Hintock Court hard by. Seeing the latter ride past in mourning clothes next day, Swetman ventured to condole with him.

"He'd no business there!" answered the other. His voice and manner showed the bitterness that was mingled with his regret. "But say no more of him. You know what has happened since, I suppose?"

"I know that they say Monmouth is taken, Sir Thomas, but I can't think it true," answered Swetman.

"Oh zounds! 'Tis true enough," cried the knight, "and that's not all. The Duke was executed on Tower Hill two days ago."

"D'ye say it verily?" says Swetman.

"And a very hard death he had, worse luck for 'n," said Sir Thomas. "Well, 'tis over for him and over for my brother. But not for the rest. There'll be searchings and siftings down here anon; and happy is the man who has had nothing to do with this matter!"

Now Swetman had hardly heard the latter words, so much was he confounded by the strangeness of the tidings that the Duke had come to his death on the previous Tuesday. For it had been only the night before this present day of Friday that he had seen his former guest, whom he had ceased to doubt could be other than the Duke, come into his chamber and fetch away his accoutrements as he had promised.

"It couldn't have been a vision," said Christopher to himself when the knight had ridden on. "But I'll go straight and see if the things be in the closet still; and thus I shall surely learn if 'twere a vision or no."

To the closet he went, which he had not looked into since the stranger's departure. And searching behind the articles placed to conceal the things hidden, he found that, as he had never doubted, they were gone.

When the rumour spread in the West that the man beheaded in the Tower was not indeed the Duke, but one of his officers taken after the battle, and that the Duke had been assisted to escape out of the country, Swetman found in it an explanation of what so deeply mystified him. That his visitor might have been a friend of the Duke's, whom the Duke had asked to fetch the things in a last request, Swetman would never admit. His belief in the rumour that Monmouth lived, like that of thousands of others, continued to the end of his days.

Such, briefly, concluded my kinsman, is the tradition which has been handed down in Christopher Swetman's family for the last two hundred years.

TRANSITION

ALGERNON BLACKWOOD

JOHN MUDBURY was on his way home from the shops, his arms full of Christmas Presents. It was after six o'clock and the streets were very crowded. He was an ordinary man, lived in an ordinary suburban flat, with an ordinary wife and ordinary children. *He* did not think them ordinary, but everybody else did. He had ordinary presents for each one, a cheap blotter for his wife, a cheap air-gun for the boy, and so forth. He was over fifty, bald, in an office, decent in mind and habits, of uncertain opinions, uncertain politics, and uncertain religion. Yet he considered himself a decided, positive gentleman, quite unaware that the morning newspaper determined his opinions for the day. He just lived from day to day. Physically, he was fit enough, except for a weak heart (which never troubled him); and his summer holiday was bad golf, while the children bathed and his wife read Garvice on the sands. Like the majority of men, he dreamed idly of the past, muddled away the present, and guessed vaguely – after imaginative reading on occasions – at the future.

"I'd like to survive all right," he said, "provided it's better than this," surveying his wife and children, and thinking of his daily toil. "Otherwise – !" and he shrugged his shoulders as a brave man should.

He went to church regularly. But nothing in church convinced him that he did survive, just as nothing in church enticed him into hoping that he would. On the other hand, nothing in life persuaded him that he didn't, wouldn't, couldn't. "I'm an Evolutionist," he loved to say to thoughtful cronies (over a glass), having never heard that Darwinism had been questioned.

And so he came home gaily, happily, with his bunch of Christmas Presents "for the wife and little ones", stroking himself upon their keen enjoyment and excitement. The night before he had taken "the wife" to see *Magic* at a select London theatre where the Intellectuals went – and had been extraordinarily stirred. He had gone questioningly, yet expecting something out of the common. "It's *not* musical," he warned her, "nor farce, nor comedy, so to speak;" and in answer to her question as to what the critics had said, he had wriggled, sighed, and put his gaudy neck-tie straight four times in quick succession. For no Man in the Street, with any claim to self-respect, could be expected to understand what the critics had said, even if he understood the Play. And John had answered truthfully: "Oh, they just said things. But the theatre's always full – and that's the only test."

And just now, as he crossed the crowded Circus to catch his bus, it chanced that his mind (having glimpsed an advertizement) was full of this particular Play, or, rather, of the effect it had produced upon him at the time. For it had thrilled him – inexplicably: with its marvellous speculative hint, its big audacity, its alert and spiritual beauty... Thought plunged to find something – plunged after this bizarre suggestion of a bigger universe, after this quasi-jocular suggestion that man is not the only – then dashed full-tilt against a sentence that memory thrust beneath his

nose: "Science does *not* exhaust the Universe" – and at the same time dashed full-tilt against destruction of another kind as well ...!

How it happened he never exactly knew. He saw a Monster glaring at him with eyes of blazing fire. It was horrible! It rushed upon him. He dodged ... Another Monster met him round the corner. Both came at him simultaneously. He dodged again – a leap that might have cleared a hurdle easily, but it was too late. Between the pair of them – his heart literally in his gullet – he was mercilessly caught. Bones crunched ... There was a soft sensation, icy cold and hot as fire. Horns and voices roared. Battering-rams he saw, and a carapace of iron ... Then dazzling light ... "Always *face* the traffic!" he remembered with a frantic yell – and, by some extraordinary luck, escaped miraculously on to the opposite pavement.

There was no doubt about it. By the skin of his teeth he had dodged a rather ugly death. First ... he felt for his Presents – all were safe. And then, instead of congratulating himself and taking breath, he hurried homewards – on foot, which proved that his mind had lost control a bit! – thinking only how disappointed the wife and children would have been if – well, if anything had happened. Another thing he realized, oddly enough, was that he no longer really loved his wife, but had only great affection for her. What made him think of that, Heaven only knows, but he *did* think of it. He was an honest man without pretence. This came as a discovery somehow. He turned a moment, and saw the crowd gathered about the entangled taxi-cabs, policemen's helmets gleaming in the lights of the shop windows ... then hurried on again, his thoughts full of the joy his Presents would give ... of the scampering children ... and of his wife – bless her silly heart! – eyeing the mysterious parcels ...

And, though he never could explain how, he presently stood at the door of the jail-like building that contained his flat, having walked the whole three miles. His thoughts had been so busy and absorbed that he had hardly noticed the length of weary trudge. "Besides," he reflected, thinking of the narrow escape, "I've had a nasty shock. It was a d—d near thing, now I come to think of it ..." He still felt a bit shaky and bewildered. Yet, at the same time, he felt extraordinarily jolly and lighthearted.

He counted his Christmas parcels ... hugged himself in anticipatory joy ... and let himself in swiftly with his latchkey. "I'm late," he realized, "but when she sees the brown-paper parcels, she'll forget to say a word. God bless the old faithful soul." And he softly used the key a second time and entered his flat on tiptoe ... In his mind was the master impulse of that afternoon – the pleasure these Christmas Presents would give his wife and children ...

He heard a noise. He hung up hat and coat in the poky vestibule (they never called it "hall") and moved softly

towards the parlour door, holding the packages behind him. Only of them he thought, not of himself – of his family, that is, not of the packages. Pushing the door cunningly ajar, he peeped in slyly. To his amazement the room was full of people. He withdrew quickly, wondering what it meant. A party? And without his knowing about it! Extraordinary! ... Keen disappointment came over him. But, as he stepped back, the vestibule, he saw, was full of people too.

He was uncommonly surprised, yet somehow not surprised at all. People were congratulating him. There was a perfect mob of them. Moreover, he knew them all – vaguely remembered them, at least. And they all knew him.

"Isn't it a game?" laughed someone, patting him on the back. "*They* haven't the least idea ...!"

And the speaker – it was old John Palmer, the book-keeper at the office – emphasized the "they".

"Not the least idea," he answered with a smile, saying something he didn't understand, yet knew was right.

His face, apparently, showed the utter bewilderment he felt. The shock of the collision had been greater than he realized evidently. His mind was wandering . . . Possibly! Only the odd thing was – he had never felt so clear-headed in his life. Ten thousand things grew simple suddenly. But, how thickly these people pressed about him, and how – familiarly!

"My parcels," he said, joyously pushing his way across the throng. "These are Christmas Presents I've bought for them." He nodded towards the room. "I've saved for weeks – stopped cigars and billiards and – and several other good things – to buy them."

"Good man!" said Palmer with a happy laugh. "It's the heart that counts."

Mudbury looked at him. Palmer had said an amazing truth, only – people would hardly understand and believe him . . . Would they?

"Eh?" he asked, feeling stuffed and stupid, muddled somewhere between two meanings, one of which was gorgeous and the other stupid beyond belief.

"If you *please*, Mr Mudbury, step inside. They are expecting you," said a kindly, pompous voice. And, turning sharply, he met the gentle, foolish eyes of Sir James Epiphany, a director of the Bank where he worked.

The effect of the voice was instantaneous from long habit.

"They are," he smiled from his heart, and advanced as from the custom of many years. Oh, how happy and gay he felt! His affection for his wife was real. Romance, indeed, had gone, but he needed her – and she needed him. And the children – Milly, Bill, and Jean – he deeply loved them. Life was worth living indeed!

In the room was a crowd, but – an astounding silence. John Mudbury looked round him. He advanced towards his wife, who sat in the corner armchair with Milly on her knee. A lot of people talked and moved about. Momentarily the crowd increased. He stood in front of them – in front of Milly and his wife. And he spoke – holding out his packages. "It's Christmas Eve," he whispered shyly, "and I've – brought you something – something for everybody. Look!" He held the packages before their eyes.

"Of course, of course," said a voice behind him, "but you may hold them out like that for a century. They'll *never* see them!"

"Of course they won't. But I love to do the old, sweet thing," replied John Mudbury – then wondered with a gasp of stark amazement why he said it.

"*I* think – " whispered Milly, staring round her.

"Well, what do you think?" her mother asked sharply. "You're always thinking something queer."

"I think," the girl continued dreamily, "that Daddy's already here." She paused, then added with a child's impossible conviction, "I'm sure he is. I *feel* him."

There was an extraordinary laugh. Sir James Epiphany laughed. The others – the whole crowd of them – also turned their heads and smiled. But the mother, thrusting the child away from her, rose up suddenly with a violent start. Her face had turned to chalk. She stretched her arms out – into the air before her. She gasped and shivered. There was anguish in her eyes.

"Look," repeated John, "these are the Presents that I brought."

But his voice apparently was soundless. And, with a spasm of icy pain, he remembered that Palmer and Sir James – some years ago – had died.

"It's magic," he cried, "but – I love you, Jinny – I love you – and – and I have always been true to you – as true as steel. We need each other – oh, can't you see – we go on together – you and I – for ever and ever – "

"*Think*," interrupted an exquisitely tender voice, "don't shout! They can't *hear* you – now." And, turning, John Mudbury met the eyes of Everard Minturn, their President

of the year before. Minturn had gone down with the *Titanic*.

He dropped his parcels then. His heart gave an enormous leap of joy.

He saw her face – the face of his wife – look through him.

But the child gazed straight into his eyes. She *saw* him.

The next thing he knew was that he heard something tinkling ... far, far away. It sounded miles below him – inside him – he was sounding himself – all utterly bewildering – like a bell. It *was* a bell.

Milly stooped down and picked the parcels up. Her face shone with happiness and laughter ...

But a man came in soon after, a man with a ridiculous, solemn face, a pencil, and a notebook. He wore a dark blue helmet. Behind him came a string of other men. They carried something ... something ... he could not see exactly what it was. But, when he pressed forward through the laughing throng to gaze upon it, he dimly made out two eyes, a nose, a chin, a deep red smear, and a pair of folded hands upon an overcoat. A woman's form fell down upon them then, and he heard soft sounds of children weeping strangely ... and other sounds ... as of familiar voices laughing ... laughing gaily.

"They'll join us presently. It goes like a flash ..."

And, turning with great happiness in his heart, he saw that Sir James had said it, holding Palmer by the arm as with some natural yet unexpected love of sympathetic friendship.

"Come on," said Palmer, smiling like a man who accepts a gift in universal fellowship, "let's help 'em. They'll never understand ... Still, we can always try."

The entire throng moved up with laughter and amusement. It was a moment of hearty, genuine life at last. Delight and Joy and Peace were everywhere.

Then John Mudbury realized the truth – that he was dead.

THE WOMAN WITH
THE GOLDEN ARM

MARK TWAIN

A traditional African American tale

ONCE UPON A TIME, a-way long ago, there was a man and his wife that lived all alone in a house out in the middle of a big lonesome prairie. There wasn't anybody or any house or any trees for miles and miles and miles around. The woman had an arm that was gold – just pure solid gold from the shoulder all the way down.

Well, by and by, one night, she died. It was in the middle of the winter, and the wind was a-blowing, and the snow was a-drifting, and the sleet was a-driving, and it was awful dark; but the man had to bury her; so he took her, and took a lantern, and went away off across the prairie and dug a grave; but when he was just going to put her in, he thought he would steal her golden arm, for he judged it couldn't ever be found out, and he was a powerful mean man.

So then he cut it off, and buried her, and started back home. And he stumbled along, and ploughed along, and the snow and the sleet swashed in his face so he had to turn his head to one side, and could hardly get along at all; and the wind it kept a-crying, and a-wailing, and a-mourning, way off across the prairie, back there where the grave was, just so: *B-z-z-z-z-z-z*. It seemed to him like it was a ghost crying and worrying about some trouble or another, and it made his hair stand up, and he was all trembling and shivering. The wind kept on going *B-z-z-z-z-z-z*, and all of a sudden he caught his breath and stood still, and leaned his ear to listen.

B-z-z-z-z-z-z goes the wind, but right along in the midst of that sound he hears some words, so faint and so far away off he can hardly make them out. *"W-h-e-r-e-'s m-y g-o-l-d-e-n a-a-a-arm? W-h-o-'s g-o-t m-y g-o-l-d-e-n a-a-a-arm?"*

Down drops the lantern; and out it goes, and there he is, in that wide lonesome prairie, in the pitch-dark and the storm. He started along again, but he could hardly pull one foot after the other; and all the way the wind was a-crying, and the snow a-blowing, and the voice a-wailing, *"W-h-e-r-e-'s m-y g-o-l-d-e-n a-a-a-arm? W-h-o-'s g-o-t m-y g-o-l-d-e-n a-a-a-arm?"*

At last he got home; and he locked the door, and bolted it, and chained it with a big long chain and put the chairs and things against it; and then he crept upstairs, and got into bed, and covered up his head and ears, and lay there a-shivering and a-listening.

The wind it kept a-going *B-z-z-z-z*, and there was that voice again – away, *ever* so far away, out in the prairie. But it was a-coming – it was a-coming. Every time it said the words it was closer than it was before. By and by it was as close as the pasture; next it was as close as the branch; next it was this side of the branch and right by the corncrib; next it was to the smokehouse; then it was right at the stile; then right in the yard; then it passed the ash hopper and was right at the door – right at the very door!

"W-h-e-r-e-'s m-y g-o-l-d-e-n a-a-a-arm?" The man shook, and shook, and shivered. He don't hear the chain rattle, he don't hear the bolt break, he don't hear the door move –

still next minute he hear something coming *p-a-t, p-a-t, p-a-t*, just as slow, and just as soft, up the stairs. It's right at the door, now: *"W-h-e-r-e-'s m-y g-o-l-d-e-n a-a-a-arm?"*

Next it's right in the room: *"W-h-o-'s g-o-t m-y g-o-l-d-e-n a-a-a-arm?"*

Then it's right up against the bed – then it's a-leaning down over the bed – then it's down right against his ear and a-whispering soft, so soft and dreadful: *"W-h-e-r-e-'s m-y g-o-l-d-e-n a-a-a-arm? W-h-o-'s g-o-t m-y g-o-l-d-e-n a-a-a-arm?*

"YOU GOT IT!"

AS COLD AS ICE

WILLIAM MAYNE

TIM WAS WAITING at the gate of his school. Anna came running to him when she saw a strange look about his face. She thought he might have gone snow-blind, because his eyes seemed to be no longer there.

"What's the matter?" she said. "What have you done?"

Tim turned towards her and put out his hands and felt his way from the gate on to the pavement. "I can't see," he said. "I can't look."

By that time Anna had got to him and found that the blank look in his eyes was indeed a sort of snow-blindness, but nothing that could not be cured by taking off his glasses and shaking them free of snow.

"Now I can see," said Tim. "But my eyes are cold."

"I should think they are," said Anna, bending down to put the glasses on him again, when she had dusted them with the fringe of her scarf.

Tim put up his hand to help the wire on to the back of his ears, under the woollen hat. "The snow doesn't go there," he said, picking up the little eye-pieces Anna had dropped in a drift. "I got them off the gate." He put them back on one of the bars of it. He had to reach up to touch it and balance the little snow-pads where he wanted them to sit.

Then he seemed to be ready to go. Anna did what she always did, looking to see whether he had on his own coat: he was likely to come home in any navy raincoat he found, even though the things in the pockets were different from those in his own.

Anna found her own name in the coat: Diana Dee. Diana had shortened itself to Anna. It was her old coat that Tim wore today at least.

"Mine," he said. "Beetle Dee's in it." Beetle Dee had been alive in the autumn, and by now he was dead, still in the pocket, tied on a blue thread. He was Tim's way of knowing the coat, if he remembered.

Tim walked ahead, as usual, sometimes bound for the same destination, stamping along the pavement, past the schoolhouse then off it and along the road, flat and white and smooth with traffic wheels. The surface was scattered with little shaped flakes from the tyres of cars.

There was no frost like it in the world. The fields below the school lay like all Antarctica, hedge-high with snow, and the river beyond was stiff as a glass log in its bed. In the houses round the green there was ice across the windows, and if water stood still in the pipes ice grew there at once.

There was no traffic through the village for a moment. There was noise on the green all the time from the close of school to teatime, daylight and dark alike, of the three toboggans of the village doing a year's work in these few biting precious days.

A door frost-tight in its frame was pulled open and someone called in the twilight for a child on the green.

"We could wait," said Tim, "a little more."

"Not at all," said Anna. "Come on."

Tim put his hands in his pockets. Anna could see him feeling for Beetle Dee, standing in the snow and thinking.

"Go on," she said.

"I'm just counting him," said Tim.

"How many?" said Anna.

"Two," said Tim. "One of him, one of me."

When that was settled, Anna pushed him along. He braced himself against her so that his feet slid, and they went down the snow-slide of the road, skidding softly and thumping with hollow wellie noise, until they turned off the road near the mill, to the bridge and the far side of the river and up the hill home.

In summer they could stay and watch the fish staring and hear the falling water where it leapt over a rock step into the pool above the bridge. In the autumn there were drifts of leaves to the water's edge on grassy banks, and mist hanging on the water. Always there was the voice of the waterfall, until this dry cold winter.

"What do the fishes drink?" said Tim.

"They're asleep," said Anna. "Let's go and look for them."

There was no need to cross the bridge now. For a week the pool had been frozen hard enough to be walked on. There could be no wet water below by now.

The ice had shifted two great rocks, each as big as a cow, that lay side by side in the middle of the pool. Swimmers could dive from them in the summer. Now the rocks had tipped uncomfortably.

There was more sliding to get to them. The ice was not smooth, but it was slippery. You slid if you walked there at all.

Anna did not let Tim stop. He would have gone on figure-of-eight circuits of the two rocks until he was lost in the dark. Anna allowed him between them, and then let him skate to the further shore. Here there was a place without snow, where the rock overhung, in a great shelf. An icicle here touched the ground, hanging from a roof higher than Anna could reach. Much taller people could have stretched up and chipped away at the top of the icicle, bent down to its foot and taken it away, nine feet long and two inches thick, a transparent candle for a keepsake.

Tim thumped the icicle. It was harder than he thought and did not break.

"Why do they put a pipe here?" he said.

"There's water inside," said Anna. She thought that water flowed in an icicle, or how did the icicle form at all? A complete icicle must be a complete tube.

The air was darkening fast under the trees. Where the banks came high and close together the waterfall hung in shapeless solid fronds over shining rock, silent in the cold sleep of water.

Anna decided to go home along the river above the waterfall, through the woods. She had never been that way with the water quiet.

There was no water above the waterfall. Here the river ran between flat rocks in deep gorges not too wide for Anna to jump but deep enough to drown Tim if he stood in them.

Now all the moving was stopped, and the turmoil in the pot-holes was no more. There was snow over everything. It was like walking along a ride in the woods, with the unknown tracks of animals in front and the known traces of wellies spoiling the wild landscape behind.

Where a beck came into the river there was another waterfall. It was only as high as a man, and it was well known for having a cave behind it. Anna had never got past the water and into the cave, or even seen it.

She saw it now, and the icicles of its waterfall made it into a cage. It was something else as well, not natural. But Tim thought it probably was. For him there was nothing odd in finding a lighted candle in a wood behind a fringe of ice. It was just more landscape to him.

If it hadn't been getting dark, Anna thought, we would not have noticed it. You do not see light until dark happens. The little flame stood clear and steady in the quiet air.

"Who lives here?" said Tim. "Why hasn't he a gate or a garden?"

"People don't always have gardens," said Anna. She was wondering who might live here. "Come on, it's time we got home." She was wondering too where this place was, if she was where she thought she was.

"Pussy," said Tim. "I want to stroke the cat."

He was standing on river ice, close by the cave, looking through into the cave, or little room beyond. Some of the icicles had been broken away and there was room for him to walk through.

"No," said Anna. He took no notice, and she followed him. Just a cat, she thought, seeing it.

Tim was not stroking it. It was too cold, and made of ice, sitting rigid on the floor.

"Like Beetle Dee," said Tim. "Has it been in a matchbox? Does it belong to a boy?"

"It'll be something else," said Anna. "Ice. It's not real, but it's natural." But that word meant nothing to Tim. This was all still landscape, more of the stuff that happened and was seen by people.

A natural cat-sculpture, Anna thought; a natural candle. But the tall candlestick must have been made, and she did not know who could have done it.

She was wondering how to get Tim away from this doubtful territory. But he said, "I'm cold. Are we home yet?"

When they got there he wanted to hang his feet out to dry, but instead got them towelled with a rough towel so that he staggered about helplessly until bedtime.

When Anna met him outside school the next day he was wearing his snow eyes once more. They were the exact same ones, he told her. "My own," he said.

"But is it your coat?" said Anna. "Is Beetle Dee in it?"

"He's not here," said Tim, not having to look. But it was his coat, marked Diana Dee. "But I know where he is. I gave him to the cat."

"You'll want him yourself," said Anna. "Our cat will lose anything."

"We'll get it for me from somewhere," said Tim. "I only lended it."

Then he just wanted to slide about in the road and thought no more about Beetle Dee.

He'll remember at some terrible time, thought Anna.

On the way home Tim wanted to climb above the big waterfall again.

"We got too wet yesterday," said Anna. "You couldn't walk about afterwards."

"Beetle Dee," said Tim. "He goes in my pocket. I want him."

"But that's the longest way home," said Anna.

"Not that cat," said Tim.

Not that candle, Anna decided. But Tim was on his way, and she could not let him go alone. But she did not want that candle in her eyes again, out of nature, out of reality. Whoever set it there might be beyond reality.

At the cave there was still a candle. There was still a cat, more real than before, as well as more unreal. There were other lumps of ice in the cave, or rock covered with ice.

"It's all right," said Tim. He was not speaking to Anna but to Beetle Dee. Beetle Dee was sitting waiting, his piece of cotton loosely tied round the cat's front leg. Beside Beetle Dee was a lump of ice that looked beetly too, but white instead of black.

The candle will be ice too, Anna decided. She made herself go into the cave and touch it. It was a common wax candle, with a warm flame. She would have preferred an ice candle.

Tim wanted to warm Beetle Dee up in his mouth, but somehow got him inside his shirt and shrieked at the way he crawled round inside so cold all the way home.

The next night Tim had forgotten cave and candle and wanted to go home the shortest way. Anna had to look again, though, and pushed him in front of her.

253

"Perhaps I don't feel well," said Tim.

"You never felt better," said Anna. "You look ever so well."

"But I've seen all that," said Tim. "You're getting snow in my wellies. Look at all where we walked yesterday."

"Some of that was Beetle Dee," said Anna. "He was here all night on his own."

The candle had burnt no lower. It had not changed. But beside it in the cave ice that had been shapeless the night before was turning into something, designs that were on the way to becoming people. There was a head on one, there were hands on the other, left holding right, right holding left; there was long hair, there was short hair; there was a knitted hat, if she looked in the right way, on the shorter figure, like Tim's knitted hat; and the whole figure becoming like Tim.

"Me?" said Tim, when she said something. "We all look like that. I keep thinking I've gone to the toilet when it's Michael who isn't there. Simple."

"You all look like that," said Anna, "Yes."

"Your name is Edward," said Tim. He was perfectly sensibly talking to the cat.

"Come on," said Anna, not wanting the cat to wake out of its ice.

The next day Tim was very obliging and went to the cave without complaint. There was fog today, and the way was quite new. Water dripped here and there. In the village sledge runners scraped on the road, and there was slush in the gutters.

"Thawing," said Anna.

"Yes," said Tim, but not wondering at all at new landscapes: they happened all the time, light, dark, yesterday, tomorrow.

At the cave the eternal candle was giving a warmer light in the softer air. Beside it were longer pieces of ice that accidentally reminded Anna of people. They now were people. The smaller one was Tim, and could not be mistaken for Michael or anyone else in Tim's class. Tim was the one with glasses there, and he was the one with glasses here.

I don't expect the other is me, Anna thought.

"It's us," said Tim. "We got our photograph." He put his hand up to feel his glasses, to see which of them, boy or statue, had them on. They each had. "Is it my coat? Has he got Beetle Dee?"

Beetle Dee was beside the cat. Beetle Dee was in Tim's pocket.

A drop of water from the beck above dropped like a tear and put out the candle. Only shadows were left.

The next day those shadows had melted in a wind as soft and warm as eiderdown.

"I can go paddling," said Tim, splashing below the fall in water that might have wasted from his own likeness in the cave.

Acknowledgements

The publisher would like to thank the copyright holders for permission to reproduce the following copyright material:

Cyril Birch: Oxford University Press for "Magicians of the Way" from *Chinese Myths and Fantasies* retold by Cyril Birch (Oxford University Press 1961); copyright © Cyril Birch 1961. **Algernon Blackwood**: A.P. Watt Ltd on behalf of Sheila Reeves for "Transition" by Algernon Blackwood; copyright © Algernon Blackwood. **Ray Bradbury**: Don Congdon Associates, Inc. for "Zero Hour" from *Planet Stories* by Ray Bradbury; copyright © Ray Bradbury 1947, renewed 1974. **Truman Capote**: Penguin Books Ltd for "Miriam" from *The Complete Short Stories of Truman Capote* by Truman Capote (Penguin); copyright © Truman Capote 1945. **Helen Cresswell**: A.M. Heath Ltd for "A Kind of Swan Song" from *Shades of Dark* by Helen Cresswell (Patrick Hardy 1984); copyright © Helen Cresswell 1984. **Jane Gardam**: David Higham Associates Ltd for "Bang, Bang – Who's Dead?" from *Beware, Beware* by Jane Gardam (Hamish Hamilton 1987); copyright © Jane Gardam 1987. **Alan Garner**: David Higham Associates Ltd for "Feel Free" by Alan Garner; copyright © Alan Garner 1967. **Elizabeth Garner**: Elizabeth Garner for "A Lesson" by Elizabeth Garner, copyright © Elizabeth Garner 1995. **Joe Hayes**: Mariposa Publishing Company for "La Llorona, the Weeping Woman" retold by Joe Hayes from *The Day it Snowed Tortillas* by Joe Hayes; copyright © Joe Hayes 1982. **Alison Lurie**: Reed Consumer Books Ltd for "The Highboy" from *Women and Ghosts* by Alison Lurie (William Heinemann Ltd 1994); copyright © Alison Lurie 1990. **Margaret Mahy**: Ashton Scholastic Ltd for "Space Invaders" from *Aliens in the Family* by Margaret Mahy (Ashton Scholastic Ltd 1986); copyright © Margaret Mahy 1986. **William Mayne**: David Higham Associates Ltd for "A Haunted Terrace," "As Cold As Ice" and "The Story of Glam" by William Mayne; copyright © William Mayne 1995. **Sorche Nic Leodhas**: McIntosh and Otis Inc. for "The Walking Boundary Stone" from *Gaelic Ghosts* by Sorche Nic Leodhas (Henry Holt & Co. Inc. 1964); copyright © LeClaire G. Alger 1964, copyright © Louis R. Hoffman 1992. **Robert D. San Souci**: Doubleday, a division of Bantam Doubleday Dell Publishing Group, Inc. for "The Hunter in the Haunted Forest" from *Short and Shivery: Thirty Chilling Tales* by Robert D. San Souci; copyright © Robert D. San Souci 1987. **Robert Westall**: Penguin Books Ltd for "The Call" from *The Call* by Robert Westall (Viking Children's Books 1989); copyright © Robert Westall 1989. **Clare Weyman**: David Higham Associates Ltd for "Cousin Edward's Cat" from *Family Tales* by Clare Weyman, copyright © Clare Weyman 1957. **Martin Wilkinson**: Artforms for "Thorns" from *The Hill Walker* by Martin Wilkinson (Insole Press, Settle); copyright © Martin Wilkinson.

Every effort has been made to obtain permission to reproduce copyright material but there may be cases where we have been unable to trace a copyright holder. The publisher will be happy to correct any omissions in future printings.